The
HANGOVER

BY EMMA NICHOLS

Britain's Next
BESTSELLER

First published in 2017 by:

Britain's Next Bestseller
An imprint of Live It Publishing
27 Old Gloucester Road
London, United Kingdom.
WC1N 3AX

www.bnbsbooks.co.uk

ISBN: 9781973391661 (PBK)

To keep in touch with the latest news from Emma Nichols and her
writing please visit:

www.emmanicholsauthor.com
www.facebook.com/EmmaNicholsAuthor
www.twitter.com/ENichols_Author

The Vincenti Series
by Emma Nichols

Whilst **The Hangover** can be read as a stand-alone novel, we would recommend you immerse yourself from the beginning of the Vincenti Series, with **Finding You**.

Thanks to...

Mu for your unwavering support and dedication to the cause. Bev the copper for your technical expertise and wicked sense of humour. To Tara and Valden for your critical input and patience. You, my readers for choosing to read what I write. I hope you love this one too.
Thank you all.

Emma x

Dedication

To Mu, because...

1.

Eva thrashed and kicked, and her sweat-soaked t-shirt clung with the desperation of a child to its mother. Adrenaline coursed through her veins, feeding her tired body. Her flailing arm made contact with something warm and soft and she jumped up into a seated position.

'Ouch,' Rosa grumbled, thrust out of a deep sleep by the accidental assault. She rubbed at the sore spot on her chest and peeked through eyes that were unwilling to open fully.

Eva blinked, momentarily stunned, as she adjusted to the unfamiliar surroundings. She was shaking physically. 'Sorry,' she said, but her voice wasn't her own, and she reached out into the darkness tentatively.

'It's okay baby. You're safe.' Rosa whispered, reaching towards Eva's wet hair, suddenly withdrawing her hand before making contact. 'You're drenched,' she said with concern. Her eyes scanned the paralysed woman and a searing pain shot through her heart.

Eva jumped involuntarily, and moved away from the woman she didn't recognise. 'Sorry... sorry... sorry,' Eva continued, stuck inside the trance that had dominated her sleep. 'Please mummy.'

The nightmares were getting worse and all Rosa could do was watch and wait, feeling helpless. She had tried to soothe Eva in the past, but that just seemed to cause even more distress, and Eva could easily lash out. She was stronger inside the nightmare and lacked any self-control. Eva would have no recollection in the morning, but the event would be deeply etched in Rosa's mind, again, and again, replaced by yet another image of her lover's pain with each recurring bad dream. She had tried to talk to Eva about it, but with no recollection of the dream world she inhabited, her response was indifferent or dismissive.

Eva sat abruptly, her body tensing, her arms reaching skywards, her eyes pleading. Time seemed to slow down as tears started to slip silently down her face. Then her eyes closed, and she fell back onto the mattress and into a deep and restful sleep.

Rosa lay awake, adrenaline pumping, and her heart pounding in her chest. She had wanted to touch Eva, snuggle close to her, and hold her until the dream subsided. She wanted the dreams not to come. And she hated the helpless feeling now residing in her gut, as she watched Eva sleeping soundly by her side. Glancing at her phone, her hand was shaking. It was 4am. She climbed slowly out of bed, being careful not to disturb Eva, and wandered towards the bathroom, rubbing her hands vigorously through her hair. She could be in work in an hour. No one would complain at her starting her shift earlier than planned.

She stepped into the shower and blasted heat onto her body, enjoying the light massage to her neck and shoulders and the gentle awakening effect that seemed to go some way to ease the burning sensation behind her closed eyes. Within a few minutes she was dressed and out the door. Stepping into the cold morning air completed the awakening process, and she moved with a sense of urgency.

*

'You're early,' Dee said, her eyes barely rising from the notes she was reading. 'Everything okay?'

'Fine, just couldn't sleep,' Rosa responded, in an effort to deflect the concern she knew Dee held for her. The absence of her charismatic smile told the story and it didn't go unmissed by Dee's eagle eyes.

Desiree Prongue had been a good friend and colleague since they had studied medicine together in Paris, some ten-years ago. Dee had specialised as an anaesthetist whilst Rosa had taken the surgical route. Short, and with a stocky build, Dee looked every bit the dyke that she was proud to be. She also had a fierce protective streak that said, *no one better mess with my Rosa*. Dee raised her eyebrows, one slightly higher than the other. Rosa ignored the questioning glare and picked up a buff file from the nurses' station. Even though her eyes scanned the pages, she hadn't registered anything by the time she put the file back down. 'So, what have we got?' she asked.

Dee looked up from her notes and eyed Rosa. Now wasn't the time to raise her concerns, but she would address the situation by the end of the day. 'It's been a busy one,' she started. 'RTC came in with seven casualties. We lost one on the table, three are in CCU and the other three are on the ward. A few more bits and bobs; I'll brief you as we walk. I've got a follow up surgery on one of the RTC patients to attend to in an hour - slow bleed on the brain. I'm sure Riccardo won't mind swapping, if you want to take the lead on it. He's had a shit night and his wife's gone into labour.'

'Sure, I'll track him down and meet you in prep,' Rosa said, nodding in affirmation at the details Dee had relayed. She was already feeling better for the distraction.

*

Eva stirred. The weight of her eyelids meant the effort of opening them almost constituted an early morning workout. She rubbed away the sticky substance from around her eyes and forced them into the light, only to close them again and bathe in the relatively soothing darkness, provided by her lids and a protective hand across her face. Rosa would have left ages ago, she mused, still reaching across into the cold space her girlfriend had left, turning away from the sunlight that was seeping through the blinds. Her smile widened as she took full stock of where she was, and she slid her body to the other side of the bed; taking in the scent of Rosa, snuffling into the soft pillow, and fully occupying *her* space in their bed. She groaned with pleasure. Rosa was special, maybe *the one*, though she tried not to think about that too much and just live each day as it came. She'd been wrong before on that topic. Her phone buzzed, jolting her out of her reverie. She ignored it, and it buzzed again. *Fuck.* She picked up the phone and read the message.

Are you coming into work today?

Mum. Damn. It really was later than she thought. She had promised Rowena she would be in work in good time to meet the new business executive she had recruited. It was nearly lunchtime and they would be heading out to eat shortly.

On my way

She tapped out her response as she leapt out of bed. She had the shower on full blast before she pressed the send button. Stepping into the shower, she took a few moments to enjoy the refreshing bergamot and thyme scent of Rosa's body wash on her skin, before drying quickly and throwing on her faded jeans, her *love is love* t-shirt, and a dark blue jumper. She was out the door within ten minutes of her mother's text, sporting a smile of contentment at her achievement, and savouring the lingering scent on her skin. With a spring in her step she exited the gated building and hailed a taxi.

*

'Hi,' Eva said, continuing to skip her way into her mum's office, with her customary offering: a box of donuts, and a beaming smile. Bouncing towards the tall woman with long blonde hair, dumping the donuts on the table as she passed, she held out her hand. 'Hi, I'm…'

'Eva,' the woman finished, shaking the offered hand, confidently. Eva couldn't help but notice the dark blue eyes contrasting with the long blonde hair, before turning her head towards her mum. 'I'm Carine Delfosse,' the woman said, in a well-spoken voice. Even the lipstick highlighting the fine lips looked expensive Eva thought, as her eyes drew back to the highly styled Parisian. Eva guessed her age to be late thirties, possibly early forties.

'Carine,' she repeated, releasing her hand, and turning to face her mum again. 'Hey mum,' she said, and before Rowena could speak Eva had taken two paces and had her wrapped in a tight squeeze. Any comment that might have been forthcoming regarding her tardiness had been buried in Rowena's layered throat. Eva wasn't prone to displays of affection towards her mum, even though they generally got on well, and certainly not in the presence of someone she didn't know. The hug had quite literally taken her mum's breath away. Rowena flustered, righted her dress even though it wasn't out of place, cleared her throat and snorted out a chuckle.

'Right, we were just about to go to lunch, but I'm guessing you knew that,' Rowena said, mock-glaring over her black rimmed glasses. There it was, that subtle dig. Eva smiled, knowing she would never change her mum and loving her just the same.

'Lunch sounds perfect,' Eva responded rubbing her hands together, before nudging her mum in the side affectionately. Carine Delfosse studied mother and daughter. She was looking forward to getting to know Eva Adams over the coming months, but she wasn't so sure that the stunning-looking daughter was fully in the picture as to her role in the

Adams family business. Lunch would be interesting, she mused.

'Sounds perfect indeed,' Carine repeated, smiling at both women. Rowena picked up her bag, threw in her phone, picked up her keys, and headed for the door, easing her overweight frame sideways to fit between the coffee table and couch. Eva and Carine followed closely to heel. Eva barely registered the light touch that lingered on her arm as they exited the office.

They took the short walk to their regular haunt in silence, and at Rowena's plodding pace. Eva felt fidgety and tapped out a text while they sauntered, only aware of Carine's eyes on her as she pocketed her phone. She cleared her throat. Carine's gaze seemed to question, but she couldn't tell if there was judgement in there too. The woman made her feel edgy in a strange way. She turned her attention to her mum.

'You okay?' Eva asked, noticing the pale colour in Rowena's puffy cheeks and the beads of sweat tracing down her temples. Rowena's eyes seemed to sit in dark pools, and suddenly appeared to lack focus. Eva's heart raced. 'Mum, are you okay?' Eva's panicked tone jolted Rowena out of the vacant state. Her breathing was fast and shallow, reminding Eva of a small fish gulping, having been out of the water for too long.

'I'm fine,' Rowena responded, waving Eva off as if she was making a fuss over nothing. She grabbed the handrail and pulled her body up the two small steps, opened the door, and entered into a room full of flavours. 'Mmm… smells wonderful… Hello Frank,' she said, without drawing breath, in complete contrast to her state just moments ago. The elderly host stepped into their path with a welcoming embrace and the zest of a thirty-year old. *Frank's,* the family run bistro, had been around as long as they had. Rowena had been one of their first clients when she set up office in Paris some twenty years ago and they had dined there at least once a week ever since. They were like family, and Frank always treated Rowena like royalty.

'Hello, my Princess. I see you have a new gorgeous lady with you today,' Frank stated in his delightfully camp tone, presenting his hand as his eager eyes scanned the tall blonde Parisian. Carine played along, took his hand lightly, and just as quickly Frank pulled away, darting towards a table at the back of the room. 'Especially for you ladies,' he said with a wicked smile. His eyes sparkled, and his cheeks bore a healthy glow that complemented his well-dressed appearance. 'I'll bring you a bottle of house wine and water to get started, while you look at the menu. Unless you'd like an aperitif?' he asked, mindful of their new guest.

'Wine is fine with me,' Carine responded. Eva nodded and shrugged her shoulders at the same time. Frank smiled, knowingly.

Eva took a seat at the rustic wooden table. Rowena took the seat opposite, and Carine sat next to her. Eva felt suddenly very self-conscious, with both women eyeing her intently. The sparsely decorated room and simple tableware only added to her feeling of nakedness. Squirming in her seat, she felt relieved to see the wine arriving. Breaking the silence, she moved to pour her mother a glass, only to find the path to the glass stopped by the warm soft hand.

'We need to talk, Eva.' Rowena moved her wine glass away and filled a tumbler with water. Carine pushed her glass towards Eva, nodded, and Eva duly poured them both a glass of wine. Suddenly, Eva was thankful Carine was joining her in a drink, though it wouldn't have stopped her if the Parisian hadn't done so.

Eva smiled tensely across the table. 'Sure,' she responded, feeling the angst between them and not really knowing what was at the root of it. She had known about

Carine's appointment some months ago, so it couldn't be about that. She hadn't been involved in the recruitment process. That was clearly her mum's decision, and rightly so in Eva's mind. But the look on her mum's face was directly related to the uncomfortable sensation developing in her gut. What was coming didn't feel good. She breathed deeply trying to control her racing heart. 'What is it you want to talk about mum?' she asked, with a hint of defensiveness in her voice. She picked up her glass and took a healthy slug of the wine, savouring the slight chill on her tongue, before her mum responded.

Rowena watched her daughter carefully, sensing her discomfort. She had no desire to hurt Eva, or upset their relationship - far from it. But the truth was, Eva wasn't on top of her work, and also, as her mother, she was concerned about Eva's lifestyle. 'I'm worried about you,' she said.

Eva choked on the wine she had just started to swallow. She hadn't expected that. She hadn't given her any reason to be concerned, had she? 'What?' she said, feeling confused.

'I'm concerned darling. You don't seem to be yourself and your work is suffering for it.' Eva rolled her eyes. Yes, she had missed a couple of deadlines in the last few months, but in those cases the client had changed direction at the last minute. She could hardly be blamed for that.

'My work's not that bad,' she challenged. Carine winced fractionally at Eva's perspective. She had seen the data for herself, and the picture didn't look pretty.

'Eva, you've missed six deadlines in the last two months alone. And before that you missed more than you hit. I've been fielding complaints for the last, I don't know how long.' Eva glared at Carine. 'It's alright, Carine is fully briefed, which brings me onto my main point.'

Eva raised her eyebrows, slumped back in the chair, and threw her arms across her chest to comfort the pain that was suddenly burning a hole in her chest. 'What point?' she asked, her voice lacking any warmth as she tried to hide the unsteadiness in her words. Rowena stared at her petulant child over the rim of her glasses, mentally confirming to herself that her decision to recruit Carine had been the right one.

'I've asked Carine to head up the business,' she said, watching for Eva's response. 'Because I'm retiring,' she added swiftly. The well-rehearsed line ricocheted around the bistro, settling in the bottle of wine on the table.

Eva picked it up and re-filled her glass, ignoring Carine's half-empty glass. She could have sworn she had seen Carine smirk as the news hit, but when their eyes locked together something quite different was present. Eva didn't know whether that was a good thing or not, so she smiled graciously at her new boss. 'Wow,' she said, raising herself in the chair, allowing the consequences of her mum's second point to register. She hadn't seen that one coming either. Silenced by Frank approaching, pad in hand, she reached out for her glass and emptied it in one long slug, unable to fully process the conversation. *Why hadn't her mum spoken to her about retiring?* That said she hadn't spoken to her mum about anything to do with the business for a long time now.

'What can I get you ladies?' Frank asked, breaking the awkwardness at the table. He cast his eyes across the three women in turn.

'I'll have the special please Frank,' Rowena responded.

'I'll have the same, please,' Carine followed.

Eva nodded to make it a third special, reached for the bottle of wine and poured another glass for herself and Carine.

'And, I'm concerned about your drinking,' Rowena said, at the point the glass rested on Eva's lips. She took another slug in defiance, before placing the glass deliberately on the table, feeling thoroughly beaten-up after the onslaught of the last few minutes.

'And I'm concerned about your weight mum, but I don't give you a hard time about it!' Eva blurted, as the rapidly rising anger met with her need to defend and protect herself. She puffed out a deep breath and fiddled with the stem of the glass, irritated that her mum was right. Though she had told herself her drinking was well within her control, deep down she knew it was a poor coping strategy. What she hadn't quite worked out was why she felt so lousy without the effect of alcohol in her system. Even work wasn't stimulating her, hence missing the deadlines, though she hadn't realised the full extent of her underachievement until now.

'I know, I know,' Rowena responded, her tone softer and her eyes lowered towards the table. 'I'm going on a diet,' she said. 'The doctor has recommended someone to help me,' she admitted before returning her eyes to her daughter.

'I didn't realise you'd seen someone,' Eva said, beginning to wonder exactly how much she had missed, and over how long.

'Yes. I didn't tell you because you're in your own world darling. Carine knows everything and that's why I've asked her to take control of the business. I trust her.' She looked towards the blonde Parisian and smiled warmly. Eva felt an unpleasant sensation rise within her, and tried to swallow it down. 'Her mum and I go back a long way,' Rowena added, with a warm smile directed at Carine. She squeezed Carine's arm and Carine placed her hand on Rowena's, holding it in place with the affection of old long-lost friends reunited. Eva nearly choked on the bile rising in her throat at the histrionic gesture. 'Anyway...'

Frank approached with three plates of food and placed them in front of the women before returning to the kitchen for a basket of sliced baguette. 'Another bottle of wine please

Frank,' Eva said. Rowena frowned. 'I'll stop in my own time,' Eva responded, as Frank returned at a pace, and placed the new bottle on the table.

'Anyway, as I was saying, you two are going to need to work very closely together until such times as I can trust you,' she said, pointing at Eva, 'to take on the business by yourself. I need to make sure it's in safe hands,' she said.

Eva studied her mum, starting to feel a swell of sadness. Aside from the insult, which was probably justified to some extent - she didn't feel equipped to look after the business. Something in her mum's eyes gave her cause for concern. 'Is everything okay? Are you okay?' she asked tentatively, reminded of her mum's struggle getting from the office to the bistro.

'I'm fine darling. Who knows what the future holds of course, and we need to be prepared. I haven't worked my arse off for this business to fold if anything happens to me,' Rowena said, with determination.

'Mum, you're scaring me. Is there something you haven't told me?'

'No darling, of course not. I'm just securing the future of my business... your business if you want it? I want to enjoy my retirement. And I need to be sure you're in the right place mentally to take it on,' she said, twirling a finger at her own temple. 'Until that time, Carine will take control, and knock you into shape... I hope,' she said with a slight chuckle.

Eva slumped back into the chair, poured another glass of wine, and sipped at it, quietly taking in the turn of events. She hadn't seen this one coming, and she wasn't quite sure how to handle it, or Carine for that matter. She looked across the table from her mum to the tall, elegant, woman. Carine smiled warmly but her eyes gave away nothing.

'See you at 9 on Monday then?' Carine said, lifting the wine glass to her lips and sipping delicately. Her face smiled but her eyes were still distant, still judging.

'Right,' Eva said, lost in the pain of the attack she had sustained over lunch. She poked at her food. She had no appetite. The joy she had felt before she entered her mother's office just a few hours earlier had disappeared, replaced by a sinking feeling and a heavy weight sitting just below her rib cage. Her heart yearned for Rosa. Rosa would make things better again, but she wouldn't be home yet.

Eva stood. 'I need to get going,' she said, and walked briskly out of the bistro and into the street. She stood on the pavement momentarily, sucked in the cold air, and braced herself against her stinging eyes. She turned swiftly and walked quickly down the street. She couldn't get away quickly enough. She turned up an alleyway and dived into the first bar she came to. It was dark, and empty. Perfect. She picked the tall wooden-topped stool and sat at the bar. Despite its dingy appearance, the surface of the bar was clean.

'Whiskey please,' she said to the approaching barman. He stopped, nodded, poured, and returned with the drink. She swilled the liquid in the glass, allowing her thoughts to torment her. *Was she really that bad?* She couldn't answer herself honestly, and pinched at the bridge of her nose to quell the rising tide of sadness that was pressing at the back of her eyes. Only the burning of the amber fluid hitting the back of her throat jolted her out of her reverie and bathed her in a comforting shield. She asked for another.

2.

'Urrgh,' Dee groaned, as her body sank heavily into the soft cushioned chair in Rosa's office. She leaned back, taking full advantage of the much-needed respite from being on her feet all day. She watched her friend intently, as she busied herself behind her desk. 'I'm starving,' she said. Rosa looked up. 'Fancy anything from the canteen?' she asked.

'Sure.' Rosa's tone was flat, her eyes returning immediately to the paperwork in front of her.

Dee pulled herself out of the brief comfort and encroached on Rosa's space, forcing her to look up again. 'Come on, what's up?' Rosa's eyes had lost their natural shine over the past couple of weeks, and in Dee's mind there was only one person who could be responsible for that, but she needed to hear it from her friend directly. Dee held Rosa's gaze.

'Let's go and eat,' Rosa said, hoping Dee could be a sounding board for the thoughts that had cast a shadow over her.

'I'm not going to let you get away with it,' Dee said, teasingly, but with a certainty that Rosa understood.

'I know, let's grab some food and chat.'

Dee breathed out deeply. *At last*, she thought, as she followed Rosa into the corridor. They took the short journey to the canteen in relative silence, simply acknowledging colleagues who addressed them as they walked past.

Rosa scanned the fridge counter and picked out a cheese baguette. She wasn't feeling very hungry, in spite of not having eaten since 8.30 that morning, after the first surgery. It was now 4.45 and although their clinical day finished a while ago, Rosa had insisted she needed to catch up on paperwork before leaving. Dee could read an excuse to not go home when she saw one, and had decided to gate crash Rosa's office until she acquiesced to the late lunch. Dee grabbed a steak sandwich, slice of apple tart, and a can of coke.

Rosa picked up a cup and placed it in the slot, pressed the coffee button and waited. 'Hungry?' Rosa asked, with a wry smile, a ray of lightness passing through her, as she watched her friend with fondness.

'Starving. And I've got a sparing session at 6.30,' Dee said.

Having paid, they made their way to a free table, avoiding the obvious patient visitors, and sat facing each other. Rosa breathed deeply and picked at the plastic wrapping housing the baguette, her attention clearly not on the task of actually eating the food.

'So?' Dee asked, biting into the steak sandwich, and devouring it in four good-sized pieces. She wiped at her mouth, pulled open the can and took a slug of the fizzy pop, belching quietly to herself as the bubbles decided to retrace their journey to her mouth. 'Hey,' she said softly, as it dawned on her that Rosa's eyes were welling up.

'I'm okay, honestly. It's just...' she faltered, and Dee kept quiet. 'I'm worried I'm going to lose her,' Rosa said with sadness, looking up to gauge Dee's response. The frown on her friend's face told her all she needed to know. 'Look, I know you don't trust her, but I do. She's not like you think. She's...' Rosa couldn't find the words. 'I think I'm in love with her,' she said, 'But I'm scared she's...'

'Not in love with you?' Dee finished, her tone more severe than she had intended. It was no secret that she hadn't warmed to Rosa's girlfriend, even though she had to admit that Eva had put the biggest smile on Rosa's face that she had ever seen. Today was not one of those days though, and today Dee would be happy to see the back of the woman she considered to be unreliable and immature.

'No, it's not that.' Rosa sighed, fiddling with the wrapper. She stopped, picked up her coffee, and took a sip. She scanned the room and locked onto the horizon beyond the plain glass window. This was one of the few areas of the building with an aspect that didn't have a building of some sort obscuring the view. Not that her attention was on the park, or the rain that was beginning to fall. 'I'm scared she'll leave me. I'm sure she loves me, but I think she's scared to commit. She's been having nightmares. She won't talk about them. I've no idea what they're about and she doesn't seem to remember anything in the morning. There's nothing I can do, and I just feel a distance growing between us.' The words streamed as her fear made its case.

Dee nodded, turning the can in her hand, and rubbed her thumb along the condensation that had formed on the outside. 'What makes you think she won't commit?' she asked.

'I don't know.' Rosa sighed, sipped at her hot drink, and held her friend's eyes. 'It's just a feeling, and maybe I'm completely wrong. I mean… we're great together. It's probably all my shit,' she added with a shrug of her shoulders.

'Rosa, I've known you for the best part of how long now? You don't have any shit… at least not this sort of shit,' she added.

'Maybe I've never been in love before,' Rosa stated, trying to raise a smile, and failing. Her eyes betrayed the seriousness behind her words, causing Dee's heart to fracture and her mouth to parch.

'Is there anything I can do to help?' Dee asked. Her mind warring between the compassion she felt for her friend and the contempt she felt towards Eva. Dee reached out and squeezed Rosa's hand. Hands that were normally so confident, capable, and nimble, when she carried out her work, seemed vulnerable and insecure in Dee's strong grasp.

'Just being here,' Rosa said, returning the squeeze unconvincingly. Dee held her friend's eyes with tenderness, allowing Rosa to process her thoughts. Rosa's sigh weighed heavily, though she felt a little lighter for sharing her concerns.

'Right, you gonna eat that thing or dance with it?' Dee asked, with her eyes fully focused on the half-unpacked snack that Rosa was still fiddling with.

'No, do you want it?'

Dee grabbed the packet, whipped the baguette out and munched into it, nodding her head in thanks. 'Fancy going out later in the week?' she asked with her mouth half-full. 'We can all go,' she added, hoping to shift the energy.

Rosa straightened her posture. 'Maybe,' she said, in as chirpy a tone as she could muster. Perhaps a night out on the town would do both her and Eva good, she thought. She hadn't been out socially with Dee and Angie for a while and maybe the change of scene would help. She and Eva had done a bit of a u-haul, and spent the last few months cooped up in her town house, making home together. Although Eva had moved a lot of her things across, she hadn't wanted to sell or rent out her own place. Maybe that was part of the problem. Eva always seemed to leave one door slightly open, as if she might need to bolt at the last minute. It left Rosa feeling slightly unnerved. She knew they were right together and felt frustrated by her own doubts, and unable to fully enjoy the time that they spent together. She smiled across the table and handed the paper napkin to Dee, pointing at the spot on her face that needed attending to.

'Thanks.' Dee took the paper and swiped it across her chin. 'So, Friday night then?' she said, tucking into her apple tart.

'Great.' Rosa smiled and finished her coffee, feeling slightly happier with her decision to go home and cook a surprise supper for Eva - and to talk to her.

'Great, Sunday 28th of Feb, 2 til 4, here at the barn. Got it, thanks.' Anna ended the call, a big grin lighting up her face. 'She can do it,' she said. Lauren's eyes smiled as she pulled Anna towards her.

'I love you,' Lauren said, closing the space between them with her own beaming smile and determined look.

'We'd best get the invitations out to...' Anna started to say, but Lauren's intensity caused her breath to hitch and her knees to buckle.

Lauren silenced her with hungry lips, her searing dark eyes causing a buzz in the centre of Anna that was of a very different quality to that elicited by the phone call. Lauren's breath was sweet, her touch tender. Anna crumbled at the vibrations building low in her womb, as their tongues played, seduced, and teased.

'Emilie...' Anna tried to speak, gasping for breath.

Lauren ignored her plea, deepening the kiss, forcing a guttural groan as her hands found their way under Anna's skirt, riding up the outside of both her legs. Lauren groaned, reaching between the thin, silky underwear and opening Anna with ease, enjoying the sensation of the soft flesh, the wet heat pulsing through her fingers.

Anna wrapped her arms around Lauren's neck in a near strangle hold, unable to get enough of her. The urgency in the clashing kiss being fuelled by the erotic sensations now filling her. She lifted her leg and wrapped it around Lauren's waist, allowing Lauren to penetrate her with depth. 'Ahhh!' she screamed as the rhythmical movements caused her insides to contract, burn, and explode, sending a spiral of fire through every cell in her body.

Lauren remained inside her until the shuddering ceased, kissing her face tenderly, savouring every part of her. 'I love you,' she said, repeating the words from a moment ago.

'I love you.' Anna's words were vulnerable, but the intensity in her eyes carried such certainty. Leaving no room for doubt, she released Lauren with a satisfied grin.

The boiling of the kettle brought Anna back to earth. She stepped across the kitchen and poured the water carefully into the two waiting cups. She handed the steaming mug to Lauren and placed an arm around her waist, just as a snuffle turned into a more vocal expression of need through the baby monitor. Both women looked at each other and laughed, recognising that just moments earlier that noise would have been an unwelcome intrusion. Now, they stood in each other's arms and watched as Emilie began to kick, her small limbs moving to turn her over.

Lauren placed her mug on the kitchen surface. 'I'll get her,' she said. She washed her hands, gave Anna a warm smile and kissed her on the cheek as she passed, and headed up the stairs two at a time. Anna sighed, feeling the warmth of affection flood her body. She watched Lauren through the monitor, hearing her soft voice coaxing Emilie as she approached the baby and pulling her up into a confident hold. She could see Emilie's arms and legs hook onto Lauren, trusting this woman unconditionally, to take good care of her, which of course, she always did. Lauren had a natural maternal side to her. Anna sipped at her tea as the screen went blank, replaced by the footsteps descending the stairs.

'Who's this?' Lauren was saying as she entered the kitchen, met by Anna, whose eyes were on a happy looking, blurry-eyed Emilie.

'Hello sweet-cheeks,' Anna said, grinning from ear to ear, gaining her daughter's attention instantly. It always delighted her that Emilie's face lit up at the sound and sight of her. Emilie's arms reached out towards her birth mother. Lauren handed her over and Anna placed a kiss on the baby's cheek. She had instantly nicknamed Emilie sweet-cheeks when she first held her in her arms, her chubby red cheeks sticking out on her otherwise pixie-like features. The term of endearment had stuck firmly, with Emilie smiling and giggling in response. 'Are you ready for some lunch?' she asked, not expecting a response. Emilie looked around as if to give one though. They had just started weaning her, introducing her to baby porridge, and Emilie had taken to it like a duck to water.

Lauren had already embarked on preparing the small meal. Like a well-oiled machine and with unspoken rules, they worked together seamlessly. Anna cooed to keep Emilie entertained, and within a few moments a cooling porridge mixture appeared at the table. Anna placed a bib around her fidgeting daughter and sat her in the highchair. She was beginning to grumble with impatience. 'Here we go, sweetheart.' Lauren blew on the food, and presented the spoon to a hungry Emilie, whose tiny mouth grappled with the implement, and its contents, most of which seemed to end up around her face and on her bib.

'Guess what?' Lauren said to Emilie as she continued to feed her. 'You're going to have a spiritual christening,' she said, in a higher pitched, singsong voice, as if that would ensure the words were more easily processed. 'Yes, we are,' she continued, sporting a big grin as she spoke.

Emilie grinned back, the soft food oozing out from between her gums and dropping from her tiny lips. Spying the wet messy substance, landing on the highchair's table, her quizzical hands reached out and started to pat enthusiastically.

'Ahhh!' Lauren groaned then began to laugh, jumping back too late to avoid the light spray landing on her white cotton shirt. Emilie stopped suddenly and held Lauren in a confused gaze. Lauren smiled broadly, 'It's okay sweetheart,' she said, scooping the porridge from the side of Emilie's mouth, before presenting another spoonful. Emilie chuckled and opened her mouth widely at the incoming food.

'Shall I take over while you get changed?' Anna offered.

'You sure?'

'Here.' Anna took the bowl and spoon and nudged Lauren out of her seat. 'Come on sweet-cheeks,' she said with a big smile.

Lauren kissed the top of Anna's head, then Emilie's. 'Right, I'll get changed then shoot into town,' Lauren said, but Anna was lost in Emilie.

'Aaaaammmmm,' Anna said, as the spoon aeroplane headed back towards a giggling Emilie. 'Okay,' she said, when her brain suddenly registered the conversation. Lauren was already at the top of the stairs by then.

3.

Rosa bounded out of the kitchen towards the front door as she heard the key turn in the lock. 'Hey. How was your day?' she beamed. Her smile faltered when she caught sight of Eva, who almost bounced off the doorframe into the open foyer.

'Hey baby,' Eva slurred with a misdirected smile. She reached for Rosa, to pull her close, and tried to place a wet kiss on her lips. Rosa jerked back from the alcoholic fumes and held Eva's swaying body by the shoulders, trying to fix her shifting eyes with her own steady gaze. Eva smiled weakly, unable to focus fully as the object of her vision seemed to move unexpectedly.

'What's happened?' Rosa asked, her stomach roiling at the response her question might provoke in her clearly intoxicated girlfriend.

'Great day,' Eva said, her head swaying with the intensity of the sarcasm in her delivery of the words. Rosa stared quizzically, waiting for the next instalment. Eva bent down, nearly toppled over, pulled her laces undone, and flicked off her brogues. When she stood again she looked pale and started to retch. She pushed past Rosa and dived into the toilet, just making the pan in time, as the contents of lunch resurfaced like a tidal wave.

Rosa sighed and looked to the ceiling, holding back the pain she felt tugging at her heart. Unsure whether to follow Eva and give her the comfort she herself needed, or leave her to her own devices. After brief consideration, she opted for the latter and returned to the kitchen. She continued chopping the vegetables she had started, the tears escaping down her cheeks having nothing to do with the onion in her hand. Raising her head, she stared out the window into the courtyard, hoping for an answer to her prayers. None came. The retching eventually ceased.

She heard the toilet door closing and waited expectantly for Eva to appear in the kitchen. She didn't. She could hear the shower running in the en-suite bathroom, further down the hallway. She tossed the idea round her head. *Should she go and help? Should she intervene?* Without answers, she turned her attention back to the ingredients lined up on the kitchen surface. The evening she had planned was ruined, but even if Eva wasn't up to it, she needed to eat. She heated the oil and started to throw the chicken and vegetables into the wok. The aroma of Thai curry wafting down the hall might entice Eva to the table. Then again, she might be better just sleeping it off.

*

'Hey baby.' The tone was soft, remorseful even. Eva stepped into the kitchen, noting the two place settings and Rosa's empty plate in front of her. Eva's hair straddled her face and stuck up in strange places. She hadn't dried it from the shower and having fallen asleep for a couple of hours it had settled into its own peculiar style.

Rosa couldn't stop the edges of her lips curling up at the sight of the bedraggled woman. Even though she felt hurt and disappointed that the evening she had planned in her mind hadn't materialised, she couldn't help but melt at the sight of Eva, with her longer hair giving her a more defenceless appearance than the harder-looking spikey-style she had when they first met. There was something quite endearing about the vulnerability, Rosa thought as she locked on to Eva's bloodshot eyes.

Eva flicked her hands through her hair and tucked it behind her ear. The fidgety behaviour reminded Rosa of a child needing to apologise but not knowing where to start.

'Hey,' Rosa responded with the tenderness she felt.

'I'm sorry.' Eva's eyes lowered, and she squirmed, unable to face the pain she knew she had inflicted on her girlfriend.

'Want to talk?' Rosa asked softly.

Eva brought her eyes upwards. 'Can we chat tomorrow. I need to sleep.' She looked tired, drained, and her words were still slightly slurred.

'Sure. I've got an early start tomorrow,' Rosa said, rising from the table and removing her plate to the dishwasher. 'You want to eat anything?' she asked, looking over her shoulder.

'No, I don't think my stomach will take it,' Eva said, her hand nursing her belly, trying to raise a coy smile. Rosa held her eyes, seeking answers. Eva sighed deeply, took in a deep breath, and looked her in the eye. 'Mum just threw a few curveballs at me today. I wasn't expecting it, that's all, and I need to adjust. Sorry... I drank too much at lunchtime.' She shrugged, looking every bit the helpless child she was in that moment. 'Can we chat tomorrow... I promise?'

'I'd like that.' Rosa's tone was sterner than she had intended. She would hold Eva to her promise though. 'I'm going to bed now.' If the hollow emptiness in Rosa's eyes bit at Eva, she didn't show it. Rosa turned her back. Her shoulders were beginning to shake as she headed for the stairs.

'Baby,' Eva pleaded, following closely, reaching out for her arm. Turning Rosa to face her.

Rosa shrugged her off and controlled her breathing. 'Tomorrow,' she said, trying to muster the confidence she lacked, and the word that came out was shaky. Eva's shoulders slumped, and her arms weighed heavily by her side. Rosa turned back around, and Eva watched her take the stairs. Eva staggered back into the kitchen to fill a glass of water. *What was she doing?* The question bounced around her fog-filled mind as she picked at the food that had been left on the stove for her. At least half an hour had passed before she too climbed the stairs. She hadn't intended to sleep in the spare room, but that's where she found herself, and, having reconciled that she didn't want to disturb Rosa, that's were she planned to stay.

*

She turned into the warmth, her arm naturally finding its way around the soft smooth waist and hip that presented itself. Her eyes flickered, but didn't open. The faded scent of bergamot and thyme, teasing her senses, both soothed and aroused her. The combination was exquisite, and she wanted to hold onto it for as long as possible. She knew she wasn't dreaming, but she also had no recollection of moving from the spare room into Rosa's bed. Maybe it was after she had been to the toilet, she wondered. Whenever it was, all that mattered was the familiarity of this warm space, next to this woman. This felt safe. This felt right.

The soft groan of pleasure caused Eva's hand to explore further as she moved in closer and started to kiss the back of Rosa's neck. Her scent was intoxicating and the sensual sounds a trigger to her clit, which had started to pulse. Rosa leaned her head back to expose her neck, and turned just enough. Eva kissed her way down to the erect nipple that was awaiting her touch.

Rosa fingered Eva's hair roughly, pulling her closer, begging for more as the tingling sensations continued to drive her lower region into spasms of delight. She bucked under the building heat, the groan emanating from her mouth stifled by Eva's sensual lips. 'Fuck me,' Rosa growled, urgently.

Eva moved swiftly, cupping Rosa between the legs, her

24

palm pressing down, whilst two fingers sought out the warm wet opening and slid effortlessly inside.

'Deeper.'

Rosa's insatiable appetite fuelled Eva's desire. She lowered herself down the bed, inserted a third finger and penetrated deeper, harder, feeling Rosa's delicious softness expanding with every thrust. Rosa groaned with the increasing intensity, as her body assumed Eva's rhythmical movement. Eva moved lower, taking Rosa's clit in her mouth as she continued to fuck her. Her fingers worked slowly and deeply, then faster and shallower - her tongue joining in the dance, taking Rosa to the edge. Eva, sensing the moment just before Rosa came, slowed her pace and teased just enough for Rosa to hold the waves of the orgasm even longer. Savouring the excitement coursing through every nerve in her body, she screamed out. Eva smiled, her confidence boosted by her ability to create such a pleasing response in another woman, and especially in this woman.

'Come here,' Rosa gasped, with a wild intensity that left no room for negotiation. Eva had intended to kiss her way up Rosa's body, but Rosa clearly had other ideas and pulled her up eagerly. Taking her girlfriend's mouth firmly with her own, she flipped Eva onto her back. Eva enjoyed the feeling of submission. She wanted to feel the weight of Rosa on top of her; wanted to feel her inside her. *This... this made everything better*. The fleeting thought was lost in a flash, as Rosa plunged into her, taking her mind into oblivion as the energy built and surged.

It wasn't long after she was spent that Eva drifted into a lazy sleep. And not long after that, Rosa slid from the bed, showered, dressed, and made her way out of the bedroom.

Rosa watched from the doorway, momentarily, enjoying the peaceful rise and fall of Eva's lean body, and the wild hair that concealed her closed eyes. The events of the previous evening seemed so long ago, but even their intimacy hadn't lifted the shadow across her heart. She eased the door shut, trod softly down the stairs, and stepped out into the dark, cold, early morning air.

*

Eva woke suddenly and grabbed for her phone. It was 9am. Disorientated, she focused her eyes on the text, her heart pounding in her chest.

We do need to talk. I'll be back about 4 x

She breathed a sigh of relief, when she realised it was Friday, not Monday, and wondered why she had reacted so badly to the idea of it being 9am on Monday morning. Carine. The woman irked her, and she didn't know why.

She rubbed at her eyes and stretched across the bed. Yes, she needed to explain to Rosa why she had arrived home so drunk. She hoped Rosa would understand; hoped Rosa would forgive her. She allowed the dark memories of the previous evening to slip easily through her mind, preferring instead to linger on the events of the early hours of the morning, and the warm feeling that their intense love making brought with the recollection. She was pulled out of her daydream by the arrival of another text.

Do you fancy going out tonight with Dee and Angie? X

She tapped her response and eased her way out of bed, heading for the shower. She didn't warm to the anaesthetist at all; hadn't liked the look of her since the first time she saw Dee and Rosa at *Le So What*, but she owed it to Rosa to go, and it had been a while since they had both been out on the town together. Now though, she would get on with some work and try to minimise the opportunity for Carine to find fault with her when she showed up on Monday.

4.

'Hello mother. Is everything okay?' Lauren asked as she took the call on her mobile, still wet from having just stepped out of the shower. Even though they were getting on well, Lauren still addressed Valerie with the more formal term. Mum just didn't seem to fit Valerie Vincenti. Valerie rarely called though, and Lauren's concern was reinforced by the distressed voice at the end of the line. Lauren wrapped the towel around her body, ignoring the water trickling down the side of her face, and wedged the phone between her ear and shoulder. She listened.

'The police have been making enquiries.' Valerie blurted in an uncharacteristically shaky voice. 'I'm at the police station now with Henri. I need your help.'

'What?' Lauren's voice rose with concern.

'Papa's death.'

Lauren's heart raced at the words, her sharp intake of breath, silencing Valerie momentarily. She began to pace the bedroom. 'What are you talking about?' Lauren asked. Valerie started sobbing, unable to speak. 'Mother, please, what's happened?' Valerie's sobs eventually trailed into a sniffle. Lauren waited patiently, trying to control the thumping in her own chest.

'Someone has suggested that we assisted Petru,' she managed, before the next wave of sobbing took her over.

'Helped him to commit suicide?'

'Yes.' The simple word was spoken more quietly than the implication of such an allegation warranted.

'Shit.' Lauren paused as she processed the information, suddenly finding answers to unasked questions. 'Did you?' she asked in a tone that was more accusatory than she had intended. Her mother's silence gave her cause for concern. 'Where are you now?' she asked.

'Ajaccio. Can you help us?' Valerie pleaded.

'I'm not a criminal lawyer mother.'

'Please?' Valerie's anxiety came across in a whimper.

'I'll get the next flight I can,' Lauren said, question after question firing through her brain. 'Is Antoine involved in this as well?' she asked. The silence came again. 'Mother.'

'I don't know.'

Fuck. 'Okay. Leave it with me. I'll get there as soon as I can.' The call ended before she removed the phone from her ear. She turned around to face a concerned looking Anna standing in the doorway.

'Everything okay?' Anna asked, registering that the answer was clearly no. She stepped across to Lauren, whose features had shifted from the cheery look of an hour ago into a tight ball of concern. 'Sweetheart, what is it?' she asked, beginning to feel the anxiety swell in her gut.

'I need to go to Corsica as soon as possible, ideally today. Mother and Henri have been taken in for questioning by the police regarding my father's death.'

Anna's eyebrows rose involuntarily as she played with Lauren's words, questioning what she had just heard. 'Jesus. I don't know what to say,' she reflected, searching for evidence in her own mind and finding none. 'I can't even begin to process that,' she admitted, shaking her head. 'Are they saying they killed your dad?' she asked, having dismissed the idea as ridiculous in her own mind.

'I don't know the details. I think they're talking about assisted suicide, which would mean a charge of manslaughter, or...' Anna took a sharp intake of breath. 'Murder,' Lauren finished.

Anna was running her fingers through her hair, trying to make sense of the shocking news. 'How? I don't understand.

He's been buried more than a year.'

'I know. That's what I don't understand.'

'Shall we come with you?' Anna offered.

'No, honestly. Hopefully they'll be released after questioning. I just need to be there, and make sure they get the best representation.' Lauren started to dress.

Anna's face began to crease with the light smile that was forming at the sight of Lauren in her dark blue jeans, light grey shirt and dark grey jacket. Distracted by the warm pulsing sensation that had started to tingle her nerve endings, 'You look hot,' she said, pulling Lauren towards her, and placing a lingering kiss on her lips. Lauren reacted to the touch, a soft moan escaping her, before she gently pulled back. 'I'll check flights,' Anna said, turning away from a lightly flushed Lauren, and heading for the stairs.

'Thanks,' Lauren mumbled. 'I'll pack.'

*

'You still okay for tonight?' Dee asked, putting on her coat as she exited the hospital building. 'You've been… quiet, all day. It's not like you and I'm worried,' she said, holding Rosa's arm as if she wanted to shake her back into her old self.

Rosa pulled her friend into a hug. 'I'm fine, honestly. Just got a lot on my mind at the moment, but yes, we'll see you at Girleze about 9.' Her smile was tired, but it was a genuine smile nonetheless.

Dee clasped Rosa's face in both hands with tenderness. Staring into her eyes, 'Good,' she said. 'Let's go let off some steam.' She pulled Rosa in and kissed her on the cheek. Rosa nudged her in the side as they stepped out from the sheltered area into the heavy rain. Quickening their pace, they dived into the Metro, threw a hug, and then headed in opposite directions.

As Rosa approached the gated entrance to her town house, her heart pounded heavily in her chest. It wasn't a feeling she enjoyed, and especially in association with her home. She was starting to wonder if she were paranoid, worrying what state she would find Eva in and whether her girlfriend would be sober enough to have a sensible conversation. But then she questioned whether she was being too harsh. Their relationship had taken off quickly. Their lovemaking was always intensely intimate, yet outside of that Eva more often than not seemed distant, cold even. Something wasn't right, but she didn't know what that something was. As she turned the key in the lock and eased the door open, she could hear Adele blasting out *Someone Like You* over the buzzing of the vacuum cleaner. She smiled at the idea of Eva cleaning, and softened a little at the homely gesture. The tension eased in her shoulders, and she released a deep breath as she entered the house.

Eva didn't hear the soft pad of Rosa's deck shoes as she approached, and jumped out of her skin as she turned into her path, nearly taking her out with the wildly swinging vacuum hose. She stopped in her tracks, holding her chest with her hand and switched off the noise. 'Hi.' She smiled, with something between remorse and affection in her eyes.

'Hi,' Rosa responded, every part of her warming to Eva in her black Lycra shorts and white string vest. The sports gear accentuated her lithe, firm, figure. She eyed her slowly from top to toe, involuntarily biting down on her lower lip, before chastising herself at her body's betrayal of her mind's concerns.

'Sorry, I've been to the gym. Thought I'd clean while I'm still grubby. I need a shower though,' Eva said, noting her sweaty body, sniffing at an armpit, and pulling her nose up at the odour. 'I'll finish up, shower, and then we can have that chat,' she said.

Rosa smiled. In that moment, she wanted to pull Eva into her arms and hold her tightly, but she refrained, allowing Eva the space to finish with the deadly machine. The noise pierced her thoughts and she headed to the bedroom to shower and change.

Rosa stood under the hot water, enjoying the refreshing feeling of the scented soap on her skin, wiping away the chemical aroma from her busy day. She couldn't stop the image of Eva; the shorts she wanted to remove from her, the vest she wanted to explore beneath. And yet she also conveyed a sense of openness and innocence that drew Rosa in, in a way that no other lover ever had. The light touch of the fingers tracing down her back caused her to gasp, but the tingling waves shooting down her spine took her attention and she turned instantly into Eva's arms. Eva's mouth was on hers before she cleared the water from her eyes, which she allowed to stay closed. The exquisite sensation fired through every cell in her body, and rendered her thoughts to a soup of explicit desire and need. Any concerns drifted with the draining water, washed away in the moment.

Eva pulled away gently and Rosa opened her eyes. Their darkened irises connected, and the intensity burned deeply in Rosa's sex. 'I'm sorry,' Eva said, her voice filled with something Rosa couldn't define.

Rosa pulled back, a sudden feeling of doubt punching her in the gut. *Was Eva about to end their relationship?* Anxiety caused her pulse to race, and not in a good way. She reached up and pushed Eva's hair behind her ear, trying to capture her eyes, which were scanning the floor, allowing the water to trickle off her nose. Rosa's hands were shaking as she resolved to handle whatever it was Eva was about to throw at her.

'I'm sorry, I've behaved like a jerk,' Eva admitted, slowly raising her head to face Rosa, noting the depth of sadness in her girlfriend's eyes. The tears were already making their way down her cheeks and Eva brushed them away with her thumbs. She pulled Rosa into her chest and held her tightly for some time, with no words passing between them and the water gently cascading over their bodies. 'I need you,' Eva said, eventually. Rosa tried to back off to give Eva the space to speak, but Eva tugged her closer. 'Please, stay here. I want to talk to you here. I feel safe. Please hold me while I explain.' Rosa's hands moved around Eva's neck and waist, holding her close, encouraging Eva to rest her head into her neck. Eva's soft breath on Rosa's ear made way for the words she needed to share.

*

Lauren stepped out of the aircraft, instantly noticing the light breeze. She shivered, but not because it was cold. Darkness had descended already, but there was still a slight warmth in the Corsican air, that was absent in Paris at this time of year. She walked towards the arrivals lounge feeling the weight of desperation in every step. She spotted Antoine before he caught sight of her, and couldn't help but notice his uncharacteristically slumped posture and tight-looking features. She almost didn't recognise him. He looked unexpectedly older. He smiled briefly as he acknowledged her, but his eyes betrayed the fact that his world had been turned upside down in the last twenty-four hours. At least he wasn't under arrest Lauren thought, as she approached him with her arms outstretched.

'Lauren. You look very well. Paris must be suiting you,' he said, his tone still carrying a gentle sing-song resonance, even though his energy seemed flat; clearly challenged by the recent change in circumstances. She pulled him into her arms, drawing a deep sigh from him, before he withdrew and reached for her hand luggage.

'How are you?' she asked, knowing the answer, as they walked towards the car park and climbed into the Outlander. Antoine fired up the car and started to drive.

'Fine,' he responded with his attention on the road, but he wasn't, not really.

'Chico?'

'He's fine... coping,' he added, with a tilt of his head as the impact on their relationship flashed across his mind. 'I've been asked to go in on Monday to assist them with their enquiries,' he said, his tone sombre. 'Valerie was released an hour ago, but they are still questioning Henri. She should be arriving home shortly,' he added.

Lauren puffed out a breath. 'I don't understand how this has come about,' she said.

'It's a vendetta.'

Lauren took her eyes off the road and turned to face Antoine as he spoke. Her attention fixed on the slight twitch in his right cheek just below his eye. 'Vendetta?' she quizzed.

Antoine shrugged as if to say, what else? He turned to face her briefly, before turning his eyes back to the road, as he started to speak. 'I was with Petru the night before he took his own life. We had a candlelit supper together, drank wine and talked... almost until dawn. He didn't want to go to bed that night, probably because he knew it would be his last.' He shrugged at his conclusion. 'He didn't share that with me of course. We had talked about going somewhere, so he could do it legally, but I think he'd played us all along with that line, so we didn't look too closely. So he could execute his plan without us really being aware of it. Henri and Valerie knew he wanted control of the end; we all did.' He smirked. 'Like he wanted control of everything, eh?' He turned again to face Lauren, a warm smile on his face. Lauren's face twitched in response.

'Take me to the police station please. I need to speak to Henri.'

Antoine nodded, and drove.

*

Lauren stood at the desk, waiting, patiently. The duty officer had been less than impressed with her request to speak to Henri, but she had positioned herself as his lawyer and through a fine display of seduction and intellect managed to get him to agree to a brief visit. Standing, still waiting, she felt like a criminal about to be charged, and that wasn't a pleasant feeling.

'Follow me please.' The young male officer, with his highly pressed uniform and military appearance opened the door into a short corridor, off which were a number of interview rooms. He stopped at room number 3 and opened the door for Lauren to enter. Lauren glanced around the room briefly, spotting another officer sat in the corner of the room and Henri who was sitting at a seat behind a metal table that had no need to be bolted to the floor.

'Lauren.' His voice lacked its jovial resonance, and his expression revealed the tension in his mind. He looked older... and very worried.

'Hi Henri.' Lauren's compassionate tone contrasted her body's sense of urgency as she rushed to take the seat opposite him, nodding briefly towards the two officers in tow. Both left the room. She looked directly into Henri's eyes. He couldn't hold her gaze and dropped his head before he started to speak.

'Many years ago, I was working in London,' he started. 'I had a cancer patient. Well, she... Karen White was her name, and she wanted to end her own life. She was only thirty-five years old, with three children under ten years of age. She couldn't stand the thought of them seeing her dying. She asked me to help her. I was younger, full of idealism... the idea of

34

personal choice... euthanasia, blah, blah.' His tone bordered on cynicism at his own, naïve, ideological outlook back then. 'Anyway, it's a long story but, thankfully, when her case went to court I was acquitted.' Lauren listened. 'I didn't help Petru,' he added, his eyes meeting Lauren's with certainty. Lauren nodded.

'Go on,' she said.

'I don't know anything else, but the police seem to be linking my past with this current situation,' he said, raising his shoulders, and letting them drop. He already looked defeated. 'They have a statement from someone.'

Lauren winced, and her chest constricted, but she tried not to show her concern regarding the potential severity of the situation. 'Okay. Well there's nothing much we can do right now. I'll see what I can find out,' she said, with as reassuring a smile as she could muster.

'Thank you Lauren,' Henri's eyes tried to reflect his gratitude, but what came across more convincingly was his deepest fear. Lauren nodded, and the door opened as she rose from the table. She glanced at the two officers re-entering the room, and nodded her head to confirm that she had finished.

'Try not to worry,' she said, looking back over her shoulder briefly before walking towards the door. The old doctor smiled weakly and muttered something inaudible.

'Right, let's go home,' she said as she stepped into the car and slammed the door shut. Antoine didn't need to ask how it went.

5.

'Well good evening ladies.' The chirpy redhead behind the bar greeted Eva and Rosa with a beaming smile. 'Sancerre?' she asked, making a move to serve the drinks before the two women confirmed their order.

Rosa pulled Eva into her side. The arm around her waist wasn't a possessive gesture in any way; it simply reflected the closeness she felt following their earlier conversation in the shower. And whilst they hadn't addressed the topic of Eva's nightmares, they had at least talked about the fact that Rowena had decided to retire and recruit a new business manager. It was a start, and Rosa was well aware that this process for Eva might be about taking small steps. Eva was a closed book, so any discussion was a bonus. She slipped her fingers down the inside of Eva's hip bone, making her jump reflexively. 'Thanks Ali,' she responded belatedly, with a light laugh as Eva squirmed at her touch.

'You guys seem in good form tonight. What's the occasion?' Ali asked as she poured.

'No occasion,' Eva responded quickly, smiling through her eyes, releasing herself from Rosa's exploring fingers. She reached into her jeans pocket and pulled out a twenty-euro note, handing it over as Ali placed the large glasses of wine on the bar. Eva held up her hand to the redhead as she took the money.

'Thanks,' Ali said, ringing the till and placing the change into a jar on the side.

Both women picked up their wine, turned to face each other, and sipped simultaneously, their eyes locking over the rim of the glass. Eva felt the sudden rush of heat dive south and settle low, below her gut. Rosa's cheeks came alive, as if she had witnessed the energetic journey with her own eyes.

'Cheers' she said, holding up her glass. Eva clinked the offered glass, her eyes never leaving Rosa's, the depth of her gaze turning Rosa's stomach inside out.

'Hello you two.' The voice came from behind Eva, but there was no mistaking the tone, or its provenance. Eva stiffened, the arousal of moments ago deserting her instantly, leaving behind a gaping hole and a disconcerted feeling in its wake. If Rosa noticed the change, she didn't let on.

'Hi.' Rosa's eyes dropped from Eva as she stepped in and hugged both approaching women briefly, before moving away from the bar.

'Hi,' Eva responded, reeling at the intrusion. There was no doubting the more reticent response to her presence from the anaesthetist, but her partner, Angie, stepped up and pulled Eva into a generous hug.

'Ignore her,' Angie whispered into her ear. 'She's feeling grumpy.'

Eva's eyebrows raised just a touch, before she turned and followed Rosa, who had spotted a vacant table and was on a mission to claim it before someone else did. Eva didn't believe Angie, but then truth be told, she didn't much care what Dee thought either. What she liked even less was the feeling she had in her gut around the woman. A feeling that told her she was both judged negatively, and being watched. It reminded her of the feeling she had around Carine. But, the feeling around Carine was a bit more complex and harder to define. Dee hated her and made no bones about it. She swallowed hard already wanting to go home. She felt on the edge of fucking up, and she knew that if she did someone would be gunning for her, someone by the name of Dee Prongue. She took a long swig of the smooth wine before placing her glass on the table and sliding into the seat on the inside of Rosa, facing Dee. *It couldn't get any worse, could it?* She focused her attention on Angie, unwilling to make eye contact with the protective anaesthetist. Rosa's hand was warm against her own which was now clammy.

'You okay?' Rosa asked with a look of concern.

'Sure,' Eva responded, trying to hide her discomfort, but the shutters were already up and they both knew it. Eva squeezed Rosa's hand before releasing it and reached for her glass, downing its contents. *It was going to be a long night*, she thought.

*

'I need the bathroom.' They had been sitting for a couple of hours, and Eva needed some space from the medical conversation that had ensued. Angie seemed quite up on their 'doctor-speak', but she and Rosa had never really had deep discussions about their work. Rosa eased out of the bench seat allowing Eva out, and teased her with her body as Eva pressed up close to pass by. Eva planted a chaste kiss on her lips, but her smile lacked any real depth. Rosa's worried look didn't go unnoticed by Dee as she seated herself again.

'What did I miss?' Rosa asked, trying to divert Dee's attention back to the chat.

Eva made her way across the bar to the ladies' room. Being away from the table had eased the feeling of pressure that had been steadily building in her chest. There were a couple of faces she recognised from previous visits and she nodded, acknowledging a familiar couple, but didn't venture to speak to them. The toilets were occupied, nothing new there, so she stood waiting, her attention suddenly directed to the text that had just appeared on her phone.

Hey, Emilie wants to see her aunty x

Eva smiled at the attached image of Emilie's face covered in food. The warm feeling that enveloped her immediately softened the tension in her neck. She studied the picture. Emilie looked the spitting image of Lauren. She wondered what it would be like; loving someone so much that you wanted to create a life together. She wondered briefly if Rosa would ever be that person to her. She had never thought about having children and an impression of the idea of her holding a baby caused a shiver to pass down her spine. She rubbed at her shoulders and tried to release a breath through the tension in her chest.

Hey, sometime soon x

She needed to catch up with Anna, having neglected her over the past months in favour of spending time with Rosa. She promised herself to visit them soon. Maybe Rosa and she could go together. The clicking sound drew her out of her thoughts as a woman exited one of the cubicles. She jumped into the space before the toilet door automatically closed, flicked the lock, pulled the lid down and sat on the toilet seat. She would pee in a minute. She flicked through Facebook and smiled at the Friday night antics that had already been posted. She jumped at the pounding on the door, unsure of how long she had been browsing.

'You coming out of there tonight?' an unfamiliar, deep voice barked.

Fucking impatient. She jumped up, pocketed her phone, flicked open the door and walked to the washbasin. She hadn't even peed and now she felt like she might need one soon, but she couldn't face getting back into a queue of people, for whom she had been the subject of an eviction. Her cheeks burned, and she coughed to clear her throat as she exited the bathroom and searched out the bar. She would get another round of drinks in.

Still pondering the idea of seeing Anna sometime, she placed the drinks on the table. 'Here goes.' She smiled warmly at the three quizzical faces, aware of the burning sensation caused by the simple sight of Rosa, and her embarrassment at the length of time she had been away from the table.

Rosa stood again to allow Eva to sit. 'Thanks for the drinks,' she whispered into Eva's ear as she passed, biting down on her earlobe. The seductive move hit the spot instantly and Eva's already flushed look darkened as goose bumps travelled down her back. She wanted out of the bar.

'Cute,' Angie commented, her doe eyes switching between Rosa and Eva, oblivious to Dee's dubious glare.

'Cheers,' Dee responded, reaching for the drinks, and placing them in front of their owners. She held up her beer in a toasting gesture, before taking a swig from the bottle.

Eva sat and leaned into Rosa. 'What did I miss?' she asked, repeating Rosa's earlier statement, not really needing an answer. 'I want to take you to bed,' she whispered into Rosa's ear, her breath teasing where it touched. 'Let's finish this and go?' She pulled away, instantly missing Rosa's scent. The fire in Rosa's eyes lingered in Eva's sex. She picked up her drink and took a long steady gulp.

Rosa groaned under her breath and sipped at her wine. She needed the throbbing sensation pulsing through her clit satiated, and that wasn't going to happen sitting opposite her best friend drinking wine. 'Right, I need to make a move, I've got work to catch up on,' she lied. The three women's smiles played out like a Mexican wave at a rugby match. 'What?' She couldn't help the grin taking over her face as she stood, pulling Eva up with her. 'Much as I love you guys, I've got better things to be doing,' she added. 'And... for the record... I do have work to do, but I might leave that until tomorrow.' She pointed at Dee as if to say, *don't start.* Dee grabbed the pokey finger and pulled herself up to stand, enjoying the tease. 'Enjoy your evening,' Rosa said, grabbing Eva's hand.

'Sweet dreams,' Dee said, sarcastically. Rosa frowned at her, and walked Eva through the bar to the exit. Dee was shaking her head and her face had contorted, reflecting her inner turmoil with her friend's relationship.

'You worry too much.' Angie said, wiping her thumb tenderly across the frown lines on Dee's forehead. She could feel the tension in her lover and her touch did nothing to release it.

'Maybe,' was all Dee could say, lost in thought. She flicked her attention back to her girlfriend and smiled. 'Right, home or party?' she asked.

Angie eyed her momentarily. 'Party,' she said with a slightly wicked smile.

*

Eva hopped from foot to foot as Rosa tapped in the key combination to the gated entrance and waited for a space wide enough to pass through. The winter chill had descended quickly as the night had progressed and she was shivering. But her trembling had as much to do with the promise, as it did the reality of the cold, damp, weather. She wanted to slow things down though. She took Rosa's hand as they walked the short distance to what had quickly become *their* front door. As Rosa reached to put the key in the lock, Eva turned her around and stopped her.

'You are gorgeous,' Eva said. She closed the gap between them, leaned into Rosa and kissed her, lightly, tenderly. Her lips were warm, inviting, and Eva could sense the urgency they both shared. Still, she wanted to slow things down. Savour the moment. Connect with Rosa, become one with her. As Eva pulled back, Rosa's eyes opened slowly. Her pupils were as dark as the night sky. Eva's breath hitched. What she saw scared the shit out of her, but she needed to be brave.

41

'You look pretty hot yourself,' Rosa croaked, taking Eva's hand in her own and opening the front door. Neither of them noticed the burst of warm air inviting them in, as their mouths clashed hungrily, and their hands worked frantically to remove the impeding articles of clothing.

'Wait, I need a pee,' Eva moaned as she pulled away and shot into the downstairs toilet.

'Do I need to get your bladder checked out?' Rosa laughed, though her body was still tingling from the feeling of Eva's hungry hands on her.

Eva had barely stepped back into the hallway and Rosa was on her naked body. Eva groaned with Rosa's heat as their bodies connected along their length. Warm flesh on warm flesh: soft silky skin on soft silky skin. The urge to dive into Rosa, push her hard against the wall, and fuck her senseless, was driving Eva's hands to work swiftly - *too fast*. She had to consciously pull back; open her eyes to see Rosa. She wanted to be present for Rosa, to be in her mind and body. To please her lover, like she had never taken the time to please any other woman. She wanted this for Rosa. She just didn't know if she had it in her to go there. To go to depths she had never been before. *What would happen if Rosa left her? What then?* She would leave, eventually. They always did. *And what if she had given her heart? Given all of herself, what then?*

Rosa's eyes opened at the subtle shift she had sensed in Eva. Rosa wanted more, and she wanted it now. Physically. She needed Eva fucking her, making her come hard. Holding her close. Consuming her. 'Fuck me Eva, please. I want you now.'

Eva's hands went to work, like a master craftsman, as she coaxed Rosa's breasts with her mouth and tongue. She teased out a willing submission and Rosa's legs struggled to hold her as an electrical charge fired through her cells, lighting every sense in her body. Eva manoeuvred her to the floor carefully, her fingers relentless in their task.

'Ahhh!' Rosa screamed. The breathy screams continued, building in intensity, slowly taking her to the edge. Eva shifted, pressed a thigh between Rosa's legs and allowed the rhythmical pressure to guide them both. She pressed her lips hard against Rosa's, and their tongues danced effortlessly, as they took all they could get - as if it might be for the last time. Eva rode her orgasm in silence; Rosa screamed wildly. As they came down, Eva kissed her lover tenderly on the lips and wiped the tears from her cheeks. They lay on the floor together for some time, no words passing between them. Rosa was the first to rise. She held out her hand. 'Come on, let's go to bed.'

Eva rose into her arms, her lips meeting Rosa's, and her hands cupping her cheeks. She pulled away holding Rosa's stare, knowing the words she really wanted to say wouldn't come. 'Take me to bed,' she said.

*

Lauren paced the living room then stopped and picked up the short glass, downed its contents, and began pacing again. She ran her fingers through her hair and sighed. Valerie sat in the high-backed chair, looking even more fragile than ever. Even the Kir Royale in her glass had hardly been touched. Her deep-set eyes and thinning skin gave her a ghostly appearance, and her demeanour was a long way removed from her confident and controlling nature.

Lauren stopped pacing again and looked directly at her mother. The older Vincenti's eyes were vacant and Lauren felt the void between them. She wished she could make her a promise, but at this point in time, it wasn't looking that good. On a positive note, her mother had been released. Although she had been allowed home, she was potentially subject to further questioning. 'Did you help father?' Lauren asked. She needed to know, even though the timing wasn't right, and she might have been considered insensitive. She needed the truth.

'No.' Valerie's tone held the determination that had gained her a reputation for so many years. 'There must be another way. We have money. We can make this problem go away… and no one is going to prison.' She was physically shaking by the time she had finished speaking her thoughts. Lauren looked at her mother intently. She hadn't answered the question. Or had she?

'Mother, are you okay?' Lauren asked, walking across to the chair, and lowering herself to her knees, addressing her mother face-to-face. 'Mother,' she said softly. Valerie's attention slowly focused on Lauren's mouth, but the words hadn't registered.

'Sorry darling, what did you say?'

'Are you okay?' Lauren asked again, searching her mother's face for something familiar and comforting to hook onto. She held Valerie's ageing hands and squeezed lightly.

'Sorry, yes I'm fine.'

Lauren admired the stoic response, knowing full well this latest incident had knocked her mother sideways. Whether Valerie's main point of concern was for her husband and herself, or whether it was all still about the Vincenti name, she hadn't quite worked out. But whatever it was, it was taking its toll. Lauren squeezed her mother's hands again and Valerie responded this time. The pressure on her own hands gave Lauren some reassurance that her mother wasn't completely consumed by the turn of events.

Valerie reached up and cupped Lauren's face and Lauren turned to kiss the soft palm. 'I love you darling.'

Lauren's eyes burned with the significance of the words she had always longed to hear. 'I know. I love you too,' she said, holding back the tears.

'Thank you for coming so quickly.' Valerie's tone had shifted to one with more assertiveness and focus. 'I didn't ask, how are my darling granddaughter and Anna?' she asked, pushing her own concerns to the back of her mind.

Lauren's heart melted at her mother's sincere interest. Her smile had depth. 'They're fine, awesome in fact.' Lauren could feel her eyes welling up again and pulled away from the intimate moment. 'I'm wondering if they should come over here while we're sorting this little problem out?' Lauren asked. She had posed the question without really giving it much thought, on the basis that the timescales could be longer than she had originally anticipated.

'I'd like that.' Valerie said. Her smile was broad and lit up her eyes.

Lauren straightened. She hadn't expected her mother to agree in that instant, but she was delighted that she had. 'If you're sure?' she asked, giving Valerie the time to adjust and maybe come to a different answer.

'I think it would be wonderful. Take our minds off this ridiculous charade,' she said, her words becoming stronger, as if she had already started to prepare for a fight. 'In fact, why don't you all stay for our first wedding anniversary and Christmas? It's only a few weeks away and I'm sure you've got plenty you could be getting on with at the vineyard.' The smile on Valerie's face had more of a pleading than controlling expression to it, and Lauren felt her head nodding in response.

'I'll text Anna,' she said.

Valerie reached for the tall glass resting on the side table. The tiny bubbles started to rise again as she moved the glass to her lips, and she savoured the sensation on her tongue. 'That's better,' she said. It was unclear to what she was referring. 'Shall we have a snack before bed?' she asked. 'I haven't eaten since lunch and that,' she held up the glass in her hand, 'has just gone straight to my head.'

Lauren sniggered, stood, and reached out to help her mother out of the chair. Valerie linked arms with Lauren until she steadied herself and they walked arm-in-arm into the dining room.

6.

Eva opened the door to her mum's office. She hadn't bothered to stop for donuts, and not because she was already late.

'Good morning Eva.' Carine's words came before Eva could see the tall blonde woman sitting in her mum's chair. She started to roll her eyes then stopped herself, hoping the Parisian hadn't seen her. She couldn't have. She was still on the other side of the door. But, that was the feeling Eva was left with in the presence of Carine Delfosse. She could see through barriers. It was an unnerving feeling that caused her mouth to parch and her mind to go numb.

Eva entered the room, which to all intents and purposes looked the same as it had done when she had left it on Friday afternoon. Except that it wasn't the same. The soft, familiar, energy that had previously filled the director's chair behind the desk had been replaced. And that change came with a sharp sensation that seemed to cut through Eva.

'Morning,' Eva said, in as chirpy a voice as she could muster, trying to ignore her disconcerting physiological response. She made a point of heading straight to the coffee machine - dumping her coat and handbag on the couch as she passed - and popping a pod into the slot, hoping the hiss and gentle aroma would settle the dark feeling sitting in her gut. She had tried not to make eye contact, but Carine's gaze had followed her every step and she couldn't fail but look up and catch her eye. Carine smiled. Eva felt the heat of assessment spread across her chest and up the back of her neck. The woman made her feel naked, and not in a good way, but there was also something else. A sort of power the woman wielded, effortlessly; a seductive force that drew you in.

'I'll have one please.' Carine said. She paused, smiled,

and for a moment Eva thought she noticed something akin to compassion in her eyes.

'Sure, how d' you take it?' Eva grabbed a cup.

'Double espresso, black, two sugars please.' Carine watched Eva attentively as she prepared the coffee. She stood, walked around the desk, and sat on the couch, her weight barely making an impact where Rowena's mark would most certainly have been felt by the leather seat. 'It might be more comfortable here,' she said, patting the cushion to her right.

For the first time since entering the room, Eva noticed the box of donuts on the table and smiled to herself. Perhaps she had misunderstood Carine, after all. She took the two coffees and placed them on the short table in front of the couch.

'That look suits you,' Carine suddenly announced. 'You didn't strike me as the dressy type,' she added, her eyes scanning down to Eva's long legs, lingering at her exposed thighs as the dress rode up her legs when she sat.

Heat invaded Eva's body, her cheeks reddening instantly. This was one of the reasons she didn't normally wear dresses. Whilst she enjoyed the attention other women paid her, a dress made her feel somehow more vulnerable. And that wasn't the most comfortable of sensations. She fidgeted the dress down a fraction, raising a slight chuckle from the Parisian whose eyes hadn't left her since she had entered the room. 'Thank you,' Eva said in a slightly hoarse voice, picking up her cup and sipping at the hot drink. The bitter taste hit the back of her throat and she shuddered. Carine smiled and reached for her coffee, sipping delicately, taking the strong coffee in her stride.

'Right, let's get down to business, shall we?' Eva nodded. 'Donuts. Help yourself,' Carine said, reaching for the box and stealing a chocolate topped one.

Eva looked on in surprise. Judging by the stick-like frame of the woman, and the fact that she had barely touched her lunch during their meeting the previous week, she had assumed nothing more calorific than a lettuce leaf would pass her lips. There was something more reassuring in the fact that she was now munching happily through the sugary, sweet cake. She smiled, comforted by the normality of eating donuts at the office, and dived into the box. 'Where d' you want to start?'

'With you.'

Eva winced, the donut poised on her lips. Her heart skipped a beat. 'What about me?'

'Everything. If I'm going to help you shape up to take over this business, I want to know what makes you tick,' she said, enjoying the power she was exerting a little too much in Eva's view.

Eva froze. The accusation regarding her incompetence was one thing, but she hadn't expected to be having any conversation about herself, and certainly not with this stranger. So, she didn't understand why, in the next moment, her mouth opened, and words spilled out. The donut remained in mid air as she spoke. 'I'm thirty-one years old and I've worked with mum since I left Uni. I studied Graphic Design, got a 2:1 and have worked on a whole load of different projects.'

'No.' Carine stopped her. 'I'm not interested in what you've done. I want to know about you. What makes *you* tick? What you like, what you don't? I know you like women for example, as do I.'

'Umm.' Eva stammered. She hoped the fire she felt inside wasn't showing through her cheeks. Carine's directness and openness sent a pulse down through her, and a warm, wet, sensation pooled between her legs. The woman was gutsy, there was no doubt about it. She knew what she wanted, and it seemed she wouldn't think twice about how to get it either.

'It's all right I don't bite. Let me tell you a bit about myself first.' Carine finished the donut, wiped her hands on a paper napkin, dabbed at her lips and sipped at her coffee. Eva watched the preparation with slight trepidation and just an ounce of amusement, relieved that Carine was willing to share her story first. Eva placed the donut in her mouth and bit down, savouring the sugar on her tongue.

'So, I'm forty-four.'

Eva's eyebrows raised, and she scanned Carine's face and neck. 'Wow.' The word escaped her before she could censor her thoughts.

'Thank you.' Carine responded confidently. Eva's eyes were instantly drawn to the bright white smile aimed at her. 'I was married to a man, until seven years ago. I now live with my partner, Tori. She is forty-two and we met three years ago when I was working on a project she was managing. My parents have both passed on now and I have no siblings. I am focused; some might say pig-headed.' She laughed, and Eva was instantly drawn to the soft lines that shaped her face.

'Well mum can be pretty determined too,' Eva added, with her own warm smile.

'You have a lovely smile,' Carine stated, her eyes lingering on Eva's lips. 'When you're not up your own arse,' she said, but with a lightness in her tone that softened the words.

Eva smiled coyly. 'You noticed.'

'Haha. Errmm… Yes. You're pretty easy to read. And I mean that in a nice way... not to freak you out,' she added, before Eva had the chance to withdraw.

Eva nodded. She'd never come across anyone saying she was easy to read. Even Rosa had never said that to her. *Was she? Maybe.* 'So, what do you see?' she asked, challenging Carine.

'Oooh… Let me see.' Carine leant towards Eva and studied her carefully, holding her eyes intently.

The tingling in Eva's gut expanded. She tried to hold Carine's gaze. She wanted to know what the tall, temptress saw… and then again, she didn't. The unnerving feeling was causing her to sweat, but at the same time she couldn't explain the excitement that was also titillating her senses. 'It's okay, you don't…' she started.

'Shhh…' Carine pressed her index finger to her lips in a move that caused a rush of electricity down Eva's back, the Parisian's eyes continuing to explore the depths of Eva's inner world.

Eva's eyes were suddenly drawn to the thin, shapely lips, delicately but perfectly painted. She cleared her throat and lifted her eyes, instantly locking onto Carine's dark blue, near black, irises. She tried to swallow but couldn't. She wanted to run, but felt rooted to the couch.

'You have pain, a lot of pain. In your past, but it's happening now too. You are frightened to love because you can't deal with being hurt. Am I close?' She asked the question with sincerity. Eva just nodded, the smallest of movements, but enough for Carine to continue. 'There's something missing in your life, but you don't know what that is. Unanswered questions. You can't settle, but you're frightened to find out the answers too. You're frozen in time. So, you drink, have casual sex, and hope it will all go away.'

Eva's jaw dropped, and her eyes widened. 'I don't have casual sex anymore,' she said, defensively, still trying to process the sweeping statements Carine had made, knowing full well that they weren't too far from the truth.

'Well, that's good to know, I guess,' Carine responded, but her smile didn't convey that she was convinced. 'You can be defensive, clearly. You isolate people and your communication sucks.'

'Okay, I get it.' Eva responded, sitting more upright, feeling something between seduced and battered by the turn in the conversation. Carine didn't stop.

'You're also kind and loving, but this rarely comes through because of your fears, and when you really care about people you will move heaven and earth for them. The last bit doesn't happen much though because you never allow yourself to get too close. I think there is a fun-loving person in you too, but again, it's suppressed.'

'Are you some psychic?' Eva retorted.

'No. I just know people. And I like you. But you are nowhere near fulfilling your potential and currently, from what I can see, pissing your life down the proverbial pan. I can spend the next few months pandering to your whim, or we can get it all out in the open now and get you up to scratch quickly. That's down to you. The reality is, unless you own yourself Eva, you'll carry on the same way as you have. It's not rocket science. Any self-help book will tell you the same thing.'

'Fuck,' Eva mumbled under her breath. 'I'm sorry, I didn't realise you'd been employed to be my therapist,' she muttered, beginning to stand.

'Wait.' Carine stood, rising above Eva to her full height of six-feet. 'I'm sorry. I didn't mean to offend you in the slightest. My interest is in getting you to a position to take over this business as quickly as possible.'

'And what about what I want?' Eva spat out the anger that had risen quickly. 'When has anyone ever asked me what I fucking want?' Her eyes burned as the feeling of rage made its presence felt.

Carine looked at her and took a step back, impressed by the passion emanating from the young woman. She had guts after all. 'You're right.' Her tone was bordering on apologetic, and Eva would have put a bet on the fact that apologetic didn't come easily to Carine Delfosse. 'I'm sorry. It's your mum who wants you to take on the business, you're right. What do you want Eva?' Carine asked with genuine interest.

Eva glanced around the office and out the window, and then towards Carine. 'I don't know what I want right now,' she said, in a tone laced with sadness. She pulled her dress down, instantly reminded of her mother's actions with her own skirt whenever she stood from a chair. 'I've got work to do,' she said, her sombre mood touching something deeper within Carine.

'Can we do lunch together?' Carine asked, stopping Eva in her tracks.

Eva was slightly taken aback by the audacity of the woman, intrigued, and irritated at the effect Carine seemed to have on her. 'Tomorrow. I'm going to work from home now. You've got my number if anything urgent comes up.' Eva picked up her coat and handbag and made her way to the door.

Carine didn't stop her, didn't speak. The door clicked, and after a moment of staring at the frosted glass panel in the door she turned towards her desk. Eva fascinated her. Yes, she had stepped over the mark, but she always knew she would. She couldn't help herself. She was like a dog with a bone, and she really wanted to get her teeth into Eva. Though she hadn't expected the athletic blonde - private, secretive almost - to touch her so deeply. Something about Eva resonated with her own past maybe? Perhaps they had a lot in common. She wanted, needed, to find out.

*

Eva walked past a tatty-looking bar on her way to the Metro. The temptation to step inside; craving the dark, solitary space, a single stool at the bar, consumed her momentarily. The place was empty, but for two older men who sat at a table by the window playing cards. *Yes - No.* The two voices battled for supremacy. It took all her will power and more to cross the street and enter the park. The rain had stopped, but she still had to skip around the shallow puddles sitting in the uneven ground. If she'd been wearing her Doc Martins she'd have kicked out her frustration and not cared about getting wet. But in her heels, she couldn't bring herself to let go in that way. She slowed her pace, trying to shake off the tension in her shoulders, all the while reflecting on Carine's words. The truth hurt. *When exactly did she let it all slip away?* She had vowed to change her life many times over the years - all empty promises it seemed. She wanted to kick herself. *Was she going mad?* She didn't know what, or even how to think any more. She tried to breathe deeply, but her chest was too constricted. She started coughing as the cool air caught in her lungs, and couldn't stop.

'You okay?' The gentle voice held clarity and a spark.

Eva looked up. She didn't recognise the face behind the question, and bent double again with the coughing. The hand that pressed on her back made her jump.

'Sorry, I didn't mean to scare you. You looked like you needed some help there.' The woman continued to rub Eva's back, firmly. Eventually the coughing subsided and Eva stood to face the well-meaning stranger. 'Hi,' she said. 'I'm Charlene.' The small-framed woman, with a pixy-cut, mousy-brown hair offered her hand. 'But people call me Charlie,' she added. Her smile was as light as her tone, effortless almost. She looked as if she didn't have a care in the world.

Eva smiled, a pained smile. 'Eva,' she said. 'Thanks for stopping. I'm fine though.'

'You look sad,' she said.

Eva rolled her eyes to herself at the honest remark. She felt sad. She tried another smile, but didn't feel it, and neither did Charlene. 'Really, I'm good. Just taking a walk in the park and got something stuck in my throat.'

'It's horrid when that happens. That sense of panic when you think you might not be able to breathe again.'

Eva spluttered. *What was it with her day?* Firstly, Carine and her assessment of her character, and now a stranger was having a conversation with her that she wouldn't even have with her own mum. 'I hadn't thought of it that way, but thanks for the insight.' Her tone was sarcastic, and Charlene giggled. Eva began to laugh, for reasons she couldn't explain. 'Well it was nice to meet you Charlie. And thanks again for stopping.'

'You're welcome. Hopefully we'll meet each other again. I walk through here every day. It's so... peaceful. Being in nature and in this beautiful city,' she clarified, as her eyes scanned the parkland.

Eva followed her eyes. 'Yes, it is,' she said, and she meant it. 'Do you live near here?' she asked, without really meaning to pursue the conversation.

'Yes, not far. You?'

'A little way out, but I work just over there.' Eva pointed to the tall building with its large glass panelled windows.

'What do you do?'

'I'm a graphic designer, of sorts.' Eva winced as her inadequacies came bounding into her mind's eye. 'You?' she asked.

'I'm a dancer,' she said. Eva grinned. 'What's funny?'

'Nothing. It just explains. You look... light, happy, fun, so it fits with what you do.' Eva winced at her feeble attempt to justify her insight.

'Oh... thank you. I think that was a compliment.' Charlie held out her hand again. 'Well it was nice meeting you Eva, and I hope whatever it was that was stuck in your throat stays unstuck.' She smiled with sincerity and Eva couldn't help but return the smile. 'Maybe you should try dancing too,' she said, handing Eva a leaflet from her pocket. 'My studio is a great place to go on a Thursday evening,' she added, 'if you like salsa that is?'

'Thanks.' Eva looked briefly at the paper in her hand before locking eyes with the cheerful dancer. 'I might just come along some time.' Charlie's hazel eyes sparkled, and Eva was drawn to the sense of joy emanating from them.

'You're welcome. I hope your day improves, by the way,' she said, heading off down the pathway.

'Thanks,' Eva said, but not loud enough to be heard. She pocketed the piece of paper and turned to continue her walk through the park. The sense of emptiness that filled her made her acutely aware that she missed the dancer's jovial presence. As fleeting as it had been, something about the dynamism emanating from Charlie had touched her and without whatever that something was, she felt incomplete. She turned and looked back, but Charlie was nowhere in sight. She followed the path back out the way she had entered the park, crossed the road and stepped into the bar. She needed time to think.

7.

Rosa turned into the cold space between the Egyptian cotton sheet and her snug, warm duvet. Her sleepy mind registered the absence of her girlfriend and her eyes opened abruptly. Her initial concern shifted to frustration as it dawned on her that Eva hadn't returned home yet. The last text she'd had from her had been at 7pm saying it was going to be a late one and not to wait up. She reached out for her phone. It was 2am. Nausea churned in her stomach, as her thoughts turned over a number of scenarios, and none of them were good. Throwing the cover off, she stepped out into the cool air, threw on a robe and padded down the stairs. The light seeping out into the hallway from the living room door caught her attention. Her heart thumped in her chest, and she chastised herself silently at her negative assumption. As she approached the door and turned the handle her chest tightened even further. Opening the door, she could hear the light tapping of fingers on a keyboard.

Eva looked up from the screen. Her eyes were bloodshot and red-rimmed, and she looked tired. 'Hi.' Her voice was soft, tender almost, and Rosa released a deep breath as her heart rate started to slow.

'I was worried,' she said, her hands beginning to tremble with the after effects of the adrenaline rush that had just passed through her, crucifying her body in its path.

Eva stood and moved towards Rosa. She pulled her casually into her body. 'Hey, I'm sorry. I didn't mean to scare you.' Rosa backed off as a wave of fumes hit her. Eva reached out and held her hands. 'Hey baby, please.'

'You've been drinking,' Rosa said. It was an accusation not a statement and the tone levied a hefty blow.

Eva's eyes lowered to the floor and she breathed out sharply, feeling the blood start to rise into her head. 'I went to the bar after work,' she said, extending the truth somewhat and feeling like a chastised child as a result.

'How long have you been back?' Rosa asked. She could tell Eva wasn't drunk, but she certainly wasn't sober either.

'I don't know. What does it matter?' Eva evaded the question, clicking a button on her laptop and closing the lid. 'Come on, let's go to bed,' she said, and moved towards Rosa again.

Rosa flinched. 'You can sleep in the spare room,' she said. 'I can't go on like this Eva.' There were no tears in Rosa's eyes, but the coldness in her glare slammed into Eva's chest. Rosa had never put up a wall between them before and Eva hadn't even considered what that would feel like. Now she knew.

Rosa turned and walked swiftly into the kitchen, poured herself a glass of water and downed it quickly, before walking back past Eva and heading back to her bedroom.

Eva watched, wanting to stop the destruction that was taking place before her eyes, but finding herself fixed to the spot. She flinched at the slamming of the bedroom door, and her eyes scanned the living room as her thoughts raced. The neat, well-designed space offered no comfort. Nothing about it felt familiar, even though she had been living here for the best part of three months now. Whatever it was she sought, she wasn't going to find here.

Rosa tossed and turned, wanting to sleep, but was prevented from doing so by the stream of consciousness whizzing through her mind. A mental switch had just flicked off as she had stared at Eva, and now she felt empty. As if her life had just come crashing down and she now had to remove the rubble brick by brick, not knowing if the next brick would bring the whole house down or be a route out of the devastation. On the one hand, Eva came with too much baggage and Rosa needed to find some respite from the negative feelings that came with being around her. But on the other hand, for some crazy and inexplicable reason, she loved her and wanted to create a life with her.

The buzzing of her phone interrupted the oscillating thoughts that had consumed her for the last two hours. She rubbed at her weary eyes; sticky from the silent tears she must have cried. Easing herself out of her bed she entered the bathroom. Glancing in the bathroom mirror, running her fingers through her hair, she cursed at the puffy bags under her eyes. 'Damn you Eva Adams,' she muttered. She watched the image of herself, allowing the tears to fall down her cheeks, providing some release from the tension behind her eyes. She picked up her toothbrush and squirted the blue and white-stripped paste across the bristles, allowing her mind to be absorbed by the inane task of brushing her teeth. Feeling too tired to direct her thoughts to anything more significant, too exhausted from trying to process her relationship, she stepped robotically into the shower. She dried and dressed in the same trance-like state; the same hollow feeling in her gut that had been with her since the early hours.

The aroma met her halfway down the stairs. The strong smell of coffee. She didn't normally take coffee before leaving for the early shift, but the scent enlivened her senses and drew her into the kitchen.

Eva had poured two mugs and handed one to Rosa as she entered the room. 'Coffee,' she said, stating the obvious.

Rosa took the coffee. Staring, assessing her girlfriend, trying to work out what she felt, she sipped at the hot drink; enjoying its warmth and instant awakening effect. She didn't know what to say, so she said nothing.

Eva's eyes searched Rosa. Needing some feedback: an accusation, an apology, or forgiveness. It didn't matter what, just something other than the silence that now sat between them. 'I'm sorry,' she said eventually, though not really knowing what she was apologising for.

She had continued to work through the night, justifying to herself the fact that she wasn't drunk, and that she had actually got a lot of stuff done since returning from the bar just after midnight. She hadn't even been drinking that much, she had reasoned to herself, though she couldn't remember how much exactly. She had just needed to be on her own, with her thoughts. She hadn't spoken to anyone. Yes, she had downed her fair share of wine and a couple of Cognacs to finish the night. But she'd also eaten lunch, though not supper, and had a couple of coffees throughout the afternoon too. Her head was beginning to pound and her eyes were tired from concentrating all night, but what cut her up the most was the look of devastation on Rosa's face. 'I'm sorry,' she said again.

Rosa continued sipping her coffee, her deep-brown eyes taking stock of Eva. It was the distance created by the stare that scared Eva the most. Rosa placed the near-empty mug onto the kitchen surface. 'Thanks for the coffee.' Turning and walking out of the room, she left Eva standing, staring vacantly.

The next thing Eva heard was the clicking of the front door.

8.

Eva knocked on the dark-blue solid-wood door to her mum's flat. She stood patiently on the doorstep, only partially protected from the heavy rain by the old-fashioned porch. She was sick of the rain already and winter had hardly begun. She shivered, the lack of sleep catching up with her, and knocked again.

'I'm coming.' She sensed the irritation in her mum's voice and huffed to herself. Eva smiled and waved at the eyehole in the door that she imagined her mum to be looking through. The door eventually clicked open.

'Did you check it was me?' she asked.

'Who else would it be?' her mum retorted, making her way back into the kitchen/diner at the back of the house.

'Mum, you should check,' Eva admonished, slowing her pace to keep a short distance between them.

'You want a coffee?' she asked, ignoring Eva's comment.

'Sure. I'll make it.'

'It's already on the go,' she said. 'Sit down.'

Eva sat at the heavy set, oak-wood table and watched her mum intently. 'So, what did the doc say?' she asked.

Rowena turned her head to look at her daughter. 'I'm fine. Got some pills for diabetes but it's not too bad, so with a change in diet, I might even be able to get off them soon. I've lost four pounds already.'

Eva nodded. She wasn't shocked in the slightest about the diabetes, but she also didn't have any idea what that meant with respect to any treatment plan, and in truth she had her own reasons for visiting. 'So, you feeling better then?' she asked.

'Yes. It's hard being off the sugar,' she said, her tone pining for the loss of her go-to treat.

'I'll bet. No more donuts then,' Eva said, teasingly.

'That word shall be banned from any conversation we have until such times as I'm back on track,' Rowena said, only partly joking. Eva could see she needed support, and nodded in agreement. Rowena placed two cups of coffee on the table and took the seat opposite her daughter. It seemed strange to be drinking coffee with no sweet treat, like some big thing they had shared together had been taken from them. They both fidgeted then smiled as it dawned on them they had been thinking the same thing. 'Anyway, how are you?' Rowena asked, breaking their reverie.

'I'm good,' Eva said, less than convincingly, her eyes on the drink moving around in her cup as she stirred in the sugar she had added.

'Right...' Rowena relaxed back into the chair and gazed at her daughter. She loved her so much and it pained her to see her so withdrawn and... unhappy. And whilst she wanted Eva to be able to talk to her, open up to her, she knew from past experience that that would only happen when Eva was ready. 'Do you want to talk?' she asked, mindful of the one-way conversation she had inflicted on Eva the last time they spoke. 'I'm sorry if I came across a bit strong when we had lunch last week,' she said. 'That was more to do with the business, but I'm also worried about you sweetheart.' The genuine concern and tenderness in her voice opened the floodgates and tears started to trail down Eva's cheeks. Rowena reached across the table, taking Eva's hands in her own. 'I love you Eva. You're the most precious thing in my world, and it kills me to see you hurting yourself this way. I've been there before, with your father, and I don't want to see you going down the same path.'

Eva's breathing stopped. Her mind stopped. The tears stopped. Suddenly, inexplicably, a penny had dropped from a serious height. She sat back in the chair, releasing her mum's hands. 'You've never spoken about him,' Eva said. She couldn't bring herself to call him dad or father. The man that had shared their life for a very short time had never been that to her, not that she remembered him in any way.

Rowena breathed in deeply and released the breath slowly. 'No. It was a very long time ago.' Her eyes glazed over, as she delved into the distant memories that had been long since buried, if not forgotten.

'I need to know about him.' Eva said, softly. Since the unexpected line of conversation with Carine on their first morning together in the office, she had pondered what might be missing in her life. Those two words, *your father*, had sparked something in her. An interest? Yes. But, more than that, she was now filled with a strong sense of needing to find out more about the man who had created her. 'Where is he?' she asked.

'I don't know. I don't even know if he's still alive. He was in the Army and the last I knew he was deployed to The Gulf, but that was some time ago now.' Rowena regarded Eva as she processed the information. Whilst Rowena felt nothing towards David Adams, and hadn't done for years, she was beginning to see the impact that his unexplained absence back then might have had on her daughter. 'I'm sorry sweetheart. Perhaps we should have talked about this before now,' she offered.

Eva shrugged. 'Tell me, why did he leave?'

'It was just adult stuff. Adult stupidity. He was a heavy drinker. They all were. It was part of the job, helped him handle the stress, I guess.' Eva nodded. 'That wasn't so bad, but one day he came back really drunk.' She paused, sipped at her coffee. 'He hit me, and I threw him out and told him not to come back. He didn't. You were three, nearly four at the time. I didn't know how I was going to cope without the money coming in, but there was no way I was going to compromise myself, or us, for the sake of having a steady income.' Rowena's face didn't change, her tone remaining matter-of-fact. Eva's eyes were wet when her mum came back out of the trance from which she spoke. 'Hey', she said, softly. She stood and stepped around the table, pulling Eva up out of her seat and into her arms.

Eva sobbed, clinging to Rowena, comforted by their physical contact. 'I feel so small,' Eva said, sniffling into her mum's shoulder.

'Hey, it's okay. It's my fault, and I'm so sorry. I didn't realise the effect not knowing would have on you.' She squeezed her daughter tightly, kissing her head, hoping to take away the sadness and pain and replace it with love.

'I didn't realise either, until just now.' Eva pulled back slightly and looked her mum in the eye. 'I don't even know why I feel this way. I didn't exactly know the man.' She shrugged, unable to reconcile her emotional response, or her need to know more. Something intangible seemed to have gripped her mind and it didn't appear that it was going to rest any time soon. She kissed her mum on the cheek, a kiss that spoke of forgiveness. A tear spilled onto Rowena's face and Eva brushed it away, softly. 'I love you mum.'

'I love you too, sweetheart.' Rowena pulled back gently and brushed at her skirt before sitting back down again. Eva sniggered lightly at the movement, cupped her mum's cheeks, and placed a kiss on her head. 'Now, tell me more about that girlfriend of yours. How is Rosa?' Rowena asked

Eva swallowed hard. Startled by the personal question, she hadn't planned to answer. She didn't really know where to start. Had her mum asked her a couple of weeks ago she would have said she was fine; they were fine. Now though, she didn't have a clear answer. 'Rosa's...' Eva started, her eyes darting around the space, not lingering on anything in particular, and deliberately avoiding her mum.

'Eva?' Rowena pushed gently for an answer.

'Rosa's lovely. It's not her, it's me.' She could feel her hands beginning to shake as she faced the truth. She started pacing the small room.

Rowena wriggled herself back into her seat. 'What about you sweetheart?' Rowena asked tentatively. Eva hesitated to speak, and stopped pacing. Her eyes began to water, and she pinched the bridge of her nose in an attempt to stop the pressure from erupting again. Rowena felt her heart break as she watched. 'I am so sorry,' she said. 'I had no idea.'

'I just feel so lost mum,' Eva said, through the well of emotion that had lodged itself in her throat. 'I just can't seem to...' She struggled to find the words, and turned to stare out of the window. 'You know I always had a thing for Anna?' she blurted.

Rowena looked away from her daughter. She wasn't sure she was ready to hear what Eva might need to say. She cleared her throat. 'I thought you were over her,' she offered, by some way of understanding.

'I was... I am... but I don't think I can take that sort of pain again. I've loved Anna since we were kids. When we left to come to Paris, and left her behind, I thought my world had collapsed...'

'I...' Rowena started.

'No. It's fine. I need to get this off my chest.' Rowena released a long breath, waiting for Eva to continue. 'I was only ten years old, but she was the second person to abandon me. The first was my... father.' Eva turned to face Rowena as she continued. 'I think I remember the night he left.' Rowena's attention piqued. 'At least I remember an argument, the door slamming. I remember the birthday cake and I remember him not being there anymore. I didn't understand it then of course. But I think I've always felt like something's been missing ever since. When Anna came into my life that loneliness disappeared. We played together. She was my best friend; fuck, she was my only friend, and when we left London I felt totally isolated.' She fidgeted her fingers. 'I know there's no logic to explain how I feel... I know what I should do, how I should behave. But that doesn't stop me feeling like shit more days than not. And when I feel like shit, I drink.' She shrugged and reached for her mug from the table, poured another coffee, holding up the pot to her mum who nodded. She filled her mum's mug and returned the pot to its stand.

'Do you love Rosa?' Rowena asked, hoping the question wouldn't make matters worse.

Eva looked up from her mug. 'I think I do. I think that's what scares me most. You know Anna and I had a...' She searched for the words to describe their brief intimate fling, 'a short time together. It wasn't a mistake, but it wasn't the right thing either. I love Anna, but I'm not in love with her and she's not in love with me.'

Rowena sighed, an involuntary release of her relief, that Eva wouldn't be destroying Anna and Lauren's life. She couldn't say she was sorry for Eva because she loved Anna like another daughter, and deep down she had always known that Eva and Anna just didn't go together. She wanted them both to be happy, and in her mind, that wasn't going to happen as a couple. And definitely not since Lauren and Emilie had entered Anna's life.

'I feel so much for Rosa, and it's different from how I felt about Anna. But something stops me from getting really close to her.'

Rowena didn't know what to do with the admission, unsure of the words that might help. 'Is there anything I can do to help?' she asked, after a moment of pondering.

'I don't know. Christ, I don't even know how to help myself,' she said, in a more upbeat and slightly cynical tone. She smiled, somewhere between helplessness and hopeful, and sipped at her coffee.

'What makes you happy? Rowena asked.

Eva studied the question as it reverberated around her mind, finding it strange that she didn't have an answer. She rubbed at her temples and yawned. 'Sorry, I'm tired,' she said. 'Bit of a shit night.'

'I can see that sweetheart. Have you seen yourself in the mirror? You look like you haven't slept in a week. Perhaps you should take a break... find yourself, or something like that.' Eva sniggered. 'You know what I mean.' Rowena flustered, frustrated at her inability to say anything of any use.

'I haven't got time for a break. Remember? I've got your right-hand woman up my ass at the moment,' she said, teasing with a smile.

'How's it going with Carine?'

'Well day one lasted about an hour in the office.' Eva rolled her eyes. 'She's ordered me in for a lunch meeting today.' She rolled her eyes again, but there was also the hint of a sparkle as she continued, 'but it's early days so I'll let you know in another week.'

'She means well, I'm sure,' Rowena said.

Eva wasn't so sure, but she didn't want to worry her mum unnecessarily. 'I'm sure', she said, picking up her phone to check the time. 'And on that note, I'd better get my head in the game and get going.'

Rowena stood, pulling Eva into her arms and holding her tightly. 'You know where I am sweetheart,' she said into her ear.

Eva pulled back and kissed her mum on the cheek. 'I'm sure I'll be fine. It was good to talk, thanks.' She winced as she caught sight of the message coming through on her phone, and held it up for her mum to see.

Don't be late

'See what you've signed me up for?' she said, starting to laugh. Rowena chuckled and ushered her out the door.

'Speak to Rosa,' were the last words she heard before the door closed behind her.

If it's not too late, Eva thought, as she stepped out into the rain.

9.

Eva hopped onto the Metro, shaking off the rain, and took the short ride back into the city. Checking her phone, she broke into a light jog to get to the bistro to meet Carine on time. She was five minutes early, so when she stepped into the warmth and scanned the room her stomach dropped at the sight of the back of the blonde head pondering a menu. There was no mistaking its owner, who turned, as if by virtue of a sixth sense, and smiled at her.

'Hi.' Carine's tone was smooth, kinder than it had been just twenty-four hours ago.

Eva's shoulders dropped. She hadn't realised she'd been carrying tension, but she felt herself relax, with the gentleness in Carine's tone. She smiled and walked towards the table. Carine stood and greeted her with a kiss on the cheek. *She hadn't even done that the first time around*, Eva noted, feeling somewhat confused by the lingering feeling of the woman's lips on her skin. They were softer than she expected, she mused, not that she had ever intended to think about Carine's lips, but apparently her body had considered the point.

Eva cleared her throat, removed her coat and rested it over the back of the chair. 'Hi,' she said, taking the seat opposite Carine, aware that she had been as near as strip-searched by the woman's eyes already. Her stomach was doing somersaults. It was the sensual sensation that she enjoyed: a feeling from which she felt at least some semblance of connection with the world. A feeling that gave her life. She picked up the menu in front of her and studied the options.

'Thanks for meeting me here,' Carine said, then dropped her eyes to read her own menu.

'I didn't think it was an option,' Eva responded, more curtly than she had intended.

'There are always options Eva.' Carine glanced over the menu, locking onto Eva's eyes, a slightly deeper resonance to her voice. 'It's not about what happens in life, it's about what we do as a result of what happens,' she continued, her gaze penetrating, her features emotionless.

'I guess,' Eva retorted. She had heard the phrase more than once in her lifetime, but dismissed it as a load of mumbo jumbo. Tiny lines appeared as Carine's eyes smiled at Eva's flippant response.

'Anyway,' she started, just as the waiter approached. 'What will you have?' she asked.

'Chicken salad, and the house white.' She closed her menu and placed it on the table with vigour.

'I'll have the same,' Carine said, directing her words to the waiter, with a smile that would be sure to have him itching in his pants.

Eva sighed as she watched, flicked her fingers through her hair, and slumped back into her chair. 'Do you always do that?' she asked as the waiter departed.

'What's *that*?' Carine asked, faking innocence. Eva noticed her eyelids flutter slightly as she spoke.

'That,' she said, pointing to Carine's eyes. 'Do you always seduce people when you speak to them?'

Carine started to laugh. 'Don't you?' she countered.

'No,' Eva responded, defensively. This was fast becoming her stock response around the charismatic Parisian and she didn't enjoy it.

'Sure you do. You're a woman. It's what women do naturally.'

'I don't.' Eva said, shaking her head.

'How many women have you taken to bed?' Carine asked, as if trying to make the point.

70

'What's that got to do with anything?'

'How many?'

'I don't know, why?'

'And you did nothing in achieving that right? Nothing to attract or encourage them? Of course you did.'

'That's different,' Eva contended.

Carine sat up in her seat. 'No, it's not Eva. It's about you using your power to get an outcome you want. Worth remembering, because unless you realise that, you can cause some serious damage to other people.' Carine picked up her phone to respond to a text. Eva watched, feeling stunned. Once again, she hadn't expected the line of conversation Carine had taken them down. 'Right, down to business,' Carine said, placing her phone back on the table. 'Do you know how much your mother's business is worth?' Have you seen the figures?'

'No.' Eva's eyes lowered to the paperwork Carine was placing on the table. Eva had never involved herself in the financial side of the business; she'd never been interested.

'Well you need to know. It might help you to decide what you want out of the next thirty-odd years of your life.' Carine's voice had shifted to something more formal, matronly even, and Eva wasn't sure if that was worse than the seductive tone of earlier.

'Right,' Eva rolled her eyes. Carine ignored the insolence and continued. She placed a sheet of paper in front of Eva. 'This is a balance sheet,' she said. 'This number, the one with a lot of numbers before the decimal point,' Eva glared at her and Carine smirked before continuing. 'This number is what the business is worth on paper, probably more if it were sold.'

Eva studied the seven-digit number for a long time, trying to register the significance of it. She wasn't used to considering more than four digits in any transaction she made.

She didn't own a car, but when she had, it had been third or fourth hand and her flat was a gift from her mum for her twenty-first birthday. She felt nothing towards the big number. 'So?' she said.

Carine's eyes closed a fraction and she released a longer breath than normal. 'Two million Euros is a lot of money.' Carine spoke slowly, accentuating each word.

Eva allowed the number to permeate. She couldn't understand how, what appeared to her to be a small operation, had amassed so much wealth. It was a big enough number for her to be unable to relate to it. 'It is,' she said, unsure of where the conversation was heading.

'Eva, this could be yours.'

Eva's gut squeezed tightly as the reality dawned. 'I don't want it,' she said, reacting instinctively to her body's desire to shut down and run.

The waiter returned, and Carine pulled the paper back, slipping it into her briefcase. Eva picked up the carafe of wine and poured them both a glass as their salads were placed in front of them.

'Looks good,' Eva said, as if the last few minute's conversation hadn't happened.

'Think about it Eva.' Carine's eyes had resumed their more seductive stance, and her smile was almost pleading. Eva took a long slug of wine, toyed with it in her mouth and swallowed hard. She didn't quite know what to think about the proposition, but found herself nodding involuntarily. Carine raised her glass. 'Cheers,' she said.

'Cheers,' Eva said, clinking her glass, lost in thought. Bringing the glass to her lips she failed to notice that she had already emptied it.

Carine took a long sip of her own wine, topped up their glasses and picked at her salad. 'There is a networking event I'd like you to attend with me on Friday evening,' she said, not looking up.

Eva prodded a piece of chicken with her fork. She hadn't attended anything of the sort before and the idea of it sent a chill through her. 'I need to check if we've got anything planned.'

'We?' Carine asked.

'My girlfriend and I,' Eva responded, feeling less than confident about using a term that could be an ex- by the time she got home.

'I didn't realise,' Carine said, with a devilish spark in her eyes. 'Tell me more.' She was starting to tuck into her salad, and Eva followed suit.

'Her name's Rosa and she's a surgeon at the *Américain de Paris*. She's originally from Corsica, and we've been together about six months now.'

'Rosa.' Carine rolled the name off her tongue. 'Are you in love with her?' she asked, watching Eva's response carefully.

Eva began coughing as the chicken caught in her throat. Intimate conversations weren't her strong point, but it seemed in the last few hours she'd bared her soul more than she had in a lifetime. She was feeling raw, exposed, and had no desire to share any more of herself, and especially not with this woman and not about her girlfriend. 'I think that's a conversation for another time,' she said, surprising herself at standing her ground.

'Of course, sorry,' Carine apologised, whilst prising Eva apart with her gaze.

Eva winced, unable to stop the sensitive parts of her body responding to Carine's intensity. She picked up her glass in an attempt to numb her senses. 'Did you get the chance to look at the work I sent across this morning?' she asked, changing the topic.

'Yes. We can pick that up back at the office, if that's okay with you. I'd hate to spoil a good lunch.'

Eva couldn't tell if the smirk was intended to be humorous, or if Carine was being facetious, so she didn't respond to the potentially sarcastic comment and carried on eating in silence. She would find out soon enough what Carine thought of her work. That thought stuck in her throat, along with the chicken she was finding hard to swallow. She took a long swig of her wine.

*

Lauren leaned against the eucalyptus tree, taking in the rising mist across the valley, sipping at her now tepid coffee. Two fresh white roses lay on Petru's grave, but it was her sister's grave drawing her attention. The small plot was well tended; all the family graves were. She crouched down, pressed her fingers to the inscription on the cold stone, and felt the tears warm her cheeks. *Hey sis,* she said to herself. *I miss you.* She looked skyward to stem the flow; to try to take control of her irrational response, then, reminded herself of the words her therapist had imparted to her time and time again. *Allow yourself to feel Lauren. Don't be afraid of the sadness, it's a good thing, and always know it will pass.* She hadn't realised until recently how much she had missed Corry: not having her in her life, not growing up together, sharing, supporting, caring. She'd never given her sister's resting place any thought until now. Knowing - accepting, owning - the fact that her small body lay here, never having the chance to grow old. The thought ripped her heart into pieces.

Impressions of Emilie stole her attention momentarily and a wave of anxiety caused her to suddenly rise from the grave. She needed to keep Emilie safe at all costs. If anything happened to her, it would surely kill her. The fiercely protective streak energised her instantly, bringing her attention into sharp focus. She threw the remains of her coffee onto the damp grass and walked back up to the house. The comforting warmth as she entered the living room tempered the fire that had roused her, and she relaxed a little.

'Mother...' Lauren paused. Valerie looked up from the armchair. Henri looked over his newspaper, from his place on the couch. He had been released, pending further investigation and had been requested not to travel until further enquires had been made. 'Do you think Phillipe could have anything to do with this?' Lauren asked.

Valerie's features drained. Her brother's name hadn't been raised in as many years as she had been married, and even before. The bile rose in her throat and she swallowed hard to prevent herself from choking. 'Why?' The question was reflective. 'Why would he be involved?' she asked, into the room.

'I don't know.' Lauren pondered. She didn't know, but she couldn't think of any of their friends or neighbours who might have done such a thing. But like her mother, she couldn't think why Phillipe would do something like this either. 'Did he know?' The question was directed towards her mother.

'Did who know what?' Valerie asked, somewhat confused.

'Did Phillipe know about dad and Antoine?' Lauren asked, her intonation deliberate.

Valerie's eyes lowered to her husband. 'What has that got to do with Henri and me?' she asked.

'Maybe this is to do with getting back at you...' Lauren said, following the train of thought Antoine had suggested. 'Did he know dad was unwell?'

'Not that I'm aware,' Valerie responded, pondering the hypothesis and dismissing it instantly. 'But then I wouldn't know. I haven't spoken to Phillipe since before Petru and I married.' She paused, in deep consideration. 'He didn't want me to marry Petru,' she said, looking straight at Lauren.

'Why?'

'I don't rightly know. Money. I always thought it was about money,' she said.

Lauren raised her eyebrows. 'Maybe,' she said, not altogether convinced.

*

Eva struggled her way through the front door, trying hard not to crush the large bouquet of fragrant flowers that had cost her a fortune. She wasn't used to buying women flowers, but reasoned that she needed to pull out all the stops after the way the morning had begun. Fighting exhaustion had been made easier with the boozy lunch, but now she was beginning to feel more than a bit jaded. She hadn't expected Rosa to be in bed already. It was only 8.30. She pondered the idea of surprising her versus letting her sleep, and couldn't decide what to do for the better. She flicked on the hall light; back heeled the door to close, and stepped into the kitchen to offload the flowers. She wandered through to the dining room. The place was in darkness. Rosa hadn't texted her all day, which wasn't unusual if she were busy with surgery, but she would normally have heard from her by late evening. Eva's enthusiasm was instantly dampened by the sight of a piece of paper on the dining room table. She picked it up tentatively, unfolded it, and read the hand-written note.

I'm struggling at work, so I'm staying at Dee's for a couple of nights. We need to talk, but firstly I need to take a break from you. I'm not sure how we move forward Eva. I love you, but I can't keep doing this, and I can't deal with us, and my schedule at the moment. Sorry, I'm off on Friday so we can chat then. Rosa x

Eva slumped into the couch, staring at the flickering note in her hand. Her eyes glassed over. The anxiety in her gut was warring with her need for sleep, and she felt utterly drained and helpless. She picked up her phone and tapped on the keys before making her way to the spare bedroom.

I'm sorry, please come home Rosa x

She could only hope that Rosa would give her another chance.

10.

Anna could see Lauren's distinctive, elegant frame as she approached the airport building. The wave of excitement lighting up her nervous system caused her to instantly blush, giving away her deepest thoughts to anyone who might be looking. She had missed her lover over the last few days, and the sense of reassurance and comfort of being able to touch her again served to enhance the fire coursing through her body as she approached the arrivals hall, with Emilie perched in one arm, the other hand carrying a small holdall.

Lauren's face radiated a mix of pure love and sheer relief. She moved swiftly towards Anna and Emilie and bundled them both into a hug, careful not to crush her smiling daughter. 'Am I pleased to see you,' she said, kissing the top of Emilie's head, and placing a lingering kiss on Anna's lips.

'Me too,' Anna responded as she pulled back from the kiss, her pupils dilated, her body responding to Lauren's touch.

'I've arranged for us to stay in Ajaccio for a couple of nights, with Carla and Francesca. I hope you don't mind. I thought of it last minute and called them on the off-chance. I think mum and Henri could do with a bit of time to themselves.' She was babbling, and Anna silenced her with a kiss.

'Perfect. How is everyone?' she asked, with concern.

'They're doing okay. At least no one's been arrested...yet,' she added, with a wry smile. She let out a deep breath.

'You look like you could do with a massage,' Anna said, watching Lauren trying to stretch out the tension in her shoulders. Lauren smirked; Anna slapped her on the shoulder. 'Later... if you're lucky,' she said, with a wink and a broad grin.

Emilie watched with muted fascination at the displays

of affection, her tiny hand reaching up, finding Lauren's face, and slowly beginning to squeeze.

'Ouch,' Lauren said, jumping back and rubbing at the sore point, teasing her daughter with a tickle. 'So, was mummy not giving you enough attention,' she said, lifting her out of Anna's arms and placing a kiss on her cheek. 'Come on. Let's get into town and get this little tot settled.' She looked back to Emilie, 'So mummy can get herself a massage, eh?' she said, nodding at a disinterested Emilie, who was already seeking Anna's arms. 'Right, I can see who's the favourite here today,' she said, trying hard not to be offended, though feeling the slight jab in her chest at the speedy rejection.

'Come on,' Anna said, making a move towards baggage reclaim. 'Before mummy gets jealous,' she added, nudging Lauren as she picked the holdall off the floor.

Lauren lifted the large red case as it moved around the belt, and wheeled it to the car park.

*

'Hey stranger,' Carla greeted Lauren with a grin. 'Anna, hi.' She leaned in and air-kissed her cheek. 'And how's our little Ems then?' she asked, smiling inanely at the dark, curly-haired infant.

'We're all good,' Lauren responded, greeting Francesca as she approached.

'Come on in.' Carla turned back into the house and they all followed. 'I'm guessing you'll want to get Ems settled first,' she said. 'We've set up a travel cot in your room. Assumed you'd rather have her in with you.'

'Thanks,' Anna said, as Carla showed them to their room and left them to settle.

'See you downstairs when you're ready,' she said, closing the door behind her. Lauren and Anna both breathed out a deep sigh, as if a whirlwind had just ceased spinning, and calmness had descended.

'Shower?' Lauren asked.

'Are you propositioning me?' Anna asked, with a seductive grin. They both looked at their daughter who was wriggling and gurgling on the king size bed. 'Let me get her bottle sorted first.'

Lauren pulled Anna into her arms. Something about the way she held Anna felt different. She felt closer than she had ever felt, and whilst that came with a touch of anxiety, the good feelings outweighed the bad. She cupped Anna's cheeks, rubbed her thumbs tenderly across the soft skin, studying Anna's steel-blue eyes, deliberately. When their lips connected, the fire in Lauren's belly sparked violently. She needed Anna, tonight. Anna's response told her that the feeling was mutual.

*

'So, what's happening in your world?' Carla asked, handing Lauren a glass of wine.

Lauren and Anna's eyes locked.

'Not another baby?' Carla asked, too enthusiastically for Lauren's liking.

'Hell no.' Anna glared at Lauren's dismissal of the possibility. 'I didn't mean that as it sounded,' she said, trying to backtrack. Anna chuckled.

Lauren's features shifted. 'What's happened?' Carla asked, feeling the slight tension, the two women shared.

Lauren explained about the allegation.

'Fuck, Lou. What are you going to do?'

'I need to find out the truth,' Lauren said.

Francesca glanced between Lauren and Carla. 'I have a friend who might be able to help,' she offered. 'She's police, she might be able to find out something.'

'We've got nothing to lose,' Lauren stated. 'Needs to happen quickly though.' Her features tightened.

Francesca shrugged. 'I can't promise anything, but I'll ask her.' Lauren nodded in appreciation and Anna squeezed her hand, aware of the impact the allegation was having on her. They would welcome any help they could get right now.

'Anyway, something smells good,' Lauren said, to try to change the topic.

'Yes, let's eat. I'm sure you need your sleep these days,' Carla said, directing her comment towards Anna.

Anna smiled. 'Yes,' she said, but her eyes were firmly fixed on Lauren and sleep was a long way from her mind.

*

'She'll be fine,' Lauren whispered, as she tiptoed into the room, with Anna running her index finger down her spine, and breathing into the back of her neck. She slowly turned Anna round to face her, closing the door softly behind them. But for the low baby-light in the corner of the room nearest Emilie, the room was pitch black. Lauren's hand moved tentatively, her fingers intertwining with Anna's as she studied her intently, as if for the first time of seeing. The adrenaline pumping through her veins was making it hard for her to make smooth movements with her fingers. The goose bumps were still standing, still tingling from Anna's earlier touch.

Anna couldn't see the depth of fire in Lauren's eyes, yet for such a delicate touch the intensity of their connection rendered her speechless, and wanting. She needed her, and at the same time there was something passing between them now that was so completely different from anything they had experienced together. Something so exquisite it caused her stomach to knot, whilst her heart pounded through her chest, as she reached out to touch Lauren across the short space separating their two bodies. Anna's heart stopped as Lauren raised her hand to delicately trace the fine lines around her eyes, down her to her jaw; tenderly brushing her thumb across her soft, swollen, lips.

Lauren stared in awe, allowing her fingers to explore every feature of the woman she loved, in slow motion. Her heart ached with the depth of feeling she held for the mother of her child. The intensity burned so fiercely she didn't know if she could sustain it. She didn't know how she could give herself so entirely to Anna, aware that at some point in time she would have to cope with the pain of loss, again. The reality cut so deeply that she knew it was already too late. She was so in love with Anna, and there was no way back. Her eyes were locked onto Anna's as she closed the space between them. And as their lips made the slightest contact, she became acutely aware that Anna too was shaking.

Anna received the tender touch of Lauren's mouth, feeling her heart swell with passion, and her focus narrowed. This woman, her lover, her friend, the mother of their daughter, was hers completely. The enormity of the realisation seemed to heighten her sensitivity to Lauren's lips on hers. She bathed luxuriously in the flow of excitement that was tripping through her body, enlivening every cell in its wake.

Lauren moved back to create a short space between them. Taking one button at a time she flipped Anna's shirt open. Her eyes penetrated Anna's as she undressed her. She studied every detail of Anna's reaction, as her fingers undid the bra supporting her still heavy breasts. Delicately, she ran her thumbs across the nipples cupping the beautiful bosom that had given life to their baby, sensing the small bumps rising, and the hitching of Anna's breath.

Anna bit down on her lower lip in response to the sensations coursing through her body, and a low groan, barely audible, escaped her. Lauren closed the space between them and claimed Anna's mouth with such tenderness the sensitivity was both excruciating and wonderful at the same time. Anna jolted. The simple reaction to every nerve ending that was beginning to fire with desire, driving her body to a wonderfully exotic place. She didn't know how much longer she could take the intensity, but she didn't want it to end.

Anna began to move her hands with a sense of urgency, pulling ferociously at Lauren's clothes, peeling them off within seconds. The sensation of Lauren's breasts pressing firmly against hers caused her to shudder and a bolt of lightning shot down her body. In the silence between them, they had spoken to each other at the deepest level of their being. Anna continued to prise off Lauren's jeans and her own until they stood together naked. Exposed, yet absent of vulnerability. Time stopped, in the stillness.

Lauren guided Anna gently backwards until her legs touched the bed. Slowly she lowered her onto the soft mattress, moving her into the middle of the large bed. Exactly where she wanted her. Her fingers traced the centre-line down Anna's body until she reached the hot wet space between her legs. The scent was intoxicating, drawing her down, and she breathed her in as her kisses followed the path down her body. Reaching the source of her temptation, she flipped over the top of Anna to expose her own shaved sex to Anna's waiting mouth.

Anna's tongue was on Lauren instantly, working frantically to satiate her own craving. Like a starved wild animal, raw, base, she consumed her lover's gift. It wasn't enough. It would never be enough.

Lauren buckled under the force of the sparks that fired through her body, zapping her of her strength. She righted herself and took Anna in her mouth, teasing her clit with her tongue before delving into her: devouring her. As Anna penetrated her with her tongue in return, Lauren's silent screams of ecstasy played out through the earthquake that rippled through her body. The aftershocks continued as Lauren took Anna to her own orgasm; both women collapsing, their heart's continuing to beat in unison through the thin layer of skin that separated them.

Moving around to face Anna, Lauren kissed her, tenderly at first, savouring the taste of her merging with her own scent on Anna's lips. Then more urgently as a wave of desire rose again, needing instant gratification. Her hands moved swiftly, and she entered Anna with three fingers, thrusting deeply, and rhythmically.

Anna tried to reach out, to find Lauren's wet heat, but the rising orgasm that now controlled every synapse in her body, stopped her attaining her target, instead drawing her into her inner world of passion and love. In that moment she gave herself completely, savouring every sensation. Lauren took her to a place she had never been before. When she came this time, she couldn't prevent the tears that flowed. She grabbed Lauren as if her life depended on it and pulled her into her chest, holding her firmly until the waves had died down.

Lauren wiped away the tears, kissed Anna's cheeks softly, kissed her neck, and then found her lips with such gentleness that Anna bucked again beneath her. Anna coaxed Lauren to sit astride her, entering her with ease. She would never tire of this feeling. The soft, wet, silky-smooth, sensation on her fingers, enticing them to dance in tune with her lover, until Lauren was spent.

11.

Eva paced up and down as she waited. Rosa had said she would be home just after 9am and it was already 9.20. The tension was turning her stomach inside out. She'd been over the situation again and again since the note, and whilst she accepted she was drinking too much, she still couldn't see why Rosa had felt the need to stay away from her. That hurt, a lot. She jumped to attention at the sound of a key turning in the lock. She couldn't stop the sinking feeling in her stomach, or the weakness in her legs. The expression on Rosa's face nearly floored her, and it took all her strength to take the couple of paces and reach out a hand. She hadn't noticed the dark rings under her lover's eyes before. Even when they had first met, and Rosa had been struggling with the death of a young child patient, she didn't look as pained as she did right now. A swathe of emotion gripped Eva and she threw her arms around the almost lifeless body of her girlfriend.

'Can we talk?' Rosa asked. The voice was familiar, but the tone was beginning to terrify Eva as she became acutely aware that her time with this woman was most likely to come to an end. She hadn't realised before this moment, the impact that reality would have on her. The worst.

'I'm sorry. Yes.' The words came out shakily and she backed off quickly, trying to regain her composure, and giving Rosa the space to lead the next step in the conversation.

'Let's go and sit down. It's been a long week.'

'Sure.' Eva scuttled towards the living room and stood by the couch until Rosa had chosen her seat. They sat at the same time, leaving a short distance between them on the couch.

'I've been thinking,' Rosa started.

Eva held her hands up. 'Please. Please don't kick me

out. I'm sorry. I'll do whatever you want. I'll stop drinking...
I'll...'

Rosa's mouth twitched slightly. She appreciated the gesture. 'I've been thinking about why I react so badly to your drinking,' she said. 'I've asked myself time and time again whether I'm over-reacting... because I care, and I can't just turn that caring off. Sometimes, I wish I could, but I can't.'

Eva lowered her gaze and closed her eyes, knowing the words that were coming next, and hating herself for causing this pain. The burning behind her eyes was reaching an intolerable level and silent tears found their way down her cheeks.

'I know you're in pain,' Rosa continued. 'That much is easy to see. Maybe that's what attracts me to you,' she admitted. 'At least in part?' she added, after a brief pause. 'I feel such a strong pull towards you. I have done since the moment I saw you in the bar.' She chuckled to herself, shaking her head at the memory. But, the sound laced in sadness and possibly regret. 'I'm not used to feeling vulnerable in this way Eva... and you were here.' She looked around the room. 'That night: the night that young girl died. You were here. I let you into my home...' she paused, 'and into my heart. And... I can't get you out of my heart Eva. Lord knows I've spent enough hours trying to work out how I might do that.' She huffed to herself at her vain attempt to rid herself of Eva, when in reality it was the last thing she wanted to happen. Eva's eyes had risen and rested on Rosa as she continued. 'I have no resistance... I feel totally exposed around you, which is why it hurts so much when you isolate yourself. When you withdraw it's like a piece of me dies inside. I know it's about self-protection. I get that. But that doesn't stop me hurting.'

Eva moved until her left knee made contact with Rosa's right thigh. She reached across and took Rosa's hand in her own. Rosa let her. 'I'm so sorry,' she said, and she really did mean it. 'I know I withdraw...' she started speaking, softly, hesitantly. 'I don't know why.' Rosa squeezed the hand in hers, lightly, urging Eva to continue. 'It's so instinctive, I don't even realise I'm doing it. I spoke to mum earlier in the week,' she said, piquing Rosa's interest. 'We talked about my father, not that he felt like a father to me,' she added. 'I was very young. I don't really remember him: just the arguing. He left one day and never came back. Then there was Anna...' she paused. 'We were best friends and then she left me too. Well actually we left, moved to Paris,' she corrected. She looked up, held Rosa's gaze. 'I've always felt abandoned, alone. I guess it's what I'm used to.' She shrugged at what she considered to be an absolute truth.

Rosa rubbed her thumb across the back of Eva's hand. 'The nightmares,' she stated.

'I think so.'

'Do you remember them?' she asked.

'Not really. I'm just left feeling like a child, vulnerable, isolated, and so very scared. When I drink, all that goes away, and I can function again.' Rosa nodded as she processed Eva's world. Eva smiled weakly, Rosa responded. 'Please don't throw me out,' Eva begged.

'I can't,' Rosa said, stroking the side of Eva's face, toying with her hair. Eva made a move towards her, but the press of Rosa's fingers to her lips prevented her making the contact she craved. 'I need you to promise to try,' Rosa said, seeking Eva's eyes for something deeper.

'I promise,' she said, and Rosa wanted to believe her.

Rosa leaned in and kissed her tenderly on the cheek, before standing and pulling Eva up to her feet. 'You need to get to work,' she said. She collected Eva's hand and pressed it to her lips. Thank you,' she said.

Eva squeezed the hand holding hers and then reluctantly released it. The last thing she felt like doing was going to work, but she would be expected and the other last thing she needed was Carine on her back. She groaned and rolled her eyes as she recalled the networking event they were scheduled to attend. 'I'll be back late tonight. We've got an event to attend. I'll pop back early afternoon for a couple of hours, and then how about brunch tomorrow?' she asked.

'Okay.' Rosa's weary tone weighed heavily on Eva. Rosa moved towards her, wrapped her arms around her, and for a brief moment Eva's world felt safe again.

*

'I'd like to nail this proposal before we go out this evening,' Carine stated, noticing Eva's edgy response. 'If that's okay with you, of course?' Her tone didn't seem to leave an option to refuse.

Eva stared at the clock on the wall. 6.10. She wasn't going to get home this side of the networking event. Her face twitched, agonisingly. She picked up her phone from the low table and tapped on the keys, sighing deeply as she pressed the send button. She had promised she would be back for a couple of hours before going out and guessed that failing on her promise wasn't going to go down too well with Rosa. Hell, it wasn't going down too well with her right now either. 'Okay,' she said, feeling more than a little dejected.

Carine reached into the desk draw and pulled out a bottle of whiskey and two glasses. 'Let's lighten the mood, eh? You want some?' The squeaking sound of the corked bottle top was enough to raise a dry smile on Eva's face.

The aperitif was a welcome distraction from the task at hand, and numbed the guilt with a warm glow as the amber liquid hit the back of Eva's throat. 'Nice,' she said, turning her attention back to the screen in front of her.

Carine poured them both another drink. 'Can you

double-check the outcomes we've promised. I think we might be missing something here.'

'Sure'. Eva studied the bullet points. 'I think the numbers are too low,' she offered. 'If we get this campaign right, they could get twice as much interest as this.' She pointed at the screen. 'It's about getting the right sales channels, then maximising the impact.'

Carine's ears pricked, and she sat taller in the chair. Eva fascinated her, amused her, and impressed her. 'So, you do know your stuff,' she said. It was a statement not a question.

Eva smirked. 'This stuff I know.'

'Change it to what you think we can achieve, as long as you also know how we will achieve it. If we over-promise and under-deliver, we'll only do business once, remember.'

Eva grimaced at the words, acutely aware of the fact that she was currently under-delivering on her own promise to Rosa. She glanced at her phone, willing a pardoning text from her girlfriend. None came. Tapping on the keys she amended the document in front of her. An hour and a half had gone by before she looked up again. Just the clicking sound, the occasional deep sigh, the glugging of drinks being poured, and the squeaking of the chair, had filled the space as both women worked. Eva leaned back and rubbed her tired eyes. As she stretched out her stiff neck she was aware of Carine watching her. 'What?' she quizzed.

'Nothing.' Carine responded, her voice slightly broken. Eva could have sworn she had spotted a colour shift in Carine's cheeks, but she ignored the observation. 'We need to get going in a bit. I need to change,' Carine said, her voice back to normal.

'Shit, I've got nothing to change into and it's too late to get home and out again.' Eva looked down at herself in her ripped jeans and oversized jumper.

Carine's eyes glanced over her too, with an altogether different kind of look. 'I don't know,' she said with a tilt of her head. 'You look pretty hot to me. Could come in handy,' she said. It took a few seconds for Eva to register that Carine was joking. 'I've got something you can borrow,' she said in a more serious tone. 'What size shoes are you?'

'Forty.'

'Mine will be too big for you, but Tori's will work though,' she said, looking at Eva's feet.

'Tori?' Eva questioned blankly.

'My partner,' Carine reminded her. She started to put on her coat and reached for her bag. 'Come on, we need to get going.'

'Ah, yes.' The vague memory of Carine mentioning her partner in their earlier conversation was coming back to her. 'Where does she work?' Eva asked, suddenly intrigued to find out more about the Parisian's private life.

'New York.' Carine's response was curt, bordering on dismissive. Eva's eyes widened. She waited for more. 'She works in New York,' Carine stated, becoming more impatient with the questioning than there was call for. 'Now, let's get going.'

'Err, right.' Eva closed her laptop, rose to her feet, and followed Carine, feeling confused by the edgy response she had just received to what she considered a simple question.

'I didn't realise you lived so close,' Eva said, as they turned right at the second street they passed, up a slight slope and right again into a small courtyard that seemed to service a number of flats. Eva felt a slight chill at the thought of this woman being able to virtually see into her mum's office from here. She followed Carine up a short flight of stairs and stopped behind her at a solid oak door. Number 4. Carine swiftly unlocked and entered the flat. Eva stepped into the foyer, taken aback at the size of the property. She would never have guessed from the outside. The entrance hall was almost as big as her entire flat. She scanned the space. The décor was perfectly balanced. The picture on the wall and the sculpture sitting on a plinth by the front door looked like original pieces. It was very chic. Totally Carine.

'This way,' Carine said, jolting Eva out of her appreciation. Carine led the way into a large bedroom with a walk-in dressing room. She flicked through the clothes on the hangers, pausing as she looked from each item to Eva and back again. 'Wear this,' she said, eventually, throwing the flimsy looking dress in her direction, before stepping into a cupboard filled with shoes. She pulled out a pair that matched perfectly with the dress and handed them to Eva. 'Shower's through there,' she pointed. 'We need to be out of here in ten. Can you do that?' she asked, exiting the room with urgency. 'You can leave your own clothes in the bathroom,' she added.

'Sure,' Eva responded, but the door had already shut before the word came out. She walked through to the en-suite, quickly undressed, and stepped into the shower, trying to avoid getting her hair wet. Within a few moments she had stepped out again, dried, and put on the silk chiffon dress and two-inch heels. She stepped out of the room and headed towards the foyer.

Eva's breath hitched in her throat as she caught sight of Carine waiting for her. It wasn't so much the long, black, fitted dress that accentuated her slim figure that caught her eye; it was more the slit up the side of the dress that revealed the extent of her toned legs. Eva swallowed hard. 'You look... stunning,' she said, before she could censor her thoughts.

Carine eyes scanned Eva from top to toe. 'You look pretty hot yourself. Take this.' She threw a matching jacket across to Eva. 'Let's go or we'll be late.' They stepped outside just as the taxi Carine had ordered pulled up. She opened the door for Eva. The devilish smile on her face didn't go unnoticed by Eva's body.

Carine talked for most of the journey, reminding Eva of the rules for the night. The event was being hosted by a local entrepreneur at a small gallery: an avid supporter of *The Arts*, and a bit of a wacko by all accounts, who's intention was to provide local businesses with the potential to connect with agencies, and other resources that might help them promote their work. This was an opportunity for them to identify new clients as well as touching base with a couple of their regulars. 'Got it?' she asked.

'Yes,' Eva responded.

12.

As the two women entered the gallery the sound in the room seemed to stop for a split second. Eva had to work hard to overcome the anxiety buzzing in her stomach, as the eyes in the room turned towards her and Carine. Carine seemed to take it all in her stride, taking two glasses of champagne from the passing waiter, handing one to Eva, before targeting someone she knew and heading straight for them.

Eva's eyes scanned the room; all her senses were telling her to run. She didn't know if she'd ever get used to this type of event, or handle this feeling. She sipped from the glass, wincing as the bubbles hit the back of her throat. It wasn't her favourite drink, but she'd make do. She was still feeling the effects of the whiskey and there was no way she was getting trashed tonight. The promise of brunch with Rosa in the morning brought a smile to her face.

'You look happier.' Eva didn't recognise the voice, but as she turned, she remembered the slight built woman with pixie-cut hair and hazel eyes from the park.

'Hi.' Eva smiled warmly. 'I wouldn't have expected to see you here,' she said, pleasantly surprised to see someone resembling a familiar face.

'Ditto. I'm Charlie,' she said, offering out her hand.

'Yes, I remember. E...'

'Eva, I remember too. What brings you here?'

'Work.' Eva shrugged. 'My mum has an agency that caters for arts based businesses,' she added.

'Is that your mum?' Charlie asked, intimating towards the back of Carine's head.

Eva burst out laughing, drawing a few pairs of eyes, then tried to duck down to avoid being identified. 'Sorry. No, that is definitely not my mum,' she said, still chuckling to herself. Her mum couldn't be more different in almost every way.

Charlie smiled. 'I didn't quite catch her, I assumed...'

'Sorry, I wasn't laughing at you, just that my mum's a lot bigger and about half as tall.' She was exaggerating with her hand to demonstrate, and Charlie chuckled. 'So, what about you?'

'Me?'

'What are you here for?' Eva asked.

Charlie seemed to stumble over words that hadn't yet been articulated, and the colour of her cheeks shifted. 'I'm... the host,' she said. Eva's mouth dropped open and Charlie laughed heartily.

Eva placed her empty flute on the passing tray and picked up two filled glasses. 'Here,' she said, holding one out to Charlie.

'I probably won't get through this one,' Charlie said, holding up her half-full glass. Eva downed one of the glasses and placed it on a low table. 'Wow!' Charlie exclaimed. 'You like a drink,' she said, but there was no judgement in her words. Eva could feel the heat of embarrassment rising to her head, nonetheless.

'What else do you do?' Eva asked, her interest in the younger woman piqued. She wouldn't have described Charlie as a wacko though.

Charlie's easy smile touched Eva and she felt suddenly happy to have the curious woman in her world. Something intangible about Charlie gave her faith in the future. It was inexplicable, but also very real. 'I'm also an energy healer and health freak,' Charlie confessed.

'Oh,' Eva grimaced acknowledging that her level of alcohol consumption was in complete contradiction with the dancer's lifestyle choices. Charlie smiled compassionately at Eva's obvious discomfort.

'It's okay. It's a personal thing for me, others are free to choose how they live,' she said, with sincerity. Somehow, the kindness of her words didn't make Eva feel any better about the habit that was beginning to consume her life. She blushed with the awareness and Charlie placed her hand on Eva's arm. Eva felt instantly calmed by the warm hand and the energy radiating from Charlie into her. She watched as Charlie released a slow breath, noticing a shift in her vision as the room moved into sharp focus.

Carine glided towards Eva, holding every inch of her six-feet in height, and towered over Charlie. 'Hi, I'm Carine,' she said, breaking the spell Charlie held over Eva. Charlie removed her hand from Eva's arm. Eva didn't know whether she felt grateful for the interruption or not. She didn't know what to think about what had just transpired between them, but she hadn't experienced anything like it in her life. She stood, entranced, and feeling puzzled.

'Charlie,' Charlie said, shaking Carine's hand firmly.

'Sorry to interrupt you both,' Carine said, aware that she had imposed on what appeared to be an intense interaction. Her fascination spiked, as did the possessive feeling that rushed to her head. 'Eva, can you make a point of speaking with Mr Dupree at some point. He's the one with the really bad hair,' she said, her eyes pointing at the dark haired, large man, who appeared to be holding court in the far corner of the room.

Eva nodded. 'Sure.'

'Right, I need to mingle.' Carine said. 'We need to seduce a few clients,' she said, more for Eva's benefit than Charlie's' Charlie laughed, and Eva rolled her eyes. 'Catch up later. It was nice meeting you, Charlie,' Carine said, though the fleeting glance told a different story. She took off at pace towards the tall, dark, tanned male beckoning her.

'That's definitely not your mum,' Charlie said. Eva chuckled at her beaming smile. She liked Charlie, a lot.

*

Eva wasn't sure when Charlie had left the event, she'd spotted her from time to time but not for a while, and she had no idea what the time was now. There were only a few hard-core punters left, from what she could see through her increasingly foggy vision. Carine seemed to be on top form, entertaining a group of men. Eva watched as the woman toyed with her adoring audience, puffing up their feathers at the same time as clipping their wings. Carine was impressive to watch. Eva glanced at her phone. No messages. As she looked up, Carine had moved again and was staring directly at her. 'Ready to go?' she asked.

Eva's heart fluttered. Carine looked a million dollars; even better than she did when they had gone out that evening. Eva tried to focus; swayed, then went to speak, but Carine stopped her, brushing her fingers across Eva's lips. The touch was exhilarating, even to her fuzzy mind.

'Shhh,' she said. 'Let's get out of here before Eric over there realises I'm still here.' Her smile was warm, and as she led Eva by the arm, the touch felt tender.

Eva allowed herself to be directed out of the building and into the taxi. She sat, for the short journey, trying to recall the events of the evening. Thoughts of Rosa filled her mind, she felt sick, and then her eyes closed.

'Are you okay,' Carine asked. She wrapped an arm around Eva's neck, allowing her to rest into her shoulder. By the time they arrived at Carine's flat, Eva was asleep. It took every effort to wake her enough to get her out of the car and into the building. 'You can't go anywhere tonight,' Carine said.

Eva mumbled something incomprehensible and Carine helped her onto the dark brown leather couch in her living room.

Leaving her there, she walked to the kitchen and returned with a glass of water. She wandered into another room and came back with a blanket, placing it over Eva, who was now slouched and snoring. Carine removed Eva's shoes, goose bumps rising at the sight of the slender legs and the feel of the taut skin of her toned calf muscles. She released a deep breath, headed to the door, and turned out the light.

*

Eva groaned at the light piercing through her closed eyes, increasing the pain in her head. The faint noise - music - in the background was soothing, but strangely unfamiliar. She tried to turn over and her hands automatically clamped her head to contain the pressure. *How much did she drink?* She could handle a lot, but she hadn't felt this bad in a long time. She tried to move again. Her head spun violently, and nausea struck, causing her to remain motionless. She didn't dare open her eyes, fearful of what she might have done, or where she might find herself. She hadn't realised the groan she'd heard, had come out of her own mouth.

'Morning.' Eva's eyes tried to open, and she groaned again. 'It's okay. Don't wake on my account. You can stay as long as you need to. I've got to go out now, but I'll be back later. Take as long as you need.'

Eva felt the brush of a soft kiss on her forehead, followed by a door clicking closed, and then darkness again. She drifted into a fitful sleep.

*

Eva's eyes opened. Momentarily disorientated, she tried to focus on the room. *Carine's place.* She released a breath and her eyes closed again, until a wave of anxiety caused her to flinch. She sat bolt upright, causing the room to spin, but this time she held her ground until the rotating stopped. *Rosa!* She picked up her phone. It took her eyes a few seconds to register the time. 12.30, and no text. *Fuck, Fuck.* Her heart sank, her stomach roiled. Jumping off the couch, she stared at the clothes she was wearing, the events of the evening coming back to her in slow motion. She wobbled on her feet, focused on the door, and staggered towards it. Exiting the room, she tried to orientate herself. She needed to find her own clothes and go back home: back to Rosa.

As Eva turned the key in the lock, she knew what she faced would rip her heart into small pieces. She also knew she had brought it on herself. Though, in her defence, she hadn't had much choice but to work through until they had gone out to the event. As she opened the door, her breathing felt tight and her heart raced. She followed her instincts and entered the living room.

Rosa looked up from the book in her hands. The red rims around her dark eyes swelled and the tears rolled freely down her cheeks. She dropped the book from her hands and placed them across her face. Unable to stop the sobbing that had consumed her since she had reckoned that Eva wouldn't be coming home.

Eva rushed over to her and knelt in front of her. 'Let me explain,' she said, but the words were empty. Rosa was shaking her head, paralysed in a world of pain.

'No. Eva. Please. I can't take this. Us. There is no us.' Her words punctuated by the sobs, caused Eva to stop in her tracks. 'I need you to leave,' she said. There was no doubting the certainty of Rosa's words, or the pain in her heart.

Eva couldn't breathe as the air in the room spiralled around her, sucking her into a world of darkness. The walls closed in instantly, and the claustrophobic feeling seemed to strangle her, as Rosa's image faded into the distance. 'Please, let me explain.' Eva's words didn't even make Rosa's ears, just an internal plea that had no substance. Eva turned and walked out of the room, her ears buzzing with the reality. She walked up the stairs and packed her clothes and toiletries, descended, and walked slowly, reluctantly, towards the front door. Closing the door softly behind her, she stepped out into the street.

13.

Eva walked into her mum's office, dropped her bag by the couch, and placed a pod in the coffee machine. She never worked at weekends, but she had no desire to go to her empty flat, and couldn't face her mum right now, so work was the only option. The building was quiet. She stood, staring out the large glass window. Ironically the sun was shining, deceptive though, as the temperature outside was cold. The half-empty bottle of whiskey attracted her attention. She grabbed it and uncorked it swiftly. Taking a long swig, she coughed at the hard smack to the back of her throat. She turned, and looked around the room as if to seek answers. Nothing. Another swig: another. Thankfully, the alcohol was dampening her obsessive thoughts, but the hollow feeling in her chest had also expanded. The buzz of her phone jump-started her attention, and for a moment her heart fluttered as she thought of Rosa. As she registered the caller's name, she had an altogether different feeling.

You okay?

Carine's text provided some reassurance that she wasn't alone, but aside from that... She took another swig from the bottle before responding.

Fine

Eva wanted to throw the bottle, but couldn't bring herself to waste its contents.

Eva, I'm worried about you. Where are you?

At the office

Eva slumped into the couch, sipped at the fiery liquid, and wondered how her world had become so fucked up. It was only a short time before the door opened and Carine entered. She moved quietly, sat down on the couch, and reached out for the, now empty bottle, resting in Eva's hands.

'My girlfriend's dumped me,' Eva said, without prompting.

'Oh.' Carine's eyes lowered, focusing on her hands, though her mind was elsewhere. Eva didn't even notice. 'Let me help you home.'

Eva didn't argue. She rose from the seat and started walking towards the door. Carine picked up her bags and followed her out of the building. Eva stood at the curb waiting for the taxi. Carine placed an arm around her waist. 'Thanks,' Eva mumbled.

'Come on,' she said, as she ushered Eva and her bags into the back seat. She waited for Eva to give the directions, and had to nudge her in the side to remind her to speak to the driver.

Eva slumped in the back seat and stared aimlessly out the window, running through her memories of the last few weeks, like a car crash happening in slow motion. The clarity of the landscape, the sharpness the sun had brought to the day, contrasted perfectly with the fog in her mind. She felt numb.

Carine watched in silence as the driver made his way to a building on the other side of town. She paid the taxi driver, pulled Eva and her bags out of the car, and pushed her up the short steps into the building. Eva fiddled with the key to her door, until Carine swiped it off her, thrust the key in the lock and opened it for her. The air was cold and damp, and a musty scent invaded her nostrils. She climbed over the pile of mail on the floor to get to a window in the living room, and opened it. 'Where's the heating switch?' she asked. Eva pointed, and Carine flicked the switch. She checked out the fridge, filled the kettle and set it to boil. 'I'll go get some milk,' she said. 'I won't be long.'

Eva watched the whirlwind of activity going on around her, suspended in the grey-mist of depression that had descended upon her. With the click of the door, she was alone.

Her eyes studied the space as if it was new to her, and she slumped back into the couch, facing the blank screen of her television. She was still there when Carine let herself back into the flat. She vaguely registered the woman's presence but didn't move.

Carine walked straight through to the kitchen and unpacked a couple of bags of provisions. Eva could see Carine from her seat, but didn't tune in to the banging of cupboards and opening and closing of the fridge. Within a moment, Carine was handing her a mug of coffee. If Carine's mouth had been moving, Eva hadn't heard the words. 'I said, are you okay?' Carine asked again.

She seemed kinder, Eva pondered. 'I don't think so,' Eva said. 'I need a drink.'

Carine stood tall. 'I don't think that's going to help. Do you want to talk?' she asked.

'No.' Eva's response was direct and clear. 'Thanks for helping me home,' she said, something in her tone saying that it was time for Carine to leave.

'Right, I'll let you get on...' she paused, assessing Eva's response to being left alone. 'If that's what you want,' she added, when none came.

Eva looked up. Nodded. 'I'll be okay. I'll see you Monday.'

'Right.' Carine stood, dropped the keys on the couch, turned slowly and walked out the door. As the door shut, Eva leaned back into the couch and allowed the tears to fall.

*

Rosa picked up her phone and dialled the English telephone number she knew by heart. 'Hello mother,' she said, before the lump in her throat prevented her from speaking.

'Rosa.' The surprised voice came back. 'Is everything okay?' Brigitte asked, genuinely concerned at the unexpected call and the uncharacteristically timid quality in her daughter's voice.

'Not really,' Rosa responded, unable to contain the sadness in her tone.

'Sweetheart, what is it? Are you ill? Is it work?' she asked, with a sense of urgency. Her daughter's sadness cut through her, causing butterflies to set flight in her stomach.

'I'm not ill and work's fine. It's just…'

The silence down the line, as Rosa paused, was excruciating. 'What is it? Do you need some help? Are you in some kind of trouble?' Brigitte was racking her brain for ideas, so she had something to go on, something for which she could provide a solution. She would take the next flight to Paris if necessary, no questions asked. There was nothing she wouldn't do for her only daughter, and the idea of her being in pain in some way… then the penny dropped. 'Is it Eva?' she asked.

Rosa started sobbing at the mention of Eva's name. 'Yes,' came the muffled response.

'I'm so sorry sweetheart.' Brigitte didn't need to know the details to realise that her daughter's relationship was over. She let out the deep breath that had built inside her with the tension, relieved that the problem wasn't a serious one, at least from a medical perspective. She spoke with kindness, 'I'm really sorry Rosa. I know how you felt about her. I thought you were getting on great together.' She was trying to help but it seemed to be coming out all wrong.

'I did too.'

Brigitte could feel the tug at her own heartstrings. A lover's broken heart could be so painful, or so she had heard. She had either never loved enough or never allowed herself to love in a way that she would suffer such a condition, she pondered. She knew of others who had though. 'I'm so sorry to hear it didn't work sweetheart.' She wanted to say not to worry, that there would be others, but it didn't feel right to do so, so she held her tongue.

'I told her to leave.'

'Oh.' Brigitte's confusion carried down the line.

'It's a long story,' Rosa said, holding back the tears enough to speak.

'Oh, right.'

'I was thinking...' Rosa took in a deep breath before continuing. 'I thought I'd take a break and come to London for a visit.' She waited to see how the words landed. Her mother was so wrapped up in her work and barely took a break herself. She had started working at the Royal Free Hospital more than fifteen-years ago following a messy divorce and was now the head of research into renal medicine. Eric Bartoli, Henri's brother, and Rosa's father, had remained in Corsica, continuing his work as a general practitioner, alongside Henri. To describe her relationship with her father as distant would be an understatement. Rosa had seen more of her uncle Henri in the last few years than she had her father, and she had only seen Henri once, which was at his wedding to Valerie last year.

'That would be lovely. When were you thinking? We're so close to Christmas now, why don't you come then for a few days?' she asked.

Rosa swallowed. She hadn't given Christmas a second thought. She'd been so engrossed in her own work, and the painful demise of her relationship, that it hadn't occurred to her that the holiday season was only a couple of weeks away. She had assumed that other than working every shift necessary, she would have been spending Christmas with Eva. Her eyes welled up as the truth bit her again. 'Yes, I'll check flights, or I may even drive,' she added, favouring the flexibility having her own car would afford her. 'Maybe I'll take a couple of weeks and do some sightseeing,' she said, without thought for the fact that it would be a busy time for her at the hospital. But, then again when wasn't it a busy time? Other than the week off with Eva in the summer, she hadn't taken a proper break for a good number of years. She was warming to the idea of time off: time away from everyone, and everything that might remind her of Eva. She would pull in a few favours and get the time off. 'I'll see what I can sort out at work,' she finally confirmed, cementing the idea in her own mind.

'That's settled then,' Brigitte said, relieved that there was a potential solution, at least in the short term. She had no doubt that her daughter would meet someone just right for her. London was a big city after all, and with a great nightlife. She was sure Rosa would be over Eva by the New Year.

*

'Thanks.' Lauren took the glass of red wine and sat on the bench seat in the open plan kitchen. She swirled the drink slowly around its glass, not that she ever doubted its quality. It was a habit. Enjoying the heat from the Aga and the aroma of freshly baked bread, she sipped the drink, savouring its complex taste, then placed the glass on the table in front of her. 'I didn't realise you liked cooking,' she said, watching as Antoine chopped onions and mushrooms with a deft hand.

He smiled. When he looked up, his eyes hinted at a sparkle. 'It is one of my passions,' he said. 'And here comes another,' he remarked, as the door opened, and a tall, dark, clean-shaven man entered. Shaking off the rain, Chico removed his coat, stepped up to Antoine and kissed him hard on the lips.

Lauren gave them their moment, sipping at the wine in her hand. Chico eventually released Antoine and turned to face her, his youthful, clean-shaven face heightened by his stunning white, perfectly straight, teeth. 'Hello Lauren,' he said, as he moved to greet her, planting a kiss on her cheek. 'How are you?' he asked.

'Good thanks. More's the point, how are you?'

He looked towards Antoine with unmistakable tenderness in his eyes. 'We're fine,' he said. 'I will be glad when all this silly accusation is over,' he added, reaching up and stroking his lover's face. Antoine shrugged him off teasingly, and began to cut up the whole chicken that had been resting on the chopping board, placing each piece in the pan in which the onions were already sizzling. 'Smells great,' Chico said, before pouring himself a glass of wine. He, too, swirled the wine in his glass, watching the trail it left around the rim. He had been working at the vineyard for the best part of a year now, having joined Antoine shortly after they got together, at Valerie and Henri's wedding. He had originally taken on the job because he considered he had outgrown lolling around the local beaches and bars and felt it would occupy his time better. He had quickly become absorbed with the process of wine making and, even more than that, he had become enamoured by the vines.

'Yes,' Lauren said, responding to Chico's desire for the ridiculous situation regarding her father to be over. 'I was hoping you might be able to help.' Both men looked towards Lauren as she spoke. 'Do you have any idea who might have made the accusation? Can you think of anyone who might have a vendetta against either of you, or Valerie, or Henri?' she asked. The men were shaking their heads. 'What do you know of Valerie's brother, Phillipe?' she asked. Antoine's face twitched at mention of the man's name.

Chico raised his shoulders and looked quizzically at his lover. 'I don't know him,' he said.

Antoine put down the knife and took Chico's hand in his, while he addressed Lauren. 'I know of him... knew of him, I should say. It was a long time ago. Just before Valerie and Petru were married.' Chico squeezed Antoine's hand before releasing it, reaching for his glass and taking a sip. Antoine continued. 'I saw them… heard them, one evening,' he corrected. 'They were stood under the eucalyptus tree drinking wine, and laughing, and then suddenly the conversation became heated and Phillipe threw down his glass and walked up the hill. They didn't know I'd seen them. When Phillipe had gone, Petru slumped to the ground and sat for a long time.' Antoine's eyes watered as he continued. 'I wanted to help him, but I was young, and I didn't know how. So, I left him. I never mentioned it to Petru. I don't know why, it just didn't seem important, until now maybe. I never saw Phillipe again after that, and Petru married your mother of course.' He shrugged as he reasoned.

'Do you know where Phillipe is now?' Lauren asked.

'No. I've never heard anything of him since then. He estranged himself from Valerie too.'

Lauren's eyebrows bunched, and she pinched the top of her nose. She had played the names of everyone else they knew through her mind, in search of a motive. Very few people had been aware of her father's failing health and those who had were fiercely loyal to the Vincenti family. Lauren stood, her face still contorted. 'I'd best get home,' she said. 'Baby bath time,' she added, the thought bringing a smile to her face. Antoine's face lit up too.

14.

Eva barely recognised her old haunt. The place had received a makeover: whitewashed walls, a newly carpeted soft-seating area, and a wooden floor around the bar and dancing area, gave the old place a completely new look. Even the barwoman had changed. The red-lipstick blonde, who couldn't take no for an answer, was nowhere in sight. She breathed a sigh of relief at that fact. She hadn't been back to *Le So What* for the best part of a year, and hoped that she wouldn't bump into Rosa or, worst still, Dee. She shivered at the thought of seeing Dee, knowing the protective anaesthetist would be gunning for her. She leaned on the bar and attracted the barwoman she didn't recognise. 'Sauvignon please. Large one.' Eva said, taking in the short pure white hair with soft pink streaks. 'Can I run a tab?' she asked, taking out her credit card.

The young woman's baby blue eyes smiled warmly as she acknowledged the order. 'Sure,' she said, taking the card and running it through the machine. As she went about her work, Eva's eyes cruised the bar. Hoping not to recognise anyone, she was pleased when she didn't.

Eva perched on the tall stool, her back to the pillar on the corner of the bar that presumably served to support the weight of the building in some way. The vantage point also afforded her the degree of obscurity she desired, hidden from view from a large portion of the room. She downed half the glass in two long slugs.

'I'm Simone, by the way,' the barwoman said.

'Eva.' She tried to raise a smile, but her eyes wouldn't comply. She took another two glugs and finished the glass. She held the glass out, her instruction clear to the intuitive barwoman.

Simone took the glass and re-filled it. 'Thirsty.' It was a comment, not a question.

Eva winced. She didn't come here for a conversation. 'Thanks,' she said, her tone indicating that the chat between them was over. She sipped from her glass, enjoying the heady effects that were already resulting in her caring less. The tension in her mind softened, the sounds merging into a blur of background noise, punctuated by the voices of those women who passed close to her seat.

'Wanna dance?'

Eva turned to face the question. The cropped dark hair and square build of the woman grabbed her attention. Fleetingly, Dee's image jumped into her thoughts, causing her pulse to race. Anxiety flew into her chest until her sluggish brain registered that Dee wouldn't be asking her to dance. She squinted, trying to study the woman further. It took even longer for her heart rate to slow down.

'Forget it.' The woman threw up a dismissive hand and moved off into the crowd that had congregated on the dance floor.

If their eyes were on Eva, she didn't notice, and she wasn't interested. She needed a pee. She hoisted herself off the stool and made her way towards the toilets. In spite of her best efforts to move in a straight line, she found herself bouncing off a couple of women: shouts of 'watch out,' trailing behind her.

She plonked herself down onto the toilet, rested her elbows on her knees and her head in her hands, and took her relief. Her thoughts drifted to Rosa and the first sighting of her, here, across the room. A surge of longing burned in her chest, but the inner voice continued its mantra - *you're not good enough for her*. She knew the truth when she heard it. She chastised herself for wishing things could be different. They couldn't.

Eva moved from the seat twice during the night; both occasions to go to the toilet. On the second time of returning to the stool at the bar, she struggled to sit. 'Can I settle the bill?' she asked as Simone passed by with a tray of glasses in her hand. Her words were slurred, and her body rocked gently from side to side.

'Sure. Are you okay? Want me to call a taxi?'

'Nah, it's okay. I'll walk, thanks.'

Simone's eyebrows rose at the idea. Eva could barely put one foot in front of the other. Against her better judgement, she put down the tray and handed Eva the card machine. Eva struggled to see the numbers, and when she'd finished pressing the digits an error message appeared. She stared at the machine, unable to read the words. She waited, still staring, unable to process what to do next.

'Do you want me to put your number in?' Simone asked softly.

Eva handed the machine over. 'Thanks. 3...8...5...6...' she said pausing between each number, repeating the whole number to ensure she remembered it correctly.

Within a few moments Simone had moved around to the front of the bar with the receipt and card in her hand. She pushed them both deeply into Eva's jeans pocket. 'Are you sure you don't need any help?' she asked, with genuine concern.

'Fine, honest.' Eva slurred, and staggered out of the bar and into the street, promising that tomorrow things would be different.

*

Lauren couldn't describe the scent hitting her nostrils. It wasn't a strong smell and it wasn't a medical one either. Yet this was a medical establishment. The echo of her heels on the slate-tiled floor reverberated around the vast entrance hall. The old house had been converted a long time ago, providing an invaluable service to the terminally ill. There was no nursing station: no reception to pass through. She looked at the visitors' book on the table, ignored it, and followed the instructions written on the piece of paper in her hand. Room 131. Orientating herself, she admired the works of art hanging on the walls, giving the place its stately-home appearance. As she walked up the wide, shallow stairs and along the corridor, the absence of sound struck her. A nurse passed her, but her movement was unhurried in every way. The place felt peaceful. She stopped outside the room; its door was open, and she could see the end of the bed from where she stood. Unsure whether to knock she entered the room.

The man in the bed turned his head, lifting it slightly so that his eyes could register her. The movement looked effortful. 'Hello,' he said, squinting to focus, trying to make out his unfamiliar guest.

'Hello Uncle Phillipe.' The man's eyes widened as he searched his memories, until a coy smile began to appear, and he rested his head back on the pillow.

'Lauren.'

'Yes.' Her voice was stern, accusing, and the old man rolled his eyes, releasing a tired breath as his body sunk deeper into the bed. 'You must have known I'd work it out,' she said. He made out as if to shrug his shoulders. 'Why?' she asked.

His eyes motioned her to sit, but her body refused to obey, and she stood her ground. 'Suit yourself,' he said. 'I always knew you were smart, like him' he said. 'But how did you...' His voice trailed as he spoke.

'Was it because you couldn't have him?' she asked, fuelled by the heat of anger rising to her head. It was the only possible explanation she had been able to find. The police contact had identified the name of the person who had given the statement of concern and it had taken a while to trace the name to anyone. But when she had, it had landed right back at Phillipe's door.

Phillipe snorted and turned his head towards the window. 'My sister was never good enough for him,' he said, the bitterness towards Valerie still present in his tone. 'And he never really loved her, at least not back then.' He continued to stare as he spoke. 'When we met in London, a long time ago - just after Corry died, I think. He was already with Antoine, so I knew he should never have married her. She only wanted him for the money... and his name.' His tone was factual yet hostile. 'At least I had a few nights with him,' he continued, a soft smile accompanying his fondest memories. Lauren's legs started to give beneath her, as the penny dropped, and she sat on the seat furthest from the bed. 'Those were the best nights of my life,' he said.

'You?' Lauren questioned. 'He contracted it from you,' she stated, feeling nothing but anger towards the vile, conceited, little man lying in the bed. He didn't respond. Lauren fought the tight ball choking the back of her throat. 'Why the accusation?' she managed to ask.

'Because it's true.' His words were confident, unwavering, and the certainty in his tone caused Lauren's breath to hitch. She took a moment to regroup her thoughts.

'You cannot prove anything,' she said.

'Maybe, maybe not,' he said menacingly. When he turned to face Lauren, his eyes were wild. 'But I also know my sister, and the last thing she will want is a *scene*.' He spat the last word with disdain. 'I'm sure we can make this problem go away Lauren,' he added. He wasn't smiling, but his message was clear. 'It's nothing personal,' he said. But Lauren could read the lie. 'I just need to make sure Alain is taken care of, after I die. We've been together a long time and he doesn't have the luxury of my sister's easy inheritance. I'm not a bad man Lauren,' he said, as if to justify his actions.

'How much?'

'Three million. I think that's fair.'

Lauren pulled the cheque out of her coat pocket, wrote out the numbers and signed it. As she stood, she threw it onto the bed. 'If the allegations aren't withdrawn by the morning I will cancel that.' She pointed to the piece of paper that lay at his chest, turned on her heels and stormed out of the room.

Her heart was still thumping when she reached the exit. She stopped at the visitors' book, before walking out the door. She stood by her car, taking the cool air into her lungs, rubbing at her stinging eyes. *Damn you*, the phrase on her tongue, but she didn't know to whom it referred.

15.

Eva knocked again on the dark-blue wooden door. She was hopping up and down with the cold, feeling impatient, and she didn't have the time to wait. She had promised Carine, and she was expected at work. She didn't want to let her down again. Though letting people down was something she seemed to be proficient at. If she were honest she'd been avoiding her mum. She hadn't even told her about Rosa and her splitting up, not that she ever did keep her mum up-to-date with her love life. Guilt prodded at her, but she pushed it down, knowing her mum understood her better than anyone. Her mum would take it all in her stride. She wouldn't judge her. Eva's head thumped as she battled with the hangover from hell. Taking out her key, she turned the lock and entered the flat.

She placed the small gift on the window ledge by the front door, while she removed her coat and placed it on the hook. 'Mum,' she shouted, leaning her head, waiting for a response. *Maybe she was at the gym?* 'Mum,' she shouted again. Silence.

She'd chosen the pendant with her mum's birthstone in it. Aquamarine, for Pisces. She was really pleased with herself and excited, because the colour matched her mum's eyes perfectly. Even though her mum didn't wear much jewellery, she hoped she would like it. She picked up the present. She'd just put it under the artificial Christmas tree that sat on her mum's low table in the living room. It would be a nice surprise for when Rowena got home, then she would pop back later and have a drink with her. It would give her mum something to look forward to, and something to open on Christmas Day. Eva hadn't thought about spending Christmas Day with her mum, until realising that she would be alone without Rosa. So she planned to make out that she wasn't available, and then surprise Rowena on the day.

She walked into the room, still shivering with the cold, the word 'mum,' on her lips. The present fell from her hand and hit the floor without a sound as her eyes registered the scene. She tried to move, but found herself rooted to the spot, while her brain continued to process the information reaching her eyes. 'Nooo,' she yelled, but only to herself. No, this wasn't right. This wasn't happening.

Rowena lay slumped backwards in the chair, her mouth and eyes slightly open, her face a ghostly white, and expressionless. The rigidity in her body was obvious even to Eva's untrained eyes. Eva's hand cupped her mouth, as the blood drained from her head. Dizziness caused her to sway, threatening her balance. She wanted to scream, wanted to cry, wanted to not believe what her eyes knew to be true. It couldn't be true. But she could do nothing. She felt nothing. Her legs gave way and she allowed herself to drop into the armchair. Staring at her mum, she fumbled for her phone and dialled the only number she could rely on.

'Yes Eva?' Carine's tone was harsh. Eva was already late, and she was still pissed at her for missing the last two deadlines and not responding to her persistent requests for information. She'd tried to get through to her, but Eva had been on a route to self-destruction, so she had backed off. Eva's low, quiet voice took her by surprise. 'Eva, what's wrong?' She stood, at the other end of the line, waiting.

'It's mum.' Eva said. 'She's dead.'

Carine gasped. 'What? Where are you?'

'At her house.'

'I'm on my way.' The silence at the end of the line triggered Eva to put her phone back in her pocket. She sat, rocking back and forth, staring at her mum. The image would stay with her forever. The blood-red sweatband around her mum's head clashed dreadfully with the natural red of her hair. It looked all kinds of wrong, Eva noted. Scanning her mum's face, she looked the most at peaceful Eva had ever seen. *She's even lost a few pounds*, Eva thought, as her eyes traced Rowena's baggy t-shirt and jogging bottoms. *So much for getting fucking fit.* The irony of the thought flew threw her mind, energised by the red mist that seemed to consume her in that moment.

The knocking on the door summoned her attention and she dragged herself to her feet and stumbled her way into the hallway. As she opened the door, Carine bundled into the space between them and pulled Eva into her arms. 'I am so sorry,' she said. The words were said slowly, each word well spaced from the last, as if the scene was being played out in slow motion.

Eva stood numbly, accepting the warmth of Carine's body against her own. She couldn't stop the tears from falling down her cheeks, and she didn't have the energy to move. Carine held her until the tears abated. 'We'll need to call an ambulance,' she said, softly. Eva stared at her, vacantly. 'Stay here,' she said.

Carine walked into the living room. As she registered Rowena, she had to bite back the tears. Phone in hand, she dialled the number.

Eva was still waiting in the hallway when the ambulance arrived, and then the police. She stood in a daze, watching the process happening around her. The fair-haired medic reasoned that Rowena had had a major heart attack. They seemed to think that she had been exercising immediately before the attack and that she wouldn't have suffered. Eva couldn't get the impression of her mum out of her mind. The image repeatedly came back to her no matter where she directed her eyes. It was just another living hell she'd need to adjust to. Knowing Rowena hadn't suffered should have provided some comfort, but it didn't.

Two police officers were busy assessing the scene and she could hear the man talking into his radio. He was unusually tall, Eva noted with detached fascination. The woman looked very young, but she was kind, and nurturing. At some point, an undertaker came and removed the body. They handed Eva a leaflet, should she need some support in the immediate future. Eva took it and put it in her pocket, without glancing at its content.

The words: coroner, registering the death and funeral, seemed to float in the space between Eva and the outside world. They didn't belong in her world; she couldn't process them. She just nodded vacantly at whomever spoke to her until eventually, the hustle and bustle quieted.

Carine placed a hand on Eva's shoulder. The touch barely registered and when Eva looked at her, the light blue eyes lacked focus. She handed her the gift she'd collected from the floor. Eva looked at it, but couldn't bring herself to reach out and take it. Carine pocketed it.

'Come on, let's go home,' Carine said, and pulled Eva into her arms again. She looked so young: so vulnerable. Eva still hadn't spoken, not since she'd made the call to Carine.

*

Eva took the coffee with shaking hands. The dark rings around her eyes highlighting the paleness in her cheeks. Her face was expressionless, and her light blue eyes had shifted to dark-grey. She stared up at Carine with a look of helplessness that had Carine's heart sinking. Nothing could be said or done to take the pain away. Eva sipped at the hot drink before sitting on the familiar couch in Carine's living room.

Carine handed her a short glass, half filled with whiskey, distracting her from her thoughts. Eva looked at the glass and then studied it with curiosity. For some inexplicable reason the last thing she wanted right now was a drink, but she took the glass and downed the burning fluid in one swift gulp. At least there was some comfort in the heat. Carine downed her drink and placed the glass on the sideboard. 'Can I get you anything?' she asked. It was past 6pm and Eva hadn't eaten since an early breakfast. 'I'll make an omelette,' Carine said, deciding before Eva had the chance to refuse.

As she returned with a plate of food, Eva was crying. 'I...' she tried to speak, but the words wouldn't come.

'It's okay.' Carine put down the plates, sat next to Eva, and put her arm around her. Eva leaned into the offered shoulder and continued to sob.

'I need to let Anna know,' Eva said, suddenly pulling out of Carine's hold and sitting bolt upright, as the thought hit her. She picked up her phone and stood up, tapping the speed dial for her old friend.

It didn't ring for long before the familiar voice at the other end, caused Eva's voice to choke in her throat. 'Eva, what's wrong?' Anna asked, immediately sensing the sorrow that permeated the airwaves. 'Eva, are you okay?' she asked, pushing words into the silence.

Eva held back the tears, but her voice was shaky. 'It's mum,' she said.

Anna's stomach flipped then landed with a heaviness that took her legs from beneath her. 'Oh no.'

Eva's head was nodding at the other end of the line and she tried to speak through the tears now tracing down her cheeks. 'She's dead.' She was sobbing by the time the words hit Anna's ears.

Anna had started to shake, and it had become obvious to the others in the room that something bad had happened.

Lauren's face had paled as she surmised, hoping the call wasn't about Lisa or Vivian. She breathed a deep sigh of relief when Anna explained that the call was from Eva, though saddened to hear that Rowena had died of a suspected heart attack.

Anna was still shaking as she fell into Lauren's arms and allowed her tears to wet the previously pristine white linen shirt. Lauren held her tightly, placing kisses on the top of her head.

Eva's tears dripped onto her phone as she stared at the now blank screen. Carine crossed the space between them, cupped Eva's cheeks and brushed away the tears. The touch was tender, compassionate, loving. She wrapped Eva in a tight embrace, pressing Eva's head into her chest. 'Do you want to lay down for a bit?' she asked.

Eva hadn't realised how tired she was, and it took all her effort to nod in affirmation. Carine released her hold and took Eva's hand, leading her through to the large double bedroom. The blue satin quilt called to Eva and when her head hit the pillow and her eyes closed, everything in the world was back in its rightful place.

*

'Do you want to go back to Paris?' Lauren asked, squeezing Anna's hand.

Anna shook her head. 'It's only three days til Christmas,' she said. Lauren nodded.

They had been celebrating the official confirmation that the allegation against Henri and Valerie had been dropped because the witness had withdrawn their statement. The senior investigating officer had driven over to the house to apologise in person for the inconvenience caused. He had assured the Vincentis that they were considering action against the witness for wasting police time. Lauren had suggested that they would all be happy just to let it go, and after the officer had downed couple of glasses of champagne, he agreed. The party had been in full swing when the call had come in about Rowena.

Now Lauren and Anna sat on the large couch in the living room, staring into the wood-burning stove, Anna expressing her disbelief at the turn of events.

'Remember when you split your head open on that fireplace?' Anna asked as her thoughts drifted.

'Yes.' Lauren smiled and tugged Anna closer, the memory bringing to mind her lover's over-zealous response and her supervision whilst Lauren took a bath. 'You were...'

'I was paranoid that you were going to die,' Anna interrupted.

'Wonderful, I was going to say,' Lauren corrected her.

'I was scared shitless,' Anna said, holding Lauren's eyes as she spoke. She moved, pressed her lips to Lauren's. 'Come to bed with me,' she said. They eased out of the couch and ambled lazily, hand in hand. Anna stopped outside the bedroom door, turned to face Lauren, and traced a finger down the side of her face. 'I love you,' she said.

Lauren leaned in to kiss Anna's lips. The touch spoke volumes.

16.

Eva paced the floor in her mum's office. Except it wasn't her mum's office any more, she reflected, battling another hot sweat and a gripping pain in her gut that nearly floored her. She wanted to scream out, but no one would hear her cries of desperation. *What was the point?* She made her way to the coffee machine, hoping the familiar hissing sound would give her mind something positive to focus on. Her mother's will sat on the table in a sealed envelope. She had collected it from the solicitor two days ago. Dying so close to the holiday season meant that the funeral couldn't be arranged until after the New Year, so she waited, in limbo until the fourth of January. Eva squeezed at her stomach as another spasm gripped her. At least the thumping in her head had eased since taking the tablets. She put in a second coffee pod and pressed the button: strong and sweet.

She glanced around the room, pausing at the director's chair, reminded of Rowena's presence. A wave of sadness passed through her. Perhaps she's still here, she thought; she wished. She'd heard about energy and spirit and wanted to believe in it, but right now all she could feel was the gaping hole that her mum had left in her life. She sipped at the strong coffee, wandered to the couch, and picked up the envelope. She knew that her mum had left her the business, and both flats, but the reality gave her no pleasure. She put the envelope down again, rubbed her fingers through her hair, and winced as her stomach tweaked again. She took a bite out of the ham baguette she had purchased on the way in. She chewed the dry contents, eventually swallowing what still felt like a large lump in her throat. The temptation was too much. She walked to the desk, opened the cabinet drawer, and pulled out the bottle of scotch. She uncorked the top and took a long swig, taking the bottle with her back to the couch. She opened her laptop and set to work, ignoring the bleeps from her phone advising her that she had a string of texts waiting.

Scrolling down the list, she checked out each profile in detail, searching for the right skills. The trouble was, she had no idea what those skills might be. Searching for a lost or missing person wasn't something she'd ever done before, and she felt a little out of her depth as to where to start. It was the name that caught her eye in the first instance, then the apparent contradiction between the name Mitch Slater and the image of a petite built, dark skinned woman, with short black curls cut tight to her scalp and a beaming white smile. She looked like an angel. She read further...

Ex police, based in Paris. If you need to find someone, I'll look for you. Give me a call.

The advert didn't give much information, but Eva felt a sudden rush of excitement as she pondered the idea that someone might be able to help her. She went to make the call, then stopped when she realised... It was Christmas Day. Surely, Mitch Slater had better things to be doing today than taking calls from a potential client. She took note of the number. The call could wait another day. She'd go to her mum's house and see what she could find. The thought caused her stomach to churn, but it needed to be done. Maybe there would be something there to help with the search: a picture, a last known address, or a social security number. Anything. Her mum must have something with David Adam's details on it, she reasoned, as she grabbed her coat and headed out the door.

*

'Merry Christmas everyone,' Brigitte announced as she plonked the large tray on the dining table. The weight brought it down with a thud, nearly spilling its contents. She picked up the sharp carving knife, and long two-pronged fork, and began slicing the large, perfectly seasoned, turkey crown.

'Merry Christmas,' came the chorus, as the other five people sat around the table responded in unison.

The aroma had been wafting through the house for the last couple of hours at least, and as Rosa spied the juices being released from the knife cutting through the tender flesh, her mouth watered. She took in the scent and her stomach complained. She took a sip of wine to quell the desire, but her belly wasn't going to be cheated by such a cheap trick. So she reached out and snatched a loose bit of turkey and threw it into her mouth, before her mum could stop her. The voices around the table protested teasingly, and Rosa moaned aloud as the flavours captivated her taste buds. 'Mmm, that's really good,' she said, to more whining noises from their guests. Brigitte worked faster, serving the turkey, and passing the plates around the table, until everyone had a dish in front of them. Groans of pleasure filled the room.

'Delicious.' Rosa said. More nods and mumbled gratitude confirmed the meal was a hit.

'Keep you waiting long enough, you'll eat anything,' Brigitte teased, taking her own seat in front of her plate.

Rosa loaded her plate with steaming vegetables, roast potatoes, and a Yorkshire pudding. She had insisted her mum make them, as they were a luxury she never got to eat when in Paris. She poured a little gravy over her meat and into the centre of the pudding, refusing the cranberry sauce that had just been offered. She picked up her knife and fork and looked up, realising for the first time that Kaye was watching her intently. She could feel the heat rise in her cheeks and tried to distract herself from the smiling eyes, tucking into her food with passion.

Kaye's smile broadened as she watched Rosa enjoying her meal. She accepted the cranberry that had now reached her and placed a small spoonful of the sauce on the side of her plate. She returned the dish to the table, and started to tuck in. 'Wow, this is fantastic,' she said, directing her words to Brigitte, whilst her eyes strayed to the younger woman who had attracted her attention.

Brigitte chewed, swallowed, and chewed and swallowed again, aware of the energy passing between her daughter and the enigmatic doctor, Kaye Bennett. Brigitte had known Kaye for five years now, having started at the Royal Free not long after finishing medical school. She was solid, dependable, and... she was single. She also figured that her daughter might think she was hot. Kaye was always drawing attention at work, even if it was from the wrong gender for her taste. Brigitte had hoped the two women would get along, and it seemed she was right. This was one of the reasons she had suggested a Christmas lunch in the first place. That, and the fact that the four colleagues she'd invited would have been eating canteen leftovers had they not had somewhere better to go. She watched with interest, as sparks fired across the table and back again. Paul and Flo, her nursing friends, were deep in their own conversation and Agnes, the oldest sister on the Renal ward, who had had one too many Gin's already, was happily tucking into the food, at a pace.

Rosa finished her plate, leaned back in her seat, and held her protruding stomach. 'I'm stuffed.'

'Me too,' Kaye said, mirroring Rosa's movement. The smile she flashed impacted Rosa quite a way below her waistline, and she wriggled in her seat to ease the sensation building between her legs. She tried to cross her legs, only to bash her knee on one of the struts of the table.

The sound of cutlery landing on plates drew Rosa's attention to the fact that others around the table had also finished eating. She excused herself, rose to her feet and began to clear away the empty plates. Kaye collected the plates from her side of the table and followed Rosa into the kitchen.

'So, are you staying here long?' Kaye asked.

Rosa rested the plates on the side, noticing her body's intense response to the simple words. 'Until after New Year,' she said, her eyes tracking the feminine figure, as Kaye placed the plates onto the pile she had started.

'Sorry,' Kaye said, as she brushed an arm across Rosa's breast, but her eyes gave away the fact that the move had been somewhat intentional.

Rosa smiled. 'It's okay.'

'Do you fancy going to a party on New Year's Eve?' Kaye asked. The question caused Rosa to flinch, though she wasn't sure why. *When did she lose her ability to flirt outrageously?* Kaye noticed Rosa's discomfort. 'As friends,' she added.

'Maybe,' Rosa said. Though not entirely convinced, she had felt a brief sense of relief pass through her when Kaye had qualified her invitation, *as friends*. Maybe it would be good for her, she pondered, as they both joined the others at the table. The atmosphere over lunch had been convivial, but a fleeting thought of Eva had dampened her mood. As crazy as it might have seemed to an onlooker, and especially to her friend Dee, she felt Eva's absence, dreadfully and painfully.

Her mother noticed and remarked. 'Everything okay sweetheart?'

'Fine, just lost in thought for a moment.' Rosa smiled weakly, and turned her attention to the banter between Paul and Flo that seemed to have the rest of the table in raptures, except for Kaye whose eyes were firmly fixed on Rosa. She seemed fully tuned in to Rosa's sadness and motioned her head as if to check that everything was okay. It wasn't.

*

'You look pensive,' Lauren said, sweeping a strand of hair from Anna's tense face. She coaxed her chin up and gazed into her eyes. 'You're worried about Eva.' It was a statement not a question, but Anna nodded all the same.

'I've texted her five times today and she hasn't responded. Her calls are going straight to answerphone.' Lauren studied the steel-blue eyes. 'She was there for me when...' Anna said.

Lauren's smile conveyed tenderness, and something else. Pride? She toyed with an errant hair sitting across Anna's eyes, pinned it behind her ear and ran her fingers down the side of Anna's face. She could feel Anna's sadness as if it were her own.

The tender touch caused a sharp prickle of discomfort and Anna averted Lauren's gaze suddenly, memories of her time with Eva riding on the wave of guilt that filtered through her mind, and settled heavily in her chest. Logically, she knew she had nothing to feel bad about. Yet, the dark-brown eyes piercing through her now, made her feel as if they had never been separated by the accident. In so many ways, it felt as if they had always been together since the time they met. The reality was, it was one year and two days since Lauren's accident, and what had happened between Anna and Eva had been left unspoken. Yet now, Anna felt as bad as if she had actually had an affair. Without questioning the timing, Anna opened her mouth.

'Eva and... we... we were intimate for a while,' she said, fighting to get the words out through the tension in her mind. As soon as the words were set free, she breathed out deeply.

Lauren stiffened as the words landed, her face tightened and her eyes withdrew into another place. She stepped away from Anna, and knelt on the floor where Emilie was playing with a soft rattle; shaking it vigorously, then

126

putting it into her mouth. Anna's heart dropped. Naively, she hadn't seen that response coming. She bent down next to Lauren and placed her hand in the small of her warm back. Lauren remained focused on entertaining Emilie. After a short while, Anna removed her hand, stood, and walked out of the living room, with the soft sounds of Emilie gurgling in the background as she closed the door quietly behind her. She pulled on her coat and stepped outside. Her breath faltered as she adjusted to the cold air.

It was already dark, but on route to the horizon, pockets of light marked the hamlets and small villages, set amid the forests that snuggled into the mountains. She wrapped her arms around herself for warmth and meandered down to the eucalyptus tree, pondering the wisdom of her confession. From the position of the tree, more lights appeared down through the valley and her eyes were drawn to a small number of moving lights close to the boundary of the vineyard. Leaning her side against the tree, she allowed her thoughts to spiral: Lauren's response, Eva's silence, and Rowena's death, and then dearest Emilie - so innocent and full of life. The pain of guilt had gone, but what had replaced it was even more excruciating. Lauren's instant withdrawal had the same crushing effect on her as the accident had this time last year. The memories came flooding back. She couldn't go there again. She fought the rising tears, but they were too insistent and left a cooling trail as they fell down her cheeks.

Lauren smiled as she watched her daughter exploring the new toy with intense interest. But she wasn't focused on the bright dark eyes, dark brown curls, and giggling smile. The tightness in her chest had a sharp feel to it, and her imagination took her on a journey she hadn't planned to make. All her logical thoughts stacked up to form the perfect argument she would be prepared to defend in a court of law, including her own transgression during the time she and Anna had been apart. But her reaction to Anna, that was something entirely different. She recognised her old self and she didn't like it. She wanted to protect herself from the pain of the truth. But she couldn't withdraw and shut herself out of the world again. She picked up Emilie and sat on the couch with her, reaching for her last bottle of the night, before bed. She'd get her settled into bed and then go and talk to Anna.

*

Eva jumped at the banging sound at her door. She wasn't expecting anyone. A pile of black and white photographs lay strewn across the floor of her living room. She had been trying to put them into some sort of order, but she didn't recognise most of the people in the pictures. The banging came again, this time more urgent. 'All right,' she shouted. Her right knee squeaked and groaned as she stood up and she rubbed her kneecap as she hobbled to the door. She'd clearly been scrunched up on the floor for too long she mused, as it dawned on her that it was long past 7pm. The thumping started again, just as she opened the door. 'All right, all right,' she said, looking directly at Carine.

'You haven't responded to your text messages all day and I was getting worried,' Carine announced, pushing her way past Eva and into the flat. She placed a sack on the kitchen side, and two bottles of wine in the fridge. 'What are you doing?' Carine asked, as her eyes scanned the images and written labels scattered across the floor.

'I need to find my father,' Eva announced. Her tone was serious, and her glare carried an intensity and determination that Carine hadn't seen in her before.

'I didn't realise...' Carine started.

'I don't know where he is, or if he's even alive, but I need to find out,' Eva interrupted, needing to justify her actions, as she immediately returned to the floor, studied an image, and placed it in its relevant pile.

Carine watched the fiercely obsessive behaviour, unsure of whether to feel concerned or simply relieved that Eva wasn't sat in a drunken stupor mourning the death of her mum. 'Can I help?' she asked, kneeling down next to Eva. She didn't recognise anyone either, so would be of little help with the sorting process. 'I'll make some supper,' she said, but Eva was too engrossed to hear the words. Carine stood, and Eva grunted some form of acknowledgement. Carine wandered through to the kitchen, opened the wine and poured them both a glass. She placed a glass on the table for Eva and then went back into the kitchen to prepare supper. She kept a curious eye on Eva as she worked.

'Did you find what you were looking for?' Carine asked. Eva looked up from the floor. The wild passion had darkened her eyes and Carine felt a bolt of lightning strike her, right between the legs. The feeling caught her by surprise and she choked down the wine she had just slurped, nearly spilling the glass in her hand.

'I think so.' Eva stood with two photographs in her hand. One, of her mum with a man in what looked like a formal Army uniform. The second was of a young child in a pink frilly dress being carried by the same man. This time he was dressed in combat uniform, but there was no mistaking the striking resemblance between Eva and her father. She held out the photos, picked up her still full glass from the table, and took a long slug.

'You have the same colour eyes,' Carine said. 'Distinctive.' She looked Eva up and down, then back to the picture in her hand. 'Same build too by the looks of it. Same fair hair.'

Eva drained her glass, picked up the bottle from the table and re-filled it. She hadn't been aware of Carine working away in the background, but the previously bare table had been dressed for Christmas: a Father Christmas patterned tablecloth, red napkins, and two posh looking Christmas crackers. Even a candle had been lit as a centrepiece, surrounded by real holly leaves together with its red berries. The scene made her smile, but a wave of sadness overwhelmed her, and she couldn't hold back the sudden rush of tears.

Carine placed the photos on the arm of the couch, deliberately out of direct sight and pulled Eva into her chest. 'It'll be okay,' she said, softly, knowing that feeling *okay* was a poor compromise for feeling alive, and happy. She pressed a kiss on the top of Eva's head and pushed the blonde straggly hair to the side of her face. The kiss to Eva's lips flowed without thought. Tender, loving, fleeting. Carine released Eva, taken aback by her own unexpected display of affection. She cleared her throat. 'Supper's ready,' she said. Her voice was broken, and she turned swiftly to avoid Eva's gaze.

Eva stood in silence, delicately brushing her index finger against her lips, not quite able to identify the feelings the brief kiss had elicited.

17.

Lauren stepped out into the cool night air, carrying two tumblers of Macallan on ice. She hoped the offering would at least spark positive memories and give her the courage to talk. The absence of any moonlight darkened the grass the further she stepped from the house, but the tree was clearly visible and the figure propping up against it, caused a tingling sensation to rise up her spine. She loved that feeling. She would get her mind to focus on that feeling and not the turmoil that Anna's honest revelation had triggered in her.

Anna turned as Lauren's footsteps infiltrated the night's silence. Lauren offered up the glass and she took it, turning her attention back to the landscape. 'It's so beautiful,' she said.

Lauren stared out into the darkness, picking up the rising mountains where they met the cloudy night sky. She still hadn't skied there with Antoine, something they had promised themselves they would do once she had recovered from her injury. *Maybe this winter?* 'It is. Spectacular, and especially when the snow comes. Over there.'

Lauren pointed into the distance and Anna's eyes followed her arm, stopping at her hand, absorbed by the long fingers, and her thoughts. She hitched her breath in her throat, forgetting to be mad at Lauren for her instant withdrawal. 'Thanks... for the drink.' Her voice revealed her longing.

'I'm sorry.' Lauren's voice was soft, deepening her naturally husky resonance.

Everything about the sound of that voice sent a pulse of heat racing from Anna's neck that weakened her knees. Her mouth had dried, and she sipped at the drink in her hand. It didn't help. She emptied the contents into her mouth and swallowed hard, adding heat to the intoxicating sensations that had already consumed her body. She could feel the ache starting to throb. In one short pace, her lips were on Lauren's, her tongue delving hungrily. Lauren responded instantly, her free hand securing Anna's head, their teeth clashing with the urgency of the kiss. 'I want you.' Anna's broken voice elicited a deep groan, increasing the frenzy between them as Lauren dropped the glass and slid her hand up Anna's bare leg and under her coat and dress. 'Jesus!' Anna cried out, allowing her glass to fall, as Lauren's fingers tracked the wet heat below her panties and penetrated her. Forcing her back against the tree for support, Lauren moved rhythmically, kissing Anna's neck, biting down on the nipples that remained covered. The goose bumps springing to life across Anna's body had little to do with the cold air; Lauren was pressed too closely for that. The orgasm peaked quickly, but the intensity blinded her, and her knees buckled. Only Lauren's weight, pressing her against the tree prevented her from crashing to the ground, as the release quaked through her.

'I love you.' Lauren said. Three small words that made everything perfect. Lauren kissed Anna's watering eyes with such tenderness that the tears tumbled in earnest. 'Hey, it's okay,' Lauren said, softly, through a slight wave of concern, until Anna's lips took hers. The languid kiss had a depth of a different quality. As they pulled out of the tender touch, Anna was shivering. 'Let's go inside,' Lauren said, brushing away the tears that had fallen down Anna's cheeks. Her own admission could wait.

*

'So, how are you planning to find your father?' Carine asked, as she sat on the couch. She was intrigued.

Eva handed her a tumbler glass, half filled with the Cognac Carine had picked up. Taking the seat next to her, she

132

sipped at her own glass. 'I found someone on the Internet. I'm gonna try and get hold of her tomorrow.'

Carine nodded as Eva spoke. 'And what are you going to do when you've tracked him down?' she asked, having been unable to fathom in her own mind what Eva might do with any information she discovered about her father.

Eva's eyes locked onto Carine's, but their expression was vacant. 'I don't know,' she admitted, her voice weak. She hadn't thought that far, she was simply responding to some force that had been driving her since the chat she'd had with her mum, before she died. The unplanned recollection of the memory, anchored itself to the fact that her mum was now deceased, and caused an overwhelming wave of grief to consume her. She started to cry.

Carine slid across the space until their bodies touched lightly. Wrapping an arm around Eva, she coaxed her to rest into her shoulder, and placed a tender kiss on the top of her head. 'I'm so sorry Eva.'

The gentle words did little to stop the recurring image of her mum on the couch presenting itself in Eva's mind's eye. Eventually, she allowed herself to fall into the warmth of the bodily contact, comforted by the scent that had become familiar to her over the past weeks. The tears fell until they dried. 'I miss her,' she said, with a child-like quality to her voice, like the young child who has lost their best friend. Eva knew that feeling too well. It haunted her, and had driven her to live recklessly for many years. As the painful sensation hit her again, she had an overwhelming need to fill the well of loneliness that seemed to stop her heart from functioning properly. She pulled out of the hold and turned her head to face Carine.

Carine sensed Eva's emotional shift and a wave of excitement coursed through her as she watched Eva's light-blue eyes darken. Her racing pulse matched her breathing, and as Eva's mouth closed the space between them, the heady feeling took her breath away. She groaned at the contact, and willingly opened to Eva's request.

Eva's sex flared instantly at the touch of Carine's lips on hers. She hadn't realised she'd missed *this*, at least not until Carine had stirred something in her earlier. Suddenly awakened, she needed more, and she needed it now. Standing suddenly, Carine gasped at the absence of her mouth. Eva pulled her to her feet and led her into the bedroom.

*

Carine woke to an empty bed. The sheets were cold, even though it was still dark outside, and she hadn't been asleep for very long. Eva's scent lingered on her. She breathed it in, drifted in thought, increasingly aware of the low throbbing sensation that was building between her legs. She turned face down and placed her hand beneath her, allowing her fingers to explore. She moaned at her own touch, unaware of Eva's intense gaze on her.

Eva stood in the doorway. She'd been seduced from her work by the sounds emanating from the room. She watched for a while, allowing the burning sensation to take hold in her own sex, before she approached the bed. Casually, she slipped her hand between the sheets. The contact caused Carine to jump, and she groaned even more deeply, opening her legs, raising her hips slightly, urging Eva on. Eva pulled back the covers and knelt on the bed. Her fingers found their target and as she thrust into Carine she slapped her hard across the arse, causing her to scream out. The intensity of the pain heightened the sensation of Carine's fingers on her own clit, and Eva's fingers pumping into her from behind. The multi-layered sensation sparked, simultaneously setting alight every cell in her body. Eva felt the wild desire build in her own sex as her fingers connected with the silky wet flesh of the woman beneath her. Familiar. Real. She moved her free hand into the robe, releasing the cord, and applied the pressure she needed to her own pulsing centre.

Carine screamed out as the orgasm sent her body into spasms, but a sense of urgency stronger than the desire to hold on to the exquisite sensation, drove her to shift herself up, turn, and throw Eva onto the bed, in one swift move. As she landed Eva on her back, she moved on top of her, hooking Eva's legs over her shoulders, immediately fucking her with her fingers, and replacing Eva's own hand with her mouth. Sucking, biting down and pumping her hard, Eva's body began to shake, until she too screamed into the early morning darkness.

Falling back onto the bed, they both lay facing the ceiling. Eva could feel her heart racing. She didn't feel satiated though; she had only just started. When she looked at Carine, her face didn't hold the smile of contentment and Carine's eyes widened as the unspoken offer dawned on her. The wicked grin on Eva's face contorted in ecstasy as Carine flipped her onto her front and entered her from behind.

*

Eva looked at her phone. 12.30. She was sure Mitch had said to meet at the small patisserie; a strange location for a meeting, with just two tables and selling cakes and bread to take away rather than eat in. But, she had grabbed one of the tables and sat, waiting for the coffee she had already ordered. She hadn't slept. Carine had been a distraction, and a pleasant diversion for her mind. She had gotten through the night without thinking about her mum, or her dad, for the first time in too many nights. She had left the house before Carine had woken, wondering how she would face the woman after what had passed between them. She didn't want Carine as a lover. It wasn't about that. She didn't want to hurt her either. Lost in thought, she didn't notice Mitch approach the table.

'You must be Eva.' The singsong voice, slightly lower in pitch than Eva had expected, invaded Eva's reverie.

Eva's head thrust upwards, her eyes immediately drawn to the light scar running down the right side of the young woman's dark brown skin, from the side of her eye to the centre of her cheek. She hadn't noticed that in the website image. The white of her eyes shone healthily around the dark pupils. Her skin looked fresh. *She looked about seventeen*, Eva thought, noting the absence of any of the normal aging factors. 'How old are you?' she asked, without intending to.

The black woman laughed, a deep, full hearted laugh that blended into a chuckle that seemed to shake her whole body, and Eva couldn't stop herself from smiling as she spotted the faint lines appear around the woman's big wide smile.

'I'm Mitch.' The woman held out her hand to introduce herself, before taking the seat opposite Eva, ignoring the question about her age.

'Hi... Mitch.' Eva pronounced the name as she studied the woman whose name didn't seem to fit her persona too well. Her quizzical tone seemed to convey her judgement.

'Long story,' Mitch responded, picking up on Eva's thoughts. She stopped speaking to allow the two coffees to be placed on the table in front of them. 'Thanks,' she said to the hostess. Eva watched with interest as the young woman winked at the dark-haired shop assistant.

'I didn't see you order,' Eva queried, plopping two cubes of sugar into the small cup.

'I didn't,' Mitch said, her eyes sparkling. She sipped from the large creamy coffee, leaving Eva waiting for further information. Nothing came for a while. Mitch savoured the coffee. 'How can I help you?' she asked, eventually.

'I want to find my father,' Eva responded, reaching into her holdall for the photos and paperwork she had managed to track down.

Mitch's eyes glanced down to where the photos rested, without moving her head. Her eyes returned to Eva. 'What do you know?' Eva shrugged, and her posture slumped slightly. Mitch noticed. She always felt for her clients, with their desperation weighing them down and preventing the flow of life.

'Not a lot really,' Eva responded in a deflated tone.

'Tell me what you got.' Mitch said, her eyes reflecting the hope that Eva needed to feel.

'Last we knew, he was serving in The Gulf.' Mitch nodded encouragingly. 'Shouldn't you be taking notes?' Eva asked.

'You said you didn't have much,' Mitch responded, matter of fact. 'My memory's not that bad for a few facts,' she added. Her smile was confident, reassuring, and Eva felt duly reprimanded.

'He's originally from Cardiff, in Wales.'

Mitch started to laugh. 'It's okay I know where Wales is... and Cardiff. I'm originally from Wales, not that you would've known that. I didn't mean to laugh,' she apologised, raising her hands in front of her face, palms towards Eva.

Eva smiled; suddenly feeling more optimistic that the person sat opposite her might actually be able to find David Adams. 'If he's still alive he would have been discharged from the Army sometime around 2008.'

'Anything else?' Mitch's eyes seem to have got whiter. 'Any siblings, grandparents, cousins?'

Eva's eyes lowered to the table. She picked up her coffee and finished it, biting back the bitter sting in her mouth. 'My grandparents on both sides are dead, my mum is...' her breath hitched in her throat and she swallowed hard. 'My mum died recently, and I don't have any siblings that I know of,' she added.

'I'm sorry to hear about your mum,' Mitch responded, genuinely touched by Eva's loss.

Eva acknowledged the empathic response, unable to prevent her eyes from glassing over. 'My dad had a brother and sister, so there may be cousins somewhere, but I've never met them.'

Mitch leaned into the table and took a long look at the images. 'Can I borrow these?' she asked.

'Sure. They're the...'

'I'll take good care of them,' she confirmed. 'You look a lot like him,' she added as she studied the picture. 'I'll find him for you,' she said. There was no mistaking the certainty in her voice, or the determination in her eyes, when she looked up from the pictures in her hand and held Eva's gaze. 'If he's alive, I'll find him. And if he's not, you'll get the closure you need.'

'Thank you.'

'I'll contact you when I have something.' Mitch downed the remains of her coffee, stood, and held out her hand. Eva stood, shook it, and held the dark eyes firmly with her own, sealing the contractual agreement between them. In a blink Mitch was gone, leaving Eva standing. Only then did she realise, she didn't get to hear the story behind her name. *Maybe another day,* she thought to herself. She had already decided she would like to know more about the woman with the engaging smile. Something about her reminded her of Charlie...

Leaving the café, the lightness Mitch had just injected into her world darkened slightly, as Eva was reminded of the fact that Carine would be waiting for her. Taking a right, instead of a left, she headed straight to the tatty bar that had become her friend. Just a couple of drinks then she'd go home. If she texted Carine to say she'd be late home, then hopefully she'd be out of the house by the time she returned from the bar.

*

Eva turned the key in her door and breathed a sigh of relief at the darkness inside the flat. Carine had vacated the place. She flicked on the living room light and walked through to the kitchen. Feeling hungry, she opened the fridge door. It was virtually empty, and she closed it again, with a deep sigh. She pulled out a short glass, cracked open a new bottle of whiskey and filled the tumbler. Walking the short distance back into the living room, she sat on the couch, listening to the ringing still intruding on her ears. There was no such thing as silence. There was always some noise, coming from somewhere, even if that was from the inside, she reflected. Maybe that was the worst kind of noise too? She was feeling restless, having restrained herself to just a couple of drinks at the bar, and with nothing much to do, the feeling was becoming oppressive. She took a hefty swig of the whiskey and debated going out to a bar. Any bar. She didn't know if she could wait for answers from Mitch. She was feeling impatient to find out about her father's existence, or not as the case may be. She sipped again, and then again. Her mind was beginning to soften, but with it came the tears. She didn't want to cry, so she stood, finished her drink and went and poured another one. She downed that one quickly, and soon after she could feel her vision fading and her thoughts beginning to merge. The sadness had gone. She staggered her way into her bedroom and fell onto the bed.

The sound of raised voices breaking the silence caused her to stir, prising her tiny eyes to open, instantly and widely. The familiarity of the deep tone, vibrated in her chest and her eyes searched into the darkness, seeking out the lines of light that seeped around the closed door. Her small frame was beginning to shake, even before she sat bolt upright. She cried silently, not wanting to add to the noises coming from out there: she didn't want to draw attention to herself. Instinctively, she reached her arms upwards, in the hope of being swept into the safety of her mother's comforting bosom. The pattern was ingrained though, and no one came. The slamming of a door caused her eyes to blink and her body to jump. She waited. Her tiny heart pumped ferociously. The male voice disappeared. Another sound occupied the space. She couldn't put a name to it, but someone was feeling sad. She continued to stare at the bedroom door. Time passed slowly. She wasn't sure when she fell asleep again, but her mummy didn't come. When she woke, the room was filled with bright light and her mummy stood over the bed, carrying boxes wrapped in pretty paper. Her mother's mouth smiled, but her eyes looked different and those eyes didn't look at her. Instead they looked at the box in her tiny hand. 'Open it,' she had said. In the afternoon they had cake with four candles on it. 'Happy birthday darling,' she had said. The man that she had called daddy didn't come back for any birthday cake.

Eva sat bolt upright, her heart thumping through her fragile frame into the darkness, and opened her eyes. She was alone. Her wild eyes scanned the room then closed again, and she fell back into the mattress.

18.

'What do you think you'll do with the business?' Carine asked tentatively. She had avoided asking the question for as long as she could. They were heading into a new year and she needed to know if she still had a place at the agency she had been brought into, to head up.

Eva looked up from the screen that had held her attention for the past hour, slightly bemused at being asked something to which the answer was obvious in her own mind. 'I don't have any plans,' she said. 'That's why you were brought in, if I remember rightly.' There was no animosity in her voice as she relayed the facts. 'I need you to carry on doing what you're doing,' Eva said without further thought. She didn't notice Carine's facial expression soften, or hear the long puff of air she released from her lungs. Eva's concentration had already diverted to an email that had just hit her in box. She needed to know its contents and didn't have time for discussing business matters with Carine. It had only been five days since she had spoken to Mitch, and with it being New Year's Eve she hadn't expected to hear anything until at least the early part of January. She clicked the icon, aware that her hands were shaking, her heart sinking with the words on the screen.

I just wanted to update you. I haven't found him yet.

'You okay?' Carine asked, noticing Eva's tension.

Eva's body softened a little as she read the second line of the email.

I'm checking out a lead. You have a cousin I believe. A Sandra Adams, your father's brother's daughter. She's 35 years old and lives in Cardiff. I'll update you when I know more.

A slight smile appeared on Eva's face. She looked up, to respond to Carine's voice. 'Sorry, did you ask me something?' she asked.

Carine studied the transformation in Eva again. 'No, that's okay. As long as you're okay?'

'Sure, I'm good.'

Eva's response was clipped, and the contradiction with the intimacy Carine experienced with her on Christmas Day was the cause of the aching sensation gripping her chest.

She had eventually decided to leave Eva's house in the early evening of Boxing Day and even though they had worked together pretty much every day since, Eva had been distant, evasive even. Carine had managed to justify the coldness as Eva dealing with her grief, and she had tried to protect herself too, but her body still yearned for the touch of the woman that had transformed her own world that night. As hard as she tried to convince herself she could and should walk away, her heart wouldn't comply. She had fallen for Eva in a way that she hadn't with any of her previous lovers.

'What are you doing tonight?' Carine asked, her tone bordering on the desperation of a lonely woman.

'I don't know,' Eva said. She hadn't given it any thought. 'Probably head to *Le So What*,' she said, having pondered the question briefly. 'What about you?' Carine had never mentioned her partner, other than to say she was working in New York, and Eva hadn't ventured to ask. But she was feeling inquisitive. 'How's Tori?' Eva asked.

The question sliced through Carine with the precision of a scalpel in a surgeon's hands. She hadn't expected Eva to ask about her partner, and her own physiological response to being asked shocked her. She didn't want to talk about Tori, and especially not now. Not since she had been intimate with Eva. There was only one way she could think to respond. 'Tori's fine. We've split up,' she said.

The words jolted Eva's attention and her eyes held Carine's momentarily. Eva wasn't deliberately searching for the truth, but when she found it, her stomach dropped. 'I'm sorry to hear that,' she offered, still knowing Carine's heart hadn't suffered from that particular fall. She wasn't in any place to take responsibility for Carine's feelings for her right now, either. In fact, she never would be. The idea of Carine falling for her caused a bubble of anxiety to burst in her gut. At the same time, she owed the woman. After all, she had been there for her at a time when her life had quite literally hit the lowest point. She smiled coyly. 'Want to come out tonight?' she asked. She'd deal with her internal struggle at some other time. Tonight was New Year's Eve after all, and no one should be alone for the start of a new year.

Carine smiled, warily. She was too old to be fooled, but too entranced not to accept the offer of spending time with Eva. 'Yes, I'd like that,' she said.

*

'I'm glad you decided to go out tonight,' Brigitte said, observing her daughter's response. 'You look gorgeous,' she said, pulling Rosa into a hug and kissing her on the cheek. Both women carried themselves well, combining sophistication with elegance. Brigitte carried the confidence her daughter had yet to discover in herself. Rosa huffed out the air in her lungs.

Rosa's apparent self-assurance - that had bordered on arrogance at times - had always served her well to disguise the insecurity she felt deep down, until Eva that was. Since Eva, her self-assurance had deserted her, and she had regressed into the reserved person she was underneath it all. She sighed deeply and looked at her reflection in the full-length mirror on the wall by the front door. 'Do you think so?' she asked.

'Of course. You look fabulous.' Brigitte spun her around, running her eyes over the classic cut of the black dress; knee length with a dipped hem and Baroque inspired embroidery. The sling back, open toe, stiletto shoes took her height to a couple of inches taller than her mum. The glum look on her daughter's face didn't inspire her that her set up would work though. 'Do you want to talk about it?' she asked.

'I just can't stop thinking about her,' Rosa blurted.

'Eva?'

'Yes.' Rosa's eyes lowered.

'Then go and get her back.' Her mother made it sound so simple.

Rosa frowned, her head shaking from side to side. 'It's not that easy,' she said.

'Of course it is. If you want her, make it work. If you don't, then let her go. Does she want to be with you?' she asked, almost as an afterthought.

'I think so.' Rosa said.

'Then what's the problem?'

'Her drinking,' Rosa admitted. 'Well it's not even that. It's the fact that she doesn't... connect,' she said after a moment's thought. 'It's like she's somewhere else, and not with me. She becomes distant and I can't get close to her.'

'She's been hurt,' Brigitte stated.

'Yes. I guess so.'

'Well, if anyone can help her, you can,' Brigitte said, cupping her daughter's face and holding her eyes with sincerity. 'And, in the meantime,' she started, in a more upbeat tone, 'how about you go out there and have yourself a wonderful New Year's Eve? You can deal with this tomorrow,' She said, pointing a light-hearted finger towards Rosa's chest.

'Thanks mum,' Rosa said, planting a kiss on her cheek, struck by a wave of confidence.

The beeping of a car horn dragged them back to now. 'That'll be the taxi,' Brigitte said, helping Rosa into her coat. 'I won't wait up,' she shouted, as Rosa dived into the back seat, her mum's front door taking the light, and her voice, with it.

*

As the taxi pulled up, Rosa spotted the short skirt and high heels that accentuated Kaye's long legs. A light flush filtered through to her cheeks as she stepped out of the car, greeting those legs up close, before standing and giving attention to Kaye's beaming smile.

'I'm so glad you made it,' she said excitedly.

'Thanks for inviting me.' Rosa responded. Kaye's appreciation was apparent as she pulled Rosa into a vice grip before linking arms with her and stepping into the elegant wine bar.

'I thought we'd get a drink before meeting the others at the restaurant,' she said. Rosa nodded and followed Kaye through to the bar, noting the distinctive artwork adorning the walls. The clean lines and clinical appearance should have made the place feel cold, but it didn't. It felt cultured, and swanky. Music played subtly in the background, and the women drinking in the bar talked at a respectful volume. Rosa's eyes scanned the space. Classy, she mused. As her eyes landed on Kaye, she became aware that the doctor had been assessing her. 'You like it?' Kaye asked.

'Yes, it's an amazing space,' Rosa responded, glancing around with approval.

'White wine?'

'Great thank you.'

Kaye ordered their drinks and pointed to a vacant table. The glass topped, small round table, hosted two high stools. Sitting brought the two women into close proximity, giving a very personal feel that felt quite intimate. A young waitress, dressed in a white shirt, black jacket and tight slacks approached their table, hovering the two glasses on the tray on her hand. She lowered the tray and placed the glasses in front of the two women, smiling courteously, and wishing them a lovely evening. Rosa flushed, and Kaye chuckled.

'You feel uncomfortable?' she asked.

'Um… no… yes, a little,' she admitted. This was the kind of place she would have liked to enjoy with Eva. The thought had crossed her mind several times already, always followed up with a wave of concern as to whether that possibility would ever arise again.

'Want to share?' Kaye asked. She lifted her glass, taking in the wine's aroma before sipping delicately.

Rosa wasn't immune to the doctor. Her energy was soft, kind, and yet strong. She was also very pretty with stunning green eyes that didn't miss a trick. Perceptive. Sensitive. Caring. And hot. There was no doubt in Rosa's mind that Kaye Bennett would make a great lover. At least that was the message her body kept pressing into her mind. But…

'It's okay. You have someone else.' Kaye said. The smile gave a hint of disappointment, but she seemed to take the idea in her stride too.

'Her name's Eva,' Rosa said, encouraged by Kaye's apparent understanding. Kaye stared at her, waiting for more information.

'We got together eight months ago and broke up three weeks and five days ago.' Rosa screwed up her face.

'Ah. You're in love with her.' It was a statement of fact.

'That obvious?' Rosa smiled weakly.

'You probably have the number of hours down too,' Kaye said, injecting humour into Rosa's despairing tone.

Rosa's smile widened. 'I do,' she said. Kaye's face was breaking into a chuckle and Rosa joined her. 'Is it really that obvious?' she asked.

'Looks pretty clear from the outside. What happened?' Kaye asked.

'You know, the more I think about it, I'm not really sure.'

A look of confusion came over Kaye's face and Rosa shrugged. 'So why did you break up?' she asked, fascinated.

'I think I expected too much of her. She's so… infuriating. One minute she's intensely intimate and the next I can't get close to her at all. It's like she has the ability to shut down to everyone, and when she does it scares the hell out of me.'

'So, when she shuts down you don't feel needed?'

The question caused Rosa to jolt, another piece of the jigsaw dropping into place. 'I hadn't thought of it that way,' she admitted, running the proposition through her mind.

'Does she love you?' Kaye asked.

'Yes. I think so.'

'Was she faithful to you?'

'Yes.'

'So, you're scared that she might leave you. I'm guessing you ended it with her?' Kaye was nodding to herself, answering the questions in her own mind as she watched Rosa still working through her memories.

'What makes you say that?' Rosa asked.

'Your fear. Looks a lot like you're protecting yourself. At least this way, you're in control, eh?' Kaye's tone was light hearted, but the point being made struck like an arrow hitting the bullseye.

Rosa wanted to argue the point, but something deep down resonated. *Had she created the issue with Eva to avoid being hurt?* Christ, she had been hurting enough these last weeks. She took in a deep breath and released it slowly, feeling a slight shift in the tension in her shoulders. She picked up her glass and took a sip of the chilled wine, her mind running on overdrive. 'Thank you,' she said, bringing her focus back to the intense, dark-green eyes across the table.

'Happy to help,' Kaye responded, a satisfied smile lighting up her face.

'Shall we go and party then?' Rosa asked, after a brief moment of adjustment and another sip at her wine. She felt as if something had lifted, and she had never been more convinced about what she needed to do. Now though, she would allow herself the freedom to enjoy the evening.

'Let's.' Kaye finished the last of her wine and the two women headed out to celebrate the coming New Year.

*

'Hi.' Simone smiled warmly as she approached the bar to greet Eva. She had a soft spot for the scraggy blonde hair and silver-blue eyes. She didn't recognise the tall blonde escort on her arm though. 'What can I get you ladies?' she asked.

'I'll have a scotch please,' the tall blonde responded.

'Simone, this is Carine; Carine, Simone,' Eva introduced them, her eyes busily scanning the room. 'I'll have...'

'Sauvignon?' Simone asked, turning her back to the two women.

'A regular then?'

'It used to be. Then I discovered Girleze, but since...' her thoughts gripped her attention, and her stomach. 'In the last couple of weeks, I've been hanging out here again.' She tried to sound grounded in her words, whilst feeling anything but.

'Is everything sorted for Wednesday?' Carine asked.

Simone placed the drinks on the bar. 'Have a great night,' she said. Both women nodded, collected their drinks, and hunted down a seat in the newly renovated comfy area.

Eva threw her coat over the arm of the chair, and lowered herself into the soft seat. The cushions embraced her body, encouraging the air out from her lungs. Suddenly, she felt tired. Drained. 'I guess so,' she said after a moment of reconciling the nauseous feeling that accompanied any thoughts of her mum's funeral service. She'd tried to bury her head, get lost in finding her father, but there was no escape. She had to face the fact, because it would be facing her on Wednesday morning at 10.30. 'I've invited the only people I know and put a note in the local newspaper. It's a cremation, with drinks in the bistro. Frank is closing the place for the day and doing the catering. I can't think of anything else.' She reeled off the actions on her mental tick list, sobered by it, conflicted by the fact that it was New Year's Eve and should be a time of celebration. All she felt like doing was running away. But, then for the most part that's all she ever felt like doing. She stared across at Carine, trying to find another feeling. Nothing came. Yes, Carine was a beautiful woman: strong, alluring, smart, caring. Yes, sex had been something else too. As Eva reflected on their night together, she felt reassured that her body sparked with interest but more than a little disgusted with herself for satisfying her needs with a woman that wasn't Rosa. Looking into the dark blue eyes across from her, she knew they were not the eyes that held her heart. Those eyes were brown: dark chocolate brown. Her hair was long, wavy and dark. Her skin was tanned, and her Italian features gave her a stately appearance. Her heart was warm, and her vulnerability touched Eva more deeply than anyone had. *She* was not the woman with the blue eyes, now staring seductively into her own blue eyes.

Eva felt the gapping space in her chest, its weight pressing down heavily, causing her stomach to turn. She took a long swig of her wine, needing the distraction, needing to numb the pain that consumed her every waking hour. She stood and walked to the bar. When she returned she was carrying an ice bucket with a bottle and a second glass. Carine didn't say no. The sombre expression on Eva's face was there for a very different reason.

'Will you continue to run the business for me?' Eva asked, aware that she hadn't formalised her earlier proposition. 'There's something I'm going to need to do, after the funeral,' she said. She was already talking more slowly, needing to concentrate harder to articulate her thoughts without allowing the negative emotional cocktail to come to the surface.

'Of course.' Carine's smile carried a sense of relief. She had planned to be around a while longer when she signed the contract with Rowena, and even though she didn't doubt her ability to attract another job, she had already invested a lot in formulating plans for the future of the agency. She enjoyed working there, and with Eva around life was also more interesting.

'Thanks.' Eva said, without expanding the conversation. Carine knew better than to ask. She would, when the time was right. 'I need the loo,' Eva said, pulling herself out of the warmth of the soft chair.

Standing waiting outside the toilet, Eva automatically studied the screen of her mobile. No messages. Not that she seriously expected any messages, at least not from the one person she wanted to hear from. Her ears registered the click of the latch and a woman exited the booth. Eva stepped forward without glancing up. The brief bodily contact brought her eyes up from her phone. The short dark-haired woman, staring back at her, sent a chill down her spine.

'Well look at what the cat dragged in.'

The words seemed unjust, but the repugnant look in Dee's dark eyes caused Eva's stomach to lurch. 'Dee.' Eva could barely get the name out of her suddenly parched mouth.

Dee moved into Eva's personal space. This wasn't a lover about to land a kiss though. Dee's face was contorted, her teeth clenched, her skin pulled tightly across her face. She was breathing fire. 'You fucking lousy bitch.'

'I...' Eva started to speak, backing off to avoid the spit flying from Dee's angry words.

'You fucking what?' Dee had her hands on her hips and even though she was a lot shorter than Eva, she looked vicious. Eva's heart was thumping through her chest. A woman exited another cubical at pace and another entered the toilets, spotted the scene and retracted her steps. Eva was alone, with Dee.

'I didn't mean to hurt her.' Eva pushed the words out, trying to hold her balance in defiance of the alcohol, and now the shock, that threatened her stability.

'You're nothing but a fucking drunk. I don't know what she sees in you. Fucking stay away from Rosa or else.' The threat was spelt out clearly, but Eva hadn't expected the punch that landed squarely on her jaw. Unable to control the fall, she hit the concrete floor, with a heavy thud.

'Fucking hell Dee.' She groaned at the searing pain in her head, which had collided with the side of the hand drier on her way down. She pressed at the tender spot and came away with blood on her hand.

Dee stared, briefly assessing the damage. Eva pondered the bright red substance on her fingers and the throbbing in her jaw. 'You'll live,' Dee said, turning away, and heading out into the bar.

Eva pulled herself to stand, stepped into a cubical and sat to pee. Her head was swimming and she closed her eyes to gather her thoughts. She stayed a while, nursing the searing pain in her head and face. *Did she deserve that beating after the way she had treated Rosa?* She allowed the tears to stream down her face in silence until they started to run dry. Relieving herself she stood slowly and staggered out of the cubicle. She splashed the cool water onto her face hoping it would help. It didn't. Leaving the bathroom, her vision seemed more blurred than it had earlier.

'What happened to you?' Carine stood sharply, reaching out for Eva as she staggered toward their seats.

'Nothing. I want to go home now,' Eva responded, unwilling to make eye contact.

'What the fuck?' Carine said, noticing the blood in Eva's hairline. She brushed a thumb over the sticky substance and Eva winced. 'Christ Eva, what fucking happened?' Carine said, with genuine concern and passion. She looked around the bar to identify a culprit.

'I fell over,' Eva lied.

Carine wasn't convinced but she was well aware that she had heard all that Eva was prepared to reveal right now. She huffed, grabbed their coats, wrapped an arm around Eva and walked her out of the bar. She hailed a taxi, and directed the driver to her flat.

Once inside, she studied Eva's head and face. 'Christ girl, who did you upset?' Carine said, making the point to Eva. Eva shrugged and tried to move away from the inspection. 'Eva.' Carine started to raise her voice. 'How did this happen?' She wasn't backing off until she'd had a proper response and she wasn't going to wait until Eva was willing to tell her of her own volition, because that time would never come.

'One of Rosa's friends.' Eva said, extending the word *friends*. Her eyes avoided Carine's as she spoke, and she tried to sound casual about the incident.

'We need to call the police,' Carine said, starting to work her mobile.

'No.' Eva's response took her by surprise. 'It's my fault. I caused this.' Eva's eyes searched skywards, fighting the tears that threatened, again. She failed, and a trail trickled down her face.

Carine pulled her into her chest and held her there until the sobbing subsided. 'It's okay baby, it's okay.' The mantra was beginning to send Eva into a trance, and Carine allowed her to sway. 'Some New Year's Eve party eh?' Carine said, softly, with more than a hint of sarcasm.

Eva sniffled then started to chuckle. 'I am so fucked up,' she said.

'No, you're not. You're just human Eva. Just like the rest of us.' Carine released Eva and poured two tumblers of whiskey, handing one to Eva. 'Cheers,' she said. 'To our fucked-up lives,' she added.

'Right,' Eva said, downing the contents in one go. She groaned with pleasure at the burning sensation in her mouth, but as her face moved when she swallowed, she became acutely aware of where the punch had landed. She cupped her chin. 'I need a shower,' she said.

'You know where it is. Use the robe on the back of the door. I'll dig out a movie.' Eva nodded, and headed for the bathroom.

19.

Eva's heart was racing as she paced up and down her living room trying to breathe normally. It was only a small space and she must have done a thousand laps already. She'd chosen a black suit, white shirt, and black tie. Her hands were sweating and with nowhere to put them, she picked at her fingers, reciting the few words of thanks she intended to say. Staring out of the window, trying to control her racing heart, the anxiety intensified at the sight of the taxi. Carine, in a black dress and long black coat, stepped out. Eva had opened her front door before Carine reached it.

'Ready?' Carine asked. Eva nodded, every cell in her body shaking in the worst way possible. Carine put an arm around her shoulder and walked her to the waiting car. Even the comfort of the familiar touch didn't help her to relax the tension that had consumed her body since the early hours of the morning.

The journey to the crematorium seemed to make time stand still, in a bubble of disbelief. As the car pulled into the grounds, the reality dawned again. Eva focused on the beautiful, natural environment. Even for winter, everything looked well attended. The barren trees reflected her feelings of emptiness. Death and destruction was followed by rebirth, apparently. She pondered the concept, staring vacantly as the car moved slowly up the long driveway to the entrance. *Nothing would bring her mum back though.* A few people had already started to gather outside, awaiting the arrival of the coffin.

Eva climbed out of the car, accepting people's condolences as she worked her way through to the front of the group, and straight into Anna's arms. No words passed between them, just a look, as they both held back the tears.

Anna squeezed her tightly and for a moment everything felt just a little bit better.

'I'm so sorry Eva,' Lauren said.

Eva released herself from Anna's firm hold. 'Thank you.' she said, maintaining her poise.

Carine stepped up behind Eva and introduced herself, immediately recognising Anna from her work with Rowena. She took Eva by the hand, and Eva let her, eliciting a slight frown from Anna as she tried to reconcile her mind's interpretation of the two women's relationship to each other.

Eva walked towards the front entrance of the chapel. Frank stood opposite her. He still had a twinkle in his eye, but his thin face looked gaunt. The remaining guests formed a line spanning from the two of them, creating a gap between the lines, leading to the main door. The pallbearers began their walk, passing the mourners with the cherry wood coffin with polished bronze handles perched on their shoulders. They moved the ornately decorated box to the front of the group, and led the way into the chapel. Eva and Frank followed immediately behind the coffin, and as they entered the chapel they peeled away to take their seats at the front. When the service began, Eva could feel her heart thump heavily through her chest and a ringing sensation in her ears. She wondered if she might faint. She watched the Civil Celebrant conducting the service, as if the proceedings were an illusion and she was having an outer body experience. Everything was happening in a blur. Until, the man's eyes landed with kindness on her, causing the scene to narrow into a fine point of focus in her mind. She stood slowly and made her way to the front, facing the congregation, and looked out across the small group of sombre faces. Most of them she didn't recognise, but their pain was evident in the glassy and downcast eyes around the room. Any smiles, were smiles of resignation, rather than happiness, and most likely intended to encourage Eva with her words of love and respect. Nothing touched her though, except her own pounding heart. She opened the sheet of paper and stared down at the words, before looking back up. Within a short moment she found herself sat back in her seat, but it was another ten-minutes or more before her heart had settled into its normal rhythm.

*

'Rowena would have loved it,' Anna said. She pulled Eva into a tight hug. The small group of friends had gathered in the bistro that had been a big part of Rowena's life in Paris.

'I hope so.' she said with a soft smile. She didn't feel the sadness she had expected to feel, more a sense of completion. Finally, it was over, and for that, she felt immense relief. She glanced around the room at the people enjoying the sumptuous spread. Carine looked to be working the room as if it were a networking meeting, but Eva was still grateful for the charismatic woman's efforts with hosting the wake. She watched people reminiscing, looking through a small selection of photos that lay on a table, surrounded by flowers and laughing at shared fond-memories of Rowena. Frank was doing the rounds with the champagne and glanced towards her every now and then, to check she was still okay.

'So, where's Rosa?' Anna asked eventually, unable to wait any longer to pose the question that had been on her lips for the past three hours. Eva held her gaze with a fatalistic look. 'Why didn't you tell me?' she said, throwing her hands in the air.

'You had enough going on,' Eva defended herself, knowing her case was a weak one.

'Even so, you're my friend for heaven's sake. You could have said something. I'll always be here for you.' Even before the words were uttered, Anna doubted their absolute truth. As much as she loved Eva, and would try to be there for her, her life was consumed with Emilie and Lauren. And, even though she felt as close to Eva as if she were family, they had only ever chatted on an ad hoc basis. She never really knew what was going on in Eva's life, any more than Eva did in hers. Eva gave her a look that said she knew as much too. 'I know,' Anna confessed, reluctantly. 'I've been busy. So, what happened?' she asked in a softer tone, though not willing to let Eva off the hook. She had seen the two women together often enough to know that there was more to their relationship than just a fling. Anna had even come to believe that Eva was falling in love with the gorgeous surgeon.

Eva updated her, including the gallant act of Rosa's friend, which received a sharp intake of breath. 'No way!' Anna's voice raised half an octave and her blood was starting to boil. As much as Eva's actions might be naïve and misguided at times, she was in no way malicious and certainly didn't deserve to be assaulted.

Eva smiled at her friend's reaction. It made her feel good, to know Anna cared, but she didn't need Anna getting upset about it. 'It's okay. I'm over that now,' she said. 'I'm trying to track down my dad,' she said, needing a distraction from the Dee saga, then realising she'd potentially just opened another can of worms.

'Your dad?' Anna questioned. She was beginning to feel as if she had just returned home from a round-the-world trip, not a three-week break in Corsica. 'Wow.' Anna's gaze rested softly on Eva's light-blue eyes, seeing for the first time the impact the last few weeks had had on her friend. She reached out and stroked Eva's arm with tenderness.

'Yeah I know. A lot has happened.' Eva raised a smile, but the sadness behind her eyes came across too strongly. 'I'll tell you about it another time,' she said, not wanting to get into that discussion until she had had more information from

Mitch. Currently, she didn't have anything to go on, and the thought had occurred to her that the whole search might come to a dead end very soon. That thought filled her with something she couldn't define, but it was an unpleasant sensation that she wanted to avoid.

'Let me know if we can help.' Anna offered.

'Thanks.' Eva said, but her voice sounded a little off key. She watched Anna observing Lauren and it struck her that they were the only people left in her life that she considered family. The thought gripped the back of her throat and she tried to swallow the lump that had started to form. 'Anyway, how have you been?' she asked with a shaky tone.

'Good,' Anna said, her eyes watching Lauren watching her. She would never tire of those dark eyes on her. Her heart fluttered, and she suppressed the adrenaline that was beginning to send a steady flow of heat to the sensitive parts of her body. *Not here, not now*, she told herself. It was the blush that gave her away to anyone in the room who might be looking.

Eva smiled kindly. 'I'm pleased for you both.' She had noticed.

'Are you coming to Emilie's christening?' Anna asked, changing the subject. '28th Feb,' she added.

'I hope so,' Eva responded, but her tone lacked certainty. 'It depends,' she said.

'On your dad?' Anna asked, softly. Eva nodded.

'Here baby,' Carine interrupted the conversation, holding out a glass of champagne for Eva.

Eva shook her head. Her body tensed as the term of endearment hit her ears. Carine had not long started calling her *baby*, and she hated it. In fact, Carine was beginning to feel like a weight on her shoulders that she didn't have the energy to carry. 'I need something stronger,' she said, excusing herself from Anna and heading to the bar.

'Hi, again,' Anna said, feeling the tension. 'I'll have that... unless you're.'

'No that's fine, here.' Carine handed over the flute, as the object of her attention knocked back a large glass of whiskey at the bar. 'Sorry,' she said, bringing her attention back to the present, and Anna. 'You're a good friend of Eva's?' she asked, already knowing the answer.

Anna smiled. 'Yes, we've known each other since we were kids,' she said, aware that Carine wasn't really interested in making conversation.

'Do we need to catch up some time regarding your work?' Carine asked, a genuine smile forming as her mind settled on something she was good at: something she could control - the business.

'Sure. I'll drop you an email and we can arrange a time.' Anna sipped at the drink before excusing herself and seeking out the dark eyes across the room.

Carine surveyed the room, halting at Eva's intent look over the top of the short glass. She watched as Eva emptied the glass, placed it on the bar and indicated for another. Carine walked slowly, deliberately, and perched on the tall bar seat next to Eva. She nodded to the bar tender for a whiskey. 'You okay?' she asked, but she wasn't referring to the events of the day, and Eva knew that too.

'Fine.' The clipped response gave away what the word concealed.

'Want to talk?' Carine asked. She didn't, just in case she heard something she didn't want to accept. Even though, as lovers they had been a once only affair to date - a simple matter of timing, of intense need and escapism - she still hoped for more. They were good together, really good. She could feel the heat rising into her chest at the thought of the intensity they had shared that night. They made a great power couple too. She just needed to give Eva time, and be there for her.

'Later,' Eva responded belatedly to the question. Picking up her drink she started to make her way around the guests to thank them all for coming. Carine felt the tightness in her chest and called for another drink. *Give her time*, she repeated the mantra in her head.

20.

'So how was London? We've missed you.' Dee asked, nodding with approval as she assessed Rosa for the answer. 'You look well,' she confirmed.

'It was good, mother was brilliant.'

Dee stared at Rosa. Judging by the sparkle in her eyes, she was expecting more information from her friend. 'And?' she asked.

Rosa wrinkled her brow momentarily, until it dawned on her that Dee had made an assumption about why she looked so happy. As she studied her friend, it also dawned on her that the decision she had taken whilst at her mother's wouldn't go down too well. She went to speak, then hesitated.

'Who is it?' Dee said, beginning to tease her, wagging a finger as if to say, she'd got the measure of what was going on.

'There isn't anyone,' Rosa responded, but the rush of blood to her face gave her away instantly.

Dee's eyebrows bunched and then her eyes widened. She knew differently, but she also figured now wasn't the time to press the point. She'd ask again after work, when they went for a drink.

'Anyway, how was your Christmas?' Rosa asked, as she put on her gown for surgery.

'Great,' Dee responded. An image of Eva lying on the toilet floor, blood on her fingers from the cut to her head, caused the doubt in her voice. She had had too much to drink and seeing Eva sitting with the tall blonde woman all evening had riled her. She hadn't intended to thump her though, and that thought sent a rush of guilt to the surface of her skin.

'So, what did you get up to then?' Rosa said, with a smirk, as she sensed Dee hiding something of interest.

'Clubbing. The usual,' she said, trying to sound unperturbed, but coming across even more deceptive. It was unlike Dee to withhold information, and in fact, she wasn't very good at it either. Dee turned her back, but Rosa picked up the tension in her shoulders and neck.

'You and Angie still good?' she asked, suddenly concerned that they had split up.

Dee looked over her shoulder. Her smile wasn't reflected in her eyes, though. 'We're fine,' she said, leaving Rosa even more confused. Dee's energy had shifted within seconds and now there was a void between them. 'Um… I don't know how to say this, and I'm really sorry, but Eva's got a new girlfriend,' she said, leaving the bomb to shed its shrapnel inside Rosa's world.

Rosa gasped, and her stomach dropped. She wished a void would take her in and not let her out again. Whilst her insides collapsed, she maintained full control of her appearances, and noted the clock on the wall. 'I've got to get going she said,' not looking back.

'Sure.' Dee watched Rosa leave the changing room, breathed deeply, and released the air slowly. She needed to know, she told herself.

*

Eva slumped into the chair in her living room. She had loosened the tie around her neck, unbuttoned the top of the shirt and opened the jacket, feeling a sense of release with every step. She swilled the light brown liquid around the glass, sipped from it, and savoured the warmth on the back of her throat. She felt strangely at peace with the silence in the room. Even her ears had stopped ringing. She lay back into the couch and allowed her eyes to close. She didn't know what the future held, but she vowed to do her best to get what she now knew she wanted more than anything. Rosa.

The light tap on her door roused her. She yawned as she stood, squinted through tired slits and plodded to the door. 'Come in,' she said, but Carine had already stepped over the threshold and before Eva closed the door she had kicked off her heels and grabbed herself a glass from the kitchen. She walked through to the living room pouring the whiskey into her tumbler, topping up Eva's glass before she slumped onto the couch.

'Fancy a movie?' Eva asked. She had no intention of anything developing between them, ever again, but she couldn't be rude and just throw the woman back onto the street, and especially after she had just helped her to get through the funeral. Carine still hadn't answered her question, but she had downed her drink and was pouring another. 'You okay?' Eva asked, suddenly aware that Carine's hand was shaking.

Carine's glassy eyes caught Eva before she could look away. 'Not really,' she said. Her voice was broken, and she had lost the Parisian elegance she had worn so well since turning up at Rowena's side.

Eva sighed. She didn't want the pressure of Carine's affections. Not now. Not ever. She thought that message had been made clear the night Dee had punched her and she had confessed her love for Rosa. What she and Carine had had together was... a moment. 'I'm sorry,' she said.

'I am too. We are great together, you know.'

Eva scanned the floor and a flush of heat rushed to her cheeks, as the memories of that night flooded her system. The residual effects were already causing her nervous system to fire, and her clit had started to pulse. She bit down on her lip to create a different type of pain; one that redirected her focus. It had the opposite effect and she cursed to herself at

163

her body's swift betrayal of her mind's intentions. As she lifted her eyes, she couldn't deny the truth. 'Yes, we were.' She puffed out a couple of breaths, collected her drink from the coffee table and took a long swig, holding the liquid in her mouth as a distraction. She wanted to feel the burn for longer. She wanted to wake up, to kick herself out of her habitual response to the events in her life. Carine's eyes pierced her, their heat weakening her resolve and fuelling her desire. Eva could feel the intensity between them sucking her in. She pinched the bridge of her nose, pressing hard into the corners her eyes, and tried to find something else to take her attention away from what she might be about to do. The duel had been set in motion, and only she could decide the part of herself that would win.

Carine stepped into Eva's space. 'I know you want this as much as I do,' she said. The lower pitch in her voice and the dark blue rings of her irises penetrated Eva's core. The tingling sensation worked its way up to her neck, causing her to shudder. She could feel the heat of Carine's breath on her ear. Carine started to run her fingers from Eva's waist up towards her breasts, causing a fire to break out across her skin.

Eva's eyes wanted to close, but doing so would leave her powerless to stop Carine's advances. She had to fight hard to keep them open, blinking quickly to break the trance. Carine's lips moved closer and Eva could feel herself groan inside. She needed that touch. She wanted *that* touch, but, not from this woman. She stepped back a fraction, away from the heat, and opened her eyes fully. 'I can't.' The words lacked conviction, but it was a start.

Carine smirked, her tongue sweeping across her lips seductively, closing the gap again. She had sensed Eva's weakness. Yes, she had had far too many to drink and she had intended to give Eva time, but she knew when a woman wanted sex with her, and Eva's body was giving off all the right signals. 'One last time,' she said. Her eyes had darkened, and her cheeks were glowing a healthy pink. 'Please fuck me?' she begged. Her clit was on fire and the only thing that was going to bring her back down was Eva, inside her.

Eva's sex reacted to the request and her mouth parched at the sight of Carine's erect nipples through her light blouse. The small pert breasts were crying out for attention. Eva's hand twitched, raring to go. She turned her head swiftly, allowing her eyes to rest on the wall, the television, and then the curtains: anything but Carine's aroused body. She could feel her heart racing and tried to calm it down. It accelerated, as she felt the heat of Carine pressing against her. She turned out of the contact, her hands clamping her head. 'No.' She hadn't realised she could shout, but she did.

Carine jumped back, shocked out of the trance that had been urging her on. Suddenly sobered, she held her hands up in front of her. 'I'm sorry,' she said, stepping even further away from Eva.

Eva turned to look at Carine, trying to control the shaking that had overtaken her. 'It's okay.' She pressed her hands to her face. 'It's okay,' she repeated, rubbing furiously at her forehead and temples, as if cleansing her thoughts through a physical ritual. When she looked up, Carine was rubbing her own hand through her hair. She appeared uncharacteristically flustered. 'It's okay,' Eva said again, wanting to make the point.

'I'm sorry. I pushed, and I shouldn't have.' Carine confessed.

Eva's head acknowledged the apology, although her body still hadn't calmed from the arousal. After a few moments a smile formed, and then a light chuckle, her nerves driving the irrational response to the delicate situation. Carine wasn't smiling. 'I know we had a thing,' Eva said. 'But, you and me...' she pointed between the two of them. 'We're... well, we're not right for each other.' She held Carine's eyes, hoping they were both on the same page. 'And, I'm in love with Rosa.' The words were said quietly, but with no lack of certainty. 'And, I intend to try and get her back,' she added.

Carine stared, unwilling to be convinced. 'Want another drink?' she asked. Something had shifted, something Eva hadn't even noticed.

'No, I don't think I do.' Eva said. Something about expressing her wishes, her desires, her intentions, had fuelled the flame of determination. 'I need to go to bed,' she explained.

Carine emptied her glass and placed it on the table. As she brushed past Eva she pressed a kiss on the side of her cheek. 'I'll see you tomorrow,' she said, before letting herself out of the door.

Eva sighed deeply, a sense of freedom filling her. The sensation was strange, yet refreshing. She picked up her phone and tapped out the message that she hoped would help her to turn her life around. The response came immediately.

Tomorrow, 10 at the studio?

Eva smiled, pleased with having taken the first step. She had already convinced herself that Charlie would be able to help her. She just didn't quite know how.

Great, see you then

Eva sipped from the glass, turning it in her hand, pondering her last drink. She felt torn. The warm feeling burning on the back of her throat as the whiskey slid effortlessly, providing comfort and reassurance, but she wouldn't miss the raging hangovers that seemed to stream from day to day. She felt a wave of anxiety sweep through her at the thought of her impending abstinence, but swiftly replaced the negative image with Rosa's smiling face. *She* was worth it. Placing her glass in the kitchen she stepped through to her bedroom, stripped and slid between the cool covers. Tomorrow was both the end, and the beginning. The rebirth.

The thought terrified and excited her at the same time, and her eyes struggled to shut long into the night as her mind battled the demons and her conditioned response, to resist the changes and run away.

*

Eva woke, feeling exhausted and wavering on her commitment to change. Having showered and dressed as if she were in a hurry, she padded through to the kitchen and popped a pod in the coffee machine. The edgy feeling didn't go away. She downed the sweet espresso in an instant. She made another, and slid two slices of bread into her toaster, before pacing around her living space. The anxiety that had been with her since the evening was becoming intolerable. She played with the idea of backing down, and enjoyed the sense of relief that the thought engendered. It would be so easy to cancel her meeting with Charlie; so easy to take a quick drink and dampen the uncomfortable sensations raging in her chest. She tried to breathe through the constricted feeling in her throat, and the sound of the toast popping caused her to jump and her heart to race.

She worked hard to control the shaking knife as she spread the butter with an unsteady hand, unable to deal with the swell of emotion building inside her. The falling tears turned to sobs, and she fell to her knees, holding her head in her hands. She rocked herself, allowing the pain of grief to consume her. The toast would wait.

Eva couldn't recall for how long she had cried, just that time had passed in a blur, and the fact that the toast would now be cold and brittle. She stood slowly, feeling entranced by the desire to survive, driven by a force she hadn't realised existed in her before. The transcendent feeling had a quality of calmness that had been absent in her earlier, more obsessive, behaviour. Something had shifted within her and for the life of her she didn't know what that something was.

Eva glanced at her phone. 9.30. She threw the toast in the bin and headed for the door. She would walk to Charlie's dance studio, and take in the fresh air. Exiting her flat, the thunderous drops descending from the dark clouds caught her by surprise. She pulled her jacket collar high up her neck and stepped into the cold rain.

Approaching the address on the crumpled-up leaflet Eva pulled out of her jacket pocket, the heavy feeling of anxiety that had rendered her paralysed earlier had been replaced with the light buzz of excitement. The smile on her lips carried through to her eyes, as she spied the name above the door. *Love to Dance*. It summed up Charlie. The door opened just as Eva's hand reached the bell. Charlie's beaming smile and gentle aura immediately caressed Eva, causing her to release a long breath. 'Thanks for...' She paused, taken aback by the depth of concern in the hazel eyes assessing her. 'Thank you for seeing me,' she said, completely oblivious to the fact that she had been followed.

'Come in.' Charlie opened the heavy metal door fully, allowing Eva to enter the studio. Shutting the door firmly, she led Eva through to the back of the building. Several rooms fed off of a long corridor, which in turn led through a locked door to a spiral staircase. Eva ascended the stairs into an open plan, light, airy space. Her eyes soaked up the converted warehouse style accommodation that seemed to house a large living space, and kitchen-dinner. She surmised that the four doors feeding off the large open room led to bedrooms and or a bathroom. The black and white décor was fitting, trendy and very unexpected. 'Would you like to sit?' Charlie asked. 'Or if you'd prefer, we can talk while you walk?' she offered waving her arm out around the room, causing Eva to raise an eyebrow, and a smile.

Eva hadn't thought about walking around, but the idea seemed to resonate well with her need to be active. Sitting still seemed to enhance the edgy feeling in her gut. 'I'm happy to keep moving,' she said.

Charlie studied Eva intently, but with softness in her gaze. She breathed in deeply, closed her eyes and breathed out, a long breath, a slow breath, before opening her eyes again. This time, when she studied Eva, her pupils were dilated, but there was nothing remotely seductive about the connection between them. Charlie's features had taken on a slightly more serious disposition, though her eyes still held their light sparkle. 'How can I help?' she asked.

'I need to get clean.' Eva said, her eyes lowering as she spoke. I have to stop drinking and I was hoping you could help,' she added, raising her eyes, pleadingly.

Charlie tilted her head a fraction, recognising the desperation in Eva's words. 'Will you follow instructions?' she asked, watching for Eva's response. Eva started to snigger, and Charlie stared at her, sternly. 'I'm serious. If you won't follow instructions, then no one can help you. I will give you all the support you need, but you need to be strong too. How much do you want to stop drinking?' she asked.

Eva's eyes shot to the tall ceiling, trying to avoid the tears that were pushing their way through. The burning pressure behind her eyes won the battle and a steady stream fell down her cheeks. 'I have to stop. I can't...' she stopped, willing the words to come. She took in a deep breath and started to speak on the flow of air she released, hoping it would drive the words. 'I can't control the drink, so I need to stop,' she said, her wet eyes holding Charlie's as she spoke. She rubbed the back of her hand across her cheeks, reached into her pocket for a tissue and blew her nose.

'I believe you,' Charlie said. The smile that was filled with compassion caused the tears to gather speed down Eva's cheeks. Charlie stepped towards Eva. 'Give me your hand?' she said. The command felt more like a request.

Eva complied and held out her right hand. Charlie took the hand, nestling the back of the hand in her own palm, turning Eva's hand palm up. She studied the lines for a while before covering the palm with her other hand. Eva could feel the red-hot heat and tried to move away, but Charlie exerted enough pressure to stop her moving. Eventually the blaze reduced. 'What did you just do?' Eva asked.

'Do you trust me?' Charlie asked softly, her gaze intense.

Eva paused. Of course she trusted Charlie, even though she didn't know why she should. It was Charlie she had been driven to reach out to. 'Yes, of course I do.'

'Follow me.' Charlie led Eva through the first door and into a softly furnished room containing a small wooden desk, a large, blue, posture-ball, a large couch seat, a smaller seat, and a clinical style bed. 'Are you okay lying on here?' she asked, tapping the clinical bed.

'Sure.'

'Take off your shoes and jacket.' Eva removed her shoes and coat, placing the coat on the arm of the couch, and climbed onto the bed. Charlie pulled out a pillow from underneath the bed and handed it to Eva as she sat, with her legs hanging off the bed. 'Have you ever had Reiki before?'

'No. What is it?' Eva asked.

'It's an energy technique, and very relaxing. I will rest my hands gently on the chakras in your body.' She indicated with her hand on her own body, 'and you'll feel heat, tingling, vibration, which is all perfectly normal. All you need to do is relax. Then we can talk about what you experienced afterwards.' She shrugged her shoulders in a matter of fact gesture, and smiled. 'Sound okay?'

'Sure,' Eva said, feeling a little trepidation. She pulled her feet up to the bed and lay down, mindful of the need to follow instructions. As soon as Charlie's hand rested on her solar plexus, Eva felt a surge of heat through her abdomen. She jolted, wide eyed, at the unexpected sensation.

'It's okay. Just relax and enjoy the feeling.'

Eva closed her eyes and tried to let go of the tension she had been holding. As Charlie moved around her body, applying heat through the slightest of touch, Eva softened. Something about the quality of the touch resonated deeply within her. She felt safe. Protected.

Eva had no idea how long she had been resting on the bed, but when her eyes fluttered and started to open, she became aware that she had a thick blanket over her. She had fallen asleep. But more than that, she felt different. Lighter. It was as if the weight she had carried for so long had been lifted, but she was also aware of the feeling of vulnerability. Light vibrations starting in her chest, flowed out to her limbs and she began to shake, her teeth chattering involuntarily. She rose to sit and stepped down onto the floor, for the first time becoming aware of Charlie who was sat in the large armchair in the corner of the room, next to the radiator. Charlie motioned for Eva to sit in the seat opposite her, and she did.

'How are you feeling?' Charlie asked. Her voice was soft, and full of compassion.

'Umm.' Eva managed through chattering teeth, even though it wasn't cold in the room. 'Good... I think.' She furrowed her brow and rubbed her hands up and down her arms before taking the seat, immediately comforted by the additional warmth coming from the radiator. Charlie smiled sweetly, and Eva copied her. 'Thank you.'

'Would you like to talk?' Charlie asked.

'Yes,' Eva responded, without hesitation.

21.

Eva had been restless for news from Mitch all week. Working with Charlie had helped her more than she would have imagined, but she still had to deal with the anxiety of not knowing whether she would be able to trace David Adams. She had visited the studio every day and always walked away feeling brighter, lighter, and stronger. She hadn't had a craving for alcohol for the past twenty-four hours, and she was beginning to enjoy the freedom that came with not needing a drink. Though, she hadn't tested herself in a social environment yet, and didn't plan to for a while.

Sitting at the small metal table, sipping the bittersweet hot drink, her legs bouncing up and down with excitement, she waited. She scanned the entrance to the small patisserie, in desperation. Inside, she felt as if she had waited all her life for this information. The reality was that it had been just a few weeks, though she had checked her in-box daily since that very first meeting. The note from Mitch on Wednesday had been brief.

I've got the information you need. Can you meet me at the café at 11 on Friday?

She re-read the email on her phone, just to make sure she'd got the right day and time. It was now 11.10, and Mitch wasn't someone who did late. She stared down at the screen. There was no text of explanation, but then Mitch had never texted her either. She sighed deeply and sipped again at the coffee, adding adrenaline to her twitching legs.

'Hi.'

Eva jumped out of her skin. Her attention had been on her phone for a split second and she hadn't seen Mitch approach. 'Hi,' she said, standing to greet the PI, unable to take her eyes off the manila wrap-around folder in Mitch's hand.

Mitch's eyes caught the attention of the barista. Eva noticed the quality of the smile that passed between the two women and felt irritated, irrationally. Mitch sat casually, and carefully placed the folder on the table. 'Expect this is what you're after,' she said, smiling at the urgency in her client's eyes. She opened the file and laid out a pile of photographs and a profile report.

Eva's eyes dived from one piece of paper to another, almost afraid to settle on something for fear of what she might discover. 'Did you find him?' she asked, hoping she had interpreted Mitch's email correctly.

'Yep,' Mitch responded, with a broad grin that took over her face, and even the small seating area inside the shop.

The barista arrived with the milky coffee that was Mitch's standard, and Eva could have sworn there had been some kind of physical exchange between them as the cup was handed over, but her eyes were so hungry for what the photos on the table would reveal, she ignored the intrusive thought.

Eva stared at the picture in her hand. The man looked older than she had expected. His hair, which had been thick and fair in the picture of him holding her as a child, looked wispy, grey and unkempt. His skin had a ruddy, weathered complexion. She picked up another, this time, a close-up of his face. Eva studied the glassy, vacant expression in the dark grey eyes staring out at her from the paper. Slowly, she placed the image back down on the table and lifted her eyes. Mitch was staring at her with a more solemn expression than when she had handed over the files and received her coffee.

'Where is he?' Eva asked. He, her father, didn't warrant the sadness Eva felt gripping her body, but it had hit her anyway. She breathed in deeply, bracing herself for the information Mitch had gathered.

Mitch stalled, and instead of answering the question directly, picked up the sheet of paper from the table and started reading, from the beginning. 'David Reece Adams, born in Wales, 13th June 1951, right?' She said, confirming the details she knew to be true. Eva's eyes blinked away the wetness forming on her eyelashes. She hadn't realised her father had a middle name. Mitch continued. 'He left the Army, a war veteran, in 91, about five years short of his end of service date. He lost his lower right leg in Desert Storm and was discharged nine months later. He went back to Cardiff, but struggled to find work, got into a bit of trouble - theft, alcohol, fighting - and ended up inside for a bit. After his release he disappeared for a while, but then turned up at a hostel in London...' Mitch looked at another piece of paper... 'Yeah, Christmas 2011. He's been on social services radar,' she said, looking up as she put the paper down. 'You're lucky. His record made him easier to track down,' she added.

Eva sat back in the chair and felt the wooden slats poke her in the back. She hadn't known what to expect, but her heart seemed to have stopped pumping the blood around her body. The prospect of finding her father had been one thing, but the idea of actually seeing him, that was something else altogether.

'You okay?' Mitch asked, noticing Eva's face pale. She reached across and placed her hand on Eva's arm. Her grip was stronger than her slight build would have intimated, and her touch was cold.

The pressure shook Eva from her reverie. She breathed deeply, her eyes darting from the picture of her aged father to the notes Mitch had just read out. 'It's a lot to take in,' Eva said, eventually.

'Want another coffee?' Mitch asked, already raising her arm to attract the attention of the woman she clearly knew. 'Thanks Estha,' she said with the same beaming smile as earlier.

'You're welcome,' Estha responded, a soothing smile appearing on her face as she glanced across at Eva. She placed the coffees on the table, turned and departed before Eva could think to respond.

'So, what are you going to do next?' Mitch asked. Her job was officially done, but she was intrigued as to what Eva would now do with the information.

'I need to see him.' Eva responded, automatically. 'Where exactly is he?' she asked, afraid of the response.

'He was sleeping on the street.' Mitch said. 'These images are from under the arches at Charing Cross Station,' she added.

Eva sipped the coffee, studying the image in detail. 'Thank you,' she said, with sincerity. She finished the last of her coffee and stood, holding out her hand. 'See you around,' she said.

Mitch stood and shook the offered hand. 'I'm sure,' she said with a broad grin. 'I hope you get what you're looking for,' she added.

'Thanks.' Right now, Eva was very tempted to take a stiff drink, but she felt even more resolved to resist the deep-rooted urge. She had work to do, and she needed to take a trip to London.

22.

Eva positioned herself at a window seat in the small coffee shop that had a vantage point down to the arches. She had walked around the area several times, trying to glance at the faces of the men who adorned the small alcoves of the closed doorways. She had watched from afar, and she had walked up close, even dropping coins in the dirty plastic cups that had the simple message *please help me*, scribbled on the side. Some of them came and went, but those who had claimed a space in a doorway didn't budge. She pondered whether they might still be alive, but that question was answered as the lump she observed shifted slightly. But, their faces remained covered in an attempt to keep out the bitter cold of winter. She ordered a cookie, but had no intention of eating it, hoping to hang out as long as possible before being politely asked by the owner if she had finished - a question that really meant, please leave so a paying guest can sit down! She watched intently, until her eyes were sore.

The afternoon was drawing in. She found herself squinting through the steamy window into the darkening dusk-sky, her view of the comings and goings down by the arches becoming obscured as every minute ticked by. Wrapping the biscuit in a napkin she stood and put on her coat. She exited the café and braced herself against the chill. She would do the circuit once again, show the recent picture of her father to anyone who might be interested, and hope that he was here.

She moved from one slumped man to another. Coming to a group of three men sat in a huddle drinking from cheap beer cans and smoking roll-ups, she stopped and took out the image. Presenting it to the group, the tiny slits of eyes and shaking heads caused a heavy feeling to settle in the pit of her stomach. She could spend days, weeks, searching. Mitch hadn't promised he could be found here, just that he had been spotted here. *Fuck.* A surge of negative energy towards the happy-go-lucky PI filled her mind with irrational rage. *What if the photos were a hoax? How did she manage to get so close? Where is he?* Question after question bounced around Eva's head as she pulled her collar up around her ears and carried on her search. It was only the third day of searching, she told herself, as she approached a man sitting inside a sleeping bag, with a mid-size black mongrel dog lying by his side. He, too, shook his head at the image.

Eva walked back to her hotel room, exhausted and shivering. She had walked for hours again, and her feet were sore. She hadn't even eaten since breakfast at the hotel. She'd given the biscuit to the man with the dog, who had apologised for not being able to help her, and he had shared it eagerly with his trusted companion. She threw off her coat and clothes and stepped into the shower, more in need of the warmth than food. As she towelled dry and pulled on a t-shirt and jeans, she opened the fridge door and stared into the mini-bar.

*

'Well, this is a treat,' Anna said, raising her glass to clink Lauren's. A night out had been a rare occurrence since the birth of Emilie, so to hit a club on a Saturday night was something akin to a luxury. 'Stop yawning,' she teased Lauren, who was fighting the sensation pulling at her jaw.

Lauren leaned in and kissed her on the lips. 'That's better. I just needed something else to occupy my mouth,' she said, in humour. 'Shall we go and sit?'

'Ha, ha. You don't want to dance then?' Anna teased.

Lauren studied her lover, wondering from where she'd gotten her sudden burst of energy. 'Maybe later,' she said.

Anna yawned, and Lauren nudged her. 'It's nice in here

since it's had a makeover,' Anna said, perusing the neatly decorated space, nudging Lauren back.

Lauren followed behind Anna. 'It's okay.' She said. She wasn't one for clubbing, preferring a meal at a table and an acoustic background that enabled two people to have a conversation without shouting. But she had agreed to Anna's suggestion as a treat. So far, it wasn't too bad. Both women made their way to the soft chairs and collapsed into the welcoming cushions. 'I don't think I'll get up from here Lauren said,' with a wry smile, before her face took on a more serious appearance.

'What's up?' Anna said, noticing the immediate change.

'I love you so much.' Lauren said. Something in her eyes was beginning to cause Anna to feel on edge. 'And I need to be honest with you.' Anna's heart was now thumping through her chest. 'As you were with me, about Eva,' she offered, by way of explanation.

Anna froze, suddenly concerned as to what was coming next. 'Yes,' she tried to say calmly, but the three letters got stuck on their way out of her mouth.

'I kissed my nurse,' Lauren said, watching for Anna's response.

Anna released the air that had stopped in her lungs, held her head in her hands and pushed back the tears that had tried to force their way out.

'I'm sorry,' Lauren apologised, leaning towards her.

'Thank God,' Anna said eventually, having gained her composure. 'I thought you were going to tell me something really serious. You scared the shit out of me,' she said, slapping Lauren across the arm. She puffed out a couple of breaths to steady herself. As her eyes locked onto Lauren's, a smile started to form. 'Is that the best you've got,' she said, jokingly.

'I just wanted to be honest with you,' Lauren said, taking both Anna's hands into her own. 'Before I...' she paused.

Anna sensed the seriousness in her tone again. 'Before what?' she asked, her voice full of concern again. She had no idea where Lauren was going with this conversation, but she needed to give her the space to get it off her chest. The emotional roller coaster was killing her though.

'Before I ask you...' Lauren swallowed deeply and focused on the hands that she was kneading to a pulp. She didn't want to see rejection. 'Before I ask you if you'll consider... having another baby with me?' Lauren's eyes pulled up slowly. She hadn't expected to see the trail of tears running down Anna's face, or the beaming smile coming at her. 'Will you?' she asked, facing the woman she loved with all her heart and soul.

'Yes.' Anna spoke the word quietly. She closed the space between them and planted a wet lingering kiss on Lauren's lips. Lauren soaked up the salty and wet warmth of Anna's mouth against her own, releasing her own tears into the mix.

'Hey, Lauren, Anna,' Rosa's voice prised them from their moment of joy.

'Hi Rosa,' Anna responded, rubbing at her eyes. She stood and pulled Rosa into her arms for a hug. 'Long time,' she said, before releasing her. Lauren repeated the ritual, a little more stiffly.

Rosa's eyes darted around the room. 'Is Eva here?' she asked with slight trepidation. Since finding out that Eva had a new girlfriend, she had dismissed any idea about them getting together. Her working hours hadn't allowed her to go out in a while, so the thought of coming across Eva hadn't occurred to her... until now. She felt torn.

'No, she's in London,' Anna responded, before it registered that there was probably a lot that Rosa didn't know.

Rosa's eyebrows rose and the enthusiasm with which she had greeted them died momentarily, replaced by melancholy at the news of Eva's absence. 'Join us,' Anna offered.

'Sure.'

'You on your own?' Lauren asked.

'I'm expecting someone, but not for a while,' Rosa said, glancing at the time on her phone. She was still trying to reconcile the fact that Eva was in London. Eva never went anywhere. It had taken all her persuasive skills to get her to go on holiday for a week late in the summer. She smiled inwardly at the exhilarating time they had spent together, reverting immediately to the painful state of today as she held Anna's gaze. 'What's Eva doing in London?' The words were expressed before she could prevent them. She wanted to know the answer, but she didn't want to appear nosy, or desperate.

Anna and Lauren looked at each other, creating a long pause. Anna turned back towards Rosa. 'Sit down,' she said.

Rosa sat, and her eyes passed from one woman to the other. 'Is she okay?' Rosa asked, the urgency in her tone an indication of her true feelings.

'She's searching for her father.' Anna said. Rosa's eyes widened. 'I'm guessing you also didn't know that her mum died, just before Christmas?' Anna asked.

Rosa gasped, a lump formed in her throat and her hands automatically covered her mouth. 'No, I didn't,' she said. She could feel the shaking in her core as it extended through to her legs. If she hadn't been sat, she would have fallen to the floor. *Poor Eva*. Her head was starting to spin with worry.

'And...' Anna was on a roll. She could sense Rosa's continued affection for her best friend - love even, and she wasn't going to let the moment pass without a few truths being told.

'And what?' Rosa held her breath. Lauren lowered her head into her hands hoping Anna wasn't going to say what she thought she was.

'And your friend Dee, punched her in the face on New Year's Eve, because she was out drinking with a friend from work.' Anna exaggerated the truth a little, and left out a few details that would only have only muddied the water.

'What?' Rosa's voice rose loudly, causing heads to turn. 'She did what?'

'Yes, nearly knocked her out.'

'Oh my God.' Rosa was shaking her head back and forth, incensed by the anger now coursing her veins. *Had Dee put one and one together and come up with five? Is that why Dee had avoided any conversations that might have led to deeper questions being asked?* Rosa could feel the fire in her belly. 'Where in London?' she asked, beginning to sound desperate. 'Is she all right? I need to find her.' Rosa said, unsure of where to put herself, as her body squirmed in the seat like a caged animal wanting to escape but not knowing how.

'She's staying at the Sumner Hotel,' Anna said. Then a thought struck her. 'I'm hoping she'll be at Emilie's christening at the end of the month. 'Will you come?'

Rosa's eyes scanned the two women. She hoped she would be as happy as they looked together, one day. The possibility of seeing Eva in three-weeks time filled her with dread, and hope, simultaneously. Though it didn't solve the immediate problem of needing to see Eva right now. 'Are you sure?' she asked.

'Of course,' Lauren said, feeling mildly guilty that Rosa had been omitted from the guest list in the first instance. Rosa might be a new - and distant - member of her family, thanks to her mother's marriage to Henri, but she was still family. 'We should have invited you before now,' she admitted.

Rosa ignored the comment, instead allowing her mind to consider new possibilities. She would deal with Dee, but she needed to calm down first, or she would be likely to do something she would regret. *How dare she?* Rosa was livid, and Dee would know about that, but more importantly she needed to find Eva. 'The Sumner,' she confirmed. Her smile was strained, but her eyes had a sparkle to them that had been absent a moment earlier. She was already working out a plan of action.

23

Eva ambled past the group of vagrant men, dropping George a latte, Ed a black coffee with two sugars, Phil a tea with milk and sugar and Jaffi a Cappuccino extra-hot. She'd come to know the men's names in the last few days. She'd bought a bag of dog biscuits for Marco, Ed's dog. She sat on the step next to the friendly, black and white terrier-looking scruff, amused as his tail thumped her repeatedly in the back. The men congregated around her, their interest piqued.

'No luck then?' George asked, assessing her, gripping the take-away cup in both hands, enjoying the heat, and sipping at the hot drink.

'I spoke to the shelter,' she said. 'They recognised him, even knew his name, but they haven't seen him since Christmas Day.'

George nodded.

'He used to come here,' Jaffi piped up. Other than asking for a cappuccino when Eva had offered, the dark-skinned man with silver curly hair hadn't spoken a word. 'Kept to himself,' he said.

Eva felt like shouting, 'Why the fuck didn't you say so,' but the old man seemed to drift in and out of moments of clarity, so the chances were this was the first time that he had remembered.

The other men shrugged. Not one of them had recognised the photo of her father when she had showed them a week ago.

'You sure Jaff?' Ed asked.

'I reckon,' he said. 'Used to sit in the yard-corner over there.' He pointed in the direction of a side alley adjoining the arches. 'Didn't speak to no one.'

She pulled out the crumpled picture and another that

had been carefully folded, unfolded the image and handed it over to Jaffi. 'You sure?' Eva asked.

The older man took the paper and looked it up and down. 'I reckon,' he said again, handing it back, sipping at his drink.

'Well, you'd know,' George said. 'You having been here the longest.'

'When did you last see him?' Eva asked, beginning to feel a rush of impatience.

Jaffi pondered. It wasn't clear whether he was searching his memories or had drifted off into another place and time. Eva waited, but her sense of urgency was causing her to fidget. 'Two, maybe - three - weeks ago,' he said, but Eva sensed that his concept of time, like his memory, wasn't to be trusted. 'Gammy leg... war vet.' he continued, receiving vacant looks from the other three men, who were listening intently.

Eva's mind started to work, testing all the possibilities. He could have moved on. He could have been locked up, and he could have been hurt in some brawl. He had a history with alcohol and violence and had done a short stretch before now. She would go to the police station and check out the local hospitals. It would be too much to search the streets, so she could only hope that if he had moved on somewhere, that he moved back again soon. Eva stood, stretched out her legs, shook herself down and began to check her phone for directions. 'I'll be back later,' she said. Marco whimpered as she walked away, and the men gathered in a huddle.

*

Rosa was shaking as she approached the Sumner Hotel. She had taken the more pleasant route through Hyde Park, making the most of the last of the winter's daylight. She had stopped by the man sitting on the bench, with two-brimming carrier bags at his side, whose begging words drifted on the light breeze. His silver-blue eyes had drawn her in, and his tone of voice - soft and kind - had touched something deep inside her. She had reached into her purse and handed over the two-pound coin, dropping it on the cloth at his feet.

'Bless you,' he had said, not taking any notice of the value of the gift. She had nodded imperceptibly, aware of his eyes on her as she continued through to the park exit, saddened by his misfortune, and humbled by his grace.

The short walk from the park to the hotel had been taken in deep reflection, the man's face being familiar in some strange way. As Rosa approached the shiny-black double-door of the Georgian terraced townhouse, she hoped she had made the right decision. A gush of heat almost took her breath away as she stepped into the foyer and approached the reservation desk. Taking in the understatedly stylish décor, she smiled weakly.

'Can I help you?' The fresh-faced young woman, with rosy cheeks and long fair hair neatly tied back, appeared from a door behind the desk. Her open-collar white shirt with a, light blue and white, stripped neck scarf, reminded Rosa of an airline hostess.

Rosa cleared her throat. 'I'm looking for Ms. Adams, Ms. Eva Adams,' she said, feeling the adrenaline lighting up her nervous system, and parching her mouth.

The young girl, whose name badge read, *Kirsty*, studied the computer screen in front of her, eyeing Rosa curiously as she punched the keyboard. 'Here we go,' she said, picking up the phone. 'Who shall I say?' she asked, waiting for Rosa's response.

Rosa breathed deeply. 'I'd like to surprise her,' she said coyly. 'She's my girlfriend.' Rosa blushed, and her eyelids fluttered slightly.

Kirsty smiled, enjoying the idea of a secret liaison. She looked around the small space, calculating. 'I shouldn't really do this,' she said, in something close to a whisper. '203, second floor on the left, it's easy to find.' Her eyes directed Rosa to the white door directly opposite the main entrance, leading to the lift.

A wide grin spread across Rosa's face and she released a long breath. 'Thank you so much,' she said. Kirsty smiled excitedly.

Rosa's heart was racing as the lift took the short rise to the second floor. By the time the doors opened, she was out of breath with the tightness in her chest and the pounding of her heart. She stepped into the short corridor, noting the brass numbers on the white painted doors. A light floral aroma filled the space, giving it a fresh, summery, feel. Standing outside room 203, she waited, listening. She couldn't hear any sounds from inside the room. She raised her hand to knock on the door, then jumped out of her skin as the door to 201 opened suddenly. The invasion, assaulting the silence, caused her head to jerk violently towards the banging sound of the closing door. Her knees tried to buckle, and she was finding it hard to control the shaking in her legs. The resident from 201 had disappeared as quickly as he appeared. She placed her hand on the solid fire-door of Eva's room for balance, closed her eyes, and focused on breathing deeply, urging her heart rate to slow. As her beat found its natural rhythm again, she stood to her full height, and banged as firmly as she could on the door with her knuckles. As she waited she could feel her pulse starting to race again. Excruciating. She waited. Banged again.

After standing for several moments, the weight of disappointment started to infiltrate her senses, and her body slumped against the wall. She fought against the rising sadness and chastised herself for the foolish idea. One last time, she banged again, this time louder, and fuelled with desperation.

Time seemed to stand still, as the rustling noises from within the room grew louder, making their way to the outside, and then Eva's voice asking her to hang on. Rosa's heart pounded at the sound of Eva's warm tones, and she could barely stand still, knowing the door would click open at any second.

It did.

Eva's eyes widened. She pulled the door fully open and stepped into the space, scanning the corridor, checking for nothing in particular; hoping she wasn't seeing an illusion. She flicked her fingers through her hair and her head bowed, unable to control the smile, or the heat, that was slowly taking over her face.

Rosa's confidence peaked, as her desire for Eva to love her was confirmed by the look in Eva's eyes, and her fidgeting feet. 'Can I come in?' she asked. Her voice was broken as she battled her instinct to pull Eva into her arms and kiss her with all the passion she possessed.

'Sure.' Eva stepped back, her eyes still avoiding the contact she wanted to make. Her heartbeat had shifted from the relaxed state of a few moments ago, resting on her bed plugged into her headphones, to the fierce pounding that had ignited the neurons in every cell in her body in a matter of seconds. The cause of that shift moved slowly into the room, and placed an overnight bag on the table opposite the bed. Eva watched every muscle carry out the simple operation, transfixed by the beautiful woman. The fizzing sensation in her stomach had sent a chain of messages around her body, all saying the same thing. The fire burned deeply, and she had no intention of allowing it to fizzle out. Rosa turned, and Eva had already closed the space between them. Her irises had darkened, and they were fixed intently on Rosa. Neither of them could be sure whose sharp intake of breath came first, or whose lips were responsible for connecting them again. And it didn't matter. The exquisite touch carried such urgency and passion that neither woman needed to breathe.

Rosa groaned as their teeth clashed and their tongues delved, reacquainting them, and more. Something intangible passed between them, then again maybe it had never really left. Rosa's hands fingered frantically through Eva's hair, pulling her closer, unable to get enough, wanting more. She had missed the taste of Eva; the sensual and intimate feeling that opened her heart with the quality of her kiss. She'd never felt it with anyone else. There was a raw essence to it that created a feeling of vulnerability, at the same time as being overcome with passion and lust. And, love.

Eva reached up and cupped Rosa's face, allowing her to disconnect from the kiss whilst keeping Rosa close. 'I've missed you,' she croaked, pressing her forehead against Rosa's, allowing her eyes to close as the scent of Rosa tantalised her senses. She felt like home and there was comfort in that. But, more than that, 'I love you,' Eva said.

Rosa pulled back, so she could make eye contact. She hadn't expected to see the tears falling down Eva's face. She brushed them away, running a thumb across Eva's swollen lips. Rosa bit down on her bottom lip, holding back, giving Eva time; giving them both time. 'I love you,' she said, softly.

The words drove Eva's eyes to lock on and Rosa gasped. Eva too, felt the sharp pain shoot through her, settling as a warm feeling in her heart. She kissed the thumb that was brushing her lips, and kissed the palm tenderly before taking Rosa's hand in her own and pressing it to her heart. Moving her other arm around Rosa's waist she pulled her close. 'Feel this?' she said. Rosa could feel Eva's heart thumping, in rhythm with her own.

'Yes.'

'*This* belongs to you. You make *this* want to beat.' Eva said.

Rosa froze as the responsibility implied in the statement hit her in the solar plexus. How could she have doubted Eva's love for her? As she looked into Eva's impassioned eyes, it dawned on her. Eva seemed stronger in some way. She couldn't identify what it was, but it was exceptionally alluring, and driving her sex crazy with desire. She moved her hand a fraction, her fingers brushing across Eva's erect nipple. Heat rose to her cheeks, and the blaze in her lower region intensified at the feeling of the tight bud against her fingers.

Eva groaned at the pulsing sensation shooting between her nipple and her clit. With the concentration of energy driving all conscious thought from her mind, her hands set to work. There was no time for finesse; this feeling was raw, fierce and in need of satiating. Clothes lay where they fell, as Eva manoeuvred Rosa to the bed, their mouths desperately searching, probing. Eva groaned as she entered Rosa, totally absorbed in the feeling of soft flesh, yielding effortlessly to her inquisitive fingers. She needed to penetrate Rosa deeper. She needed to delve into her soul.

Rosa cried out, as the exquisite sensation started to build, causing her hips to rise, craving more. She could feel herself opening to Eva's touch, but she wanted to feel her lover too. Suddenly thrashing wildly, Eva backed off in surprise, far enough for Rosa to slide down the bed and find the heat she sought. As she penetrated Eva again and again, Eva collapsed under the flood of sensation coursing through her.

Eva's mouth captured Rosa's breast, causing her to writhe beneath her, but the steady rhythmical thrusts into her own sex were causing Eva to lose the relationship between her mind and body. She struggled to coordinate her hands and mouth as wave after wave flooded her system and rendered her motionless. The flaming intensified, and Eva screamed out as the orgasm peaked and her hips bucked against the strong fingers inside her. 'Fuck!' she screamed repeatedly, while her body continued to reel from the aftershocks. Opening her eyes, she locked on to Rosa's dark stare, her fingers resuming their place inside the beautiful woman lying beneath her.

Rosa's eyes remained open, her teeth biting down on her lower lip, completely entranced by the tingling warmth building at Eva's deft touch. The scream that emanated was of a lower pitch, guttural, and it resonated with something deep inside Eva. That same shooting pain she experienced earlier penetrated her heart again and settled, with glowing warmth. She lowered herself onto Rosa. Rosa's residual shocks continued to play out on the leg Eva had resting between her thighs.

Rosa wrapped her arms around Eva and held her tightly, their bodies connected along their length. 'Want to talk?' Rosa asked.

'In the morning,' Eva responded, snuggling into Rosa's breast. 'I haven't finished with you yet,' she growled.

24.

Eva stepped out of the bathroom, tiptoed across the room, and threw on her jeans, t-shirt and jumper. She scribbled a note and left it on the bedside table. It was still early, and she didn't want to disturb Rosa. She took stock of the wavy mass of hair and distinctive Italian features, and smiled. The void had been filled, and she hoped it would be a permanent feeling. They would talk later. But for now, she had work to do. Pulling on her coat she closed the door quietly behind her. She walked on air, from the hotel down to Marble Arch, collecting the boys' early morning drinks from Caffe Nero's as she passed by. As she approached Ed, he looked uncharacteristically downcast. He sat, running his fingers rhythmically through Marco's scraggly coat, his eyes fixed longingly on his scruffy companion. She handed him the cup with his name on it. 'Everything okay?' she asked, sensing things weren't at all okay. She placed the bag of croissants on the floor beside him, Marco's nose twitching at the scent drifting past him. Her heart was beginning to race with her thoughts latching onto Ed's concerned features.

'Old Jaffi,' he said in a whisper, cupping the drink, and sipping from it before he continued. Eva's heart skipped a beat. 'Ambulance took him away last night.'

'What happened?' Eva's genuine concern for the old man she'd come to know appeared in the lines that had formed on her face.

'Dunno. No one's said nothing,' Ed said looking up, his eyes glistening from his own disconcerting thoughts.

'Where're George and Phil?' Eva asked, her eyes scanning the still dark street, trying to spot their silhouettes near the lampposts.

'Phil's pitched over there.' He pointed down the road leading to the park. 'And George's gone over Peckham way for a bit.'

'Oh.' Eva's voice betrayed her surprise. They hadn't said anything about moving on, but then she guessed they probably never did. She plonked herself down next to the young boy feeling as deserted as he must have felt, and sipped at George's latte, grimacing as the thick sticky drink worked its way slowly down her throat, leaving a film of grease on her tongue. She winced. 'What about you?' she asked.

'What?'

'What will you do?'

Ed scanned the street, up and down, and sighed. His long blonde hair was as straggly as his dog's. He had a strong jaw line, and beneath the scruffy, worn out clothes, laid a toned, athletic form. 'Nothin,' He sipped from the cup in his hands. Marco didn't even twitch, and remained curled up at his side. Eva watched the pair with interest. She wanted to ask questions, but didn't have the courage to broach a personal topic with this stranger. She sat for a while, reluctantly finishing the milky coffee, staring out at the early morning passers-by.

'I'll see if I can find out where Jaffi is,' she said. Ed nodded and reached inside the bag for the food. 'I'll pop back later.' Eva stood, leaving Phil's tea for Ed to drink.

'Thanks for breakfast,' he responded, but Eva was out of earshot, buried in the noise of the early morning traffic.

*

Eva crossed the wooden floor of the hotel sitting room and beamed a smile at Rosa resting on the deep-set couch. The heat from the fire created a soft glow in her cheeks, deepening her naturally tanned skin. 'Hi.' The movie of their night together filtered through her mind as she locked onto Rosa's gaze. Rosa noted the time on the clock above the fireplace. Eva had returned as she said she would, 11am on the dot.

Rosa reached up, grabbed Eva's hand, and pulled her down. Rosa jolted slightly as the cold lips met her warm skin. 'Hi,' she said, clearing her throat. She cupped Eva's chilled cheeks in her warm hands.

A hungry moan escaped, before Eva silenced herself by taking Rosa's mouth with her own. The soft warmth of Rosa's lips had already triggered heat in other areas of her body. She pulled back. 'Have you had breakfast?' she asked.

'Some. You?'

'Kind of,' Eva said, not meaning to be evasive. She swivelled around and sat down on the couch, next to Rosa.

'Want to tell me about it?' Rosa asked in a serious tone.

Eva nodded then began to speak.

By the time she had finished Rosa had stopped trying to hold back the tears and let them flow. Tears of joy, merged with tears carrying the deepest sense of grief, as Eva explained all that had happened and all that she had discovered in the last few weeks. 'I'm so sorry,' Rosa said, rubbing her thumb over the hand she was holding. Eva shrugged trying to shake off the truth, but her eyes were glassy. She pulled Rosa into her arms and held her tightly.

'I don't know where else to look?' Eva confessed, kissing the top of Rosa's head that was resting in her shoulder.

Rosa pulled away and sat upright. 'I've got to head back first thing tomorrow, but I can help.' Eva traced the fine features of Rosa's face with a tender touch that connected them both. 'Do you have a picture?' she asked, suddenly filled with a sense of purpose.

Eva pulled out the image and handed it over. Rosa's hand cupped her mouth. Eva's eyes dropped to Rosa's fingers wrapped around the image. She had been shocked too when Mitch had given her the pictures. 'You look... so, similar,' Rosa said, her eyes scanning repeatedly between the photo and Eva. Eva released the breath she had been holding, pleased that Rosa hadn't negatively judged the man's shoddy appearance. Rosa traced the printed features with her index finger, as if trying to connect to some energetic source that would reunite this man with his daughter. Whether it was her mind playing tricks on her, or her overwhelming desire to help Eva, something about the man she had passed on her walk from the station to the hotel niggled at the back of her mind. There must be hundreds of men sleeping rough, and many more places Eva's father might have moved on to. She studied the picture again, imagining what his voice might sound like, trying to compare it with the timbre of the man in the park. When she looked back towards Eva, she was convinced it was David Adams. 'I think I saw this man last night.'

Eva's eyes widened, and her mouth dropped open. 'What? Where?'

'Hyde Park. He was sitting on a bench. I gave him some money,' she said, as Eva jumped to her feet and pulled Rosa with her. Rosa could feel the twisting in her gut and hoped that she wasn't wrong.

'You coming with me?' Eva asked, holding Rosa's hand firmly.

'Would you like...?' The firm kiss to her lips gave her the answer. 'I need to get my coat,' Rosa said, when she came up for air.

'Sure,' Eva said, marching out of the room, and heading for the lift.

Eva took Rosa's hand and they walked down the main road, through the Queen Elizabeth gates into Hyde Park. The vast green space, carrying its barren winter coat, was more open, and breezier than the streets, and wouldn't offer much respite from the gripping weather. Eva strained to take in every slight movement as her eyes scrutinised the area. She increased her pace, hoping every step would bring her closer to him: to her father, David Adams.

'This seat,' Rosa said, pointing to the empty bench on the edge of the lake, within direct sight of the Serpentine Bridge. The seat was empty and there was no sign of the life that had sat there the previous afternoon.

Rosa could feel Eva's despondence and pulled her closer, as they continued walking arm in arm. They followed the lake around to the bridge, grabbing a snack and coffee from the café stand. They ate as they walked, crossed the bridge and headed towards Victoria Gate and back around the outer edge of the park. They circled the route again, taking alternative paths, leading in the same direction, ending at the Queen Elizabeth Gates. By the fourth time around, night was drawing in and the temperature had dropped significantly. Eva's expression weighed heavily in her feet as they trudged their way back up the road.

'I'm sorry,' Rosa said, Eva's sadness ripping through her heart as if it were her own.

'I just need to grab some drinks,' Eva said, diving into Nero's. Rosa followed her, grateful for the sudden injection of warmth. 'I've been getting the guys drinks and food this last week,' she said, by way of explanation. Rosa frowned, not wanting to point out the obvious question of what would happen when Eva was no longer there? 'I know,' Eva said. 'I don't know what I'll do when I leave,' she said, answering the unasked question.

'It's okay,' Rosa responded, squeezing Eva's arm reassuringly. 'We'll work something out,' she said, without knowing what that might be.

As they wandered up towards the arches carrying the drinks, Eva could see that the number of men gathered had increased again. Ed still sat with Marco in the locked entrance to what looked like a derelict building, and George stood beside him, fiddling with a roll-up paper and tobacco. Phil was still nowhere in sight, but another man obscured by George's torso, was laughing, and drinking from a bottle. Eva shuddered.

'Are you okay?' Rosa asked.

'There's someone here I haven't seen before,' Eva said. Her heart was racing with optimism and trepidation as she drew closer. Ed's eyes diverted towards her. He was laughing and revealing his missing first molars on the right side of his mouth.

'Hi Eva,' he said, his face settling into a smile that crowded his face. The other two men turned, and Eva's heart skipped a beat as she came face-to-face with the man with scraggly, thinning hair, ruddy cheeks and silver-blue eyes.

She stopped in her tracks as David Adams held her stunned expression with his own soft, glazed, eyes.

'Is this your man? George asked, taking the drinks from Eva's hands. 'I found him on my way to Peckham, so thought I'd bring him back here, in case you showed up again.

Eva was lost for words. Of course she was going to show up again. She hadn't said she wouldn't. But then she remembered, life was like that on the streets, never really knowing what would happen from one day to the next. Rosa put an arm around Eva's waist to remind her she was there for her. Eva didn't need to take out the picture in her pocket to know that the man staring at her was her father. She tried to clear her throat, reached into her pocket, and took out the image of her as a small child sitting on her father's lap. She handed it to the man with the silver eyes.

He scanned the image and his head moved back and forth. He brought the image closer to his face, studied it in more detail, looking back at Eva before returning to the picture. 'This is you,' he said. His voice was softly spoken, though his words were slightly slurred.

Eva realised he was swaying and her heart sunk as the very real possibility struck her, that he might not be able to remember her. Time seemed to drag, as she waited for another response from him. Her stomach in knots, she leaned into Rosa's hold, thankful for the strength she provided.

'And this is me?' he asked.

Eva cleared her throat. 'Yes.' Her eyes were sore with the pressure of the tears she was holding back. She looked away, turned her attention to the other two men in the group. All eyes were on her. She diverted her attention to the passers-by. Even they were glancing quizzically at the two women in deep conversation with the group of vagrant men. When she looked back towards the man with the ruddy cheeks, they were wet, and he was rubbing a partially gloved hand across them.

'Eva,' he said, but the word was barely audible, and his voice had broken.

Eva stood motionless, unable to stem the tears that were gathering pace down her cheeks. She stared. Rosa pulled her closer, her own tears starting to fall. Even George pressed his fingers into his eyes, as if to swat away the emotion. Only Ed beamed a smile, and rubbed Marco's back with the vigour of success.

'David. My name's David,' he said, taking a step towards Eva and holding out his hand.

Eva took the hand, noting the callused skin, surprised by the warmth in the exposed fingers. 'You're my father,' she said, watching for his response. His glassy-eyes lit up and a smile grew on his face as he processed her statement. She moved a step closer and held out her arms, their two bodies colliding in a fierce hold. Rosa rubbed her eyes and sniffled as she watched father and daughter reconcile a lifetime in one short embrace. No words passed between any of them. As Eva pulled back from David, she turned and remembered Rosa.

'This is Rosa,' she said to the group. 'My girlfriend.' Rosa melted at the smile in Eva's eyes. Ed and George beamed.

David approached Rosa, Eva still tucked under his left arm and held out his right hand. Within a moment he had both women in a triple embrace. 'Thank you,' he said.

*

Rosa had returned to the hotel and Eva could see the boys celebrating with a beer in the alleyway. The story would be passed down the streets for some time to come, feeding hope to those in need, and cynicism to those who'd been around long enough to know better. Eva sat, transfixed by her father's weathered face. The warmth of the coffee shop deepened the red in his cheeks. She had placed the photos on the table and he had given them careful consideration, his mind working hard to place them in time and space. He had shed a silent tear at the news of Rowena's death and Eva had fought hard to challenge the lump blocking her throat as she watched him grapple with a new reality. His hands were still shaking as he picked up the china cup and drank the hot milky drink. 'I can set you up,' she said, in a tone full of hope.

David shook his head. 'My place is here,' he said. His solemn stare bore no resentment or desire for change. Eva's chest tightened as an overwhelming sense of loss cut through her heart. She hadn't reckoned on him refusing her offer of help. His silver eyes held a level of contentment that Eva dreamed of, yet was seemingly impossible for her to attain. Her eyes lowered, and David reached out a hand across the table. Eva took it, savouring the sensation of his hand in hers, knowing it would probably be the first and last time. 'Can I keep these?' he asked. Eva couldn't hold back the sadness as it welled up from somewhere deeper than her mind could fathom, and shed more tears down her cheeks. She had never cried so much in such a short space of time. She looked skyward to gain her composure, catching the glint in his smile. 'I'll be fine. This is my home,' he said, looking out the window.

They sat in relative silence, until David's discomfort became apparent in his fidgeting. Eva smiled, reminded of her own propensity to wriggle when her mind had reached saturation for something. 'I'd best let you get on,' she said, standing, giving him permission to move freely. He stood, facing her. 'Please, take this,' she said, handing him two twenty-pound notes. 'It's all I've got on me. I'll get some more for tomorrow,' she said, feeling a little embarrassed.

'Eva.' Her name locked their eyes. 'I don't need your money. I do just fine,' he said. He reached out for her and when she fell into his arms he closed them around her, and kissed the top of her head. She could feel his heart beating slow and strong through his thick coat.

'Please take it,' she begged. 'For me.' She moved out of the hold and held his eyes pleadingly. Tenderness passed between them and he nodded his head in agreement. She placed the money in his hand and he pocketed it, before turning and leaving the café. 'Will you be here tomorrow?' she asked.

'Yes,' he said. Turning he walked over to the step, watched by the men sipping beer. He'd made some new friends today and for that he was grateful. *They would all eat and drink well tonight*, he thought. When he reached Ed and George he looked back over his shoulder. Eva had disappeared.

25.

'Thank you for being there with me.' Eva said, peaking over the menu in her hand, watching Rosa as she scanned the food options hungrily. She'd lost her appetite but wanted to enjoy what little time she had with Rosa before she returned to Paris.

Rosa lowered her menu and held Eva with a compassionate gaze. They had talked for hours since Eva had returned from the café. Eva had cried a lot and Rosa had comforted her. There was little more she could do. But she knew she would be there for Eva, no matter what. 'I love you, Eva,' she said, as if that was the only thing that mattered, and in many ways, it was.

Eva smiled mournfully through a resigned sigh. She lowered her menu and started shaking her head.

'What?' Rosa asked.

'I know I'm very lucky,' she said, leaning across the table and planting a tender kiss on Rosa's lips. 'I just didn't expect him to not want any help,' she added, still processing her dad's response.

'I guess this...' she pointed out the window, 'this is what he knows and is comfortable with,' Rosa offered. She could only imagine how difficult it must be for Eva to have to face the fact that her father would rather stay on the street than in a warm, dry flat. It was hard enough for her to relate to, and it wasn't personal, although she had instantly warmed to Eva's father, with his gentle energy and pragmatic approach. He certainly seemed happy.

Eva released another long breath, allowing the truth to permeate her illusion. 'Yes. I guess,' she said, before turning her attention back to the menu.

The waiter approached. 'What can I get you ladies to drink?' he asked.

'Wine?' Rosa asked.

'No, water's fine for me,' Eva responded, continuing to ponder the food choices, unaware of the slight frown that had appeared on Rosa's face.

'A bottle of water please,' Rosa said, addressing the waiter, who repeated the order and then left, returning swiftly with the drink and a platter of poppadum and dips.

Eva dived into the crispy bread. 'What are you having?' she asked.

'I'm going to try the Chicken Shathkhora. I haven't had that before,' Rosa responded. 'You?'

'Chicken Tikka Masala,' Eva said, with certainty.

A smile appeared on her face as she looked up from the menu. Its depth sent a warm feeling through Rosa's chest and down to her legs. 'I'm the lucky one by the way,' she said with a sparkle in her eyes.

Eva felt the heat rise to her cheeks, softened by the tenderness within which Rosa's eyes held her. 'I love you,' she said.

'No wine tonight?' Rosa asked, as Eva picked up the tall glass and filled it with water.

'No. I stopped drinking,' she said. 'It's early days, but I know what I need to do, and if I could get through the last two weeks without it, I figure I can get through anything.'

Rosa's eyes had glassed over with the gravity of Eva's words. A blaze sparked in her chest. She moved across the table in an instant and this time the kiss between them lingered. 'I'm so proud of you,' she said, after she released Eva's swollen lips, and re-seated herself. She picked up a poppadum, dipped it in the relish and bit down. Even though the move wasn't intended to be seductive, it hit the spot and Eva gulped. She picked up her glass and took a sip of the water, watching Rosa intently. Their moment was interrupted by the waiter approaching, pad and pencil in hand.

'Are you still hungry?' Eva asked.

Rosa's dark eyes lifted from the menu with a glint that only said one thing. She was hungry, but not for the food on offer.

*

Eva pulled Rosa into the room. She hadn't been able to down her meal quickly enough, with her mind being fully occupied by the sexy woman whose body she wanted to feel naked against her own in a warm bed. Her mouth clashed against Eva's, and their tongues danced together, with an insatiable appetite that they both shared. Rosa pulled back to gain her breath before pouncing again and biting down on Eva's lower lip, pulling and tweaking it, teasing out a groan. Passionately kissing, parting only to remove their own clothes, they staggered, naked, to the bed and fell onto the soft mattress.

Eva's mouth ventured to Rosa's neck, nipping and biting her way down to the centre of Rosa's breasts. She eyed the taut nipples and settled on the left side, her thumb and finger teasing the right breast. Rosa arched at the contact, and groaned when Eva parted her and settled in between her legs. The warm wet sensation pressed into Eva's sex and Rosa's scent gently tantalised her senses. The intimate rhythmical motion they shared, increased in pace and pressure. Eva's sex was starting to burn. It was too much, too soon. She lowered herself down Rosa's sleek frame, kissing and licking down her belly, savouring the spot just short of Rosa's clit, her tongue pulling up on the fleshy tip, sending a shiver of lust that caused Rosa to buck uncontrollably. Lower still her tongue dived between the silky wet lips, savouring the taste, the warmth, and the certainty of what was to come.

Rosa cried out as wave after wave of sensation turned her inside out and back again. She wanted the ride to never end, the rise to climb higher and the edge to drive the most exquisite drop into the abyss of happiness. And when it came, it delivered, causing a flood of tears as the depth of emotion ripped her in two. Her greatest fear was losing the woman she had now truly found. Yet the feeling of joy, and the ecstasy of being around Eva, was equally as punishing to her sense of vulnerability. She wept, and Eva held her.

*

'I don't want to leave you.' Rosa exclaimed, packing the last of her things.

'I know.' Eva said, kissing her tenderly. 'I'm coming home soon,' she added. Her smile was soft, caressing, and her eyes held their future in them. Rosa had never seen the same quality of sparkle in Eva's eyes as she did right now. 'I just need to sort out a couple of things here and I'll be back. I promise.' Rosa believed her.

Rosa's eyes blinked in acknowledgement of the closure Eva needed with her father. 'Will you...' she hesitated, took a deep breath, and started again. 'Will you come and live with me?' she asked, feeling more than a little insecure at the possibility of rejection.

Eva closed the space between them and eyed Rosa carefully. 'I'd like that,' she said, causing a sudden intake of breath from Rosa, who started squealing with excitement.

'Let's go and get some breakfast,' Rosa said, feeling lighter and more confident.

Eva took her hand and walked them down to the breakfast room.

Eva sauntered down to the arches with the drinks, including the extra-hot latte for her father. She was a lot later than her normal early morning visits, in part due to seeing Rosa off, but also because she had needed to wait until the shops were open, and on a Sunday, that wasn't until 10am. The men were sat around smoking and chatting, and greeted her enthusiastically as she handed out the drinks. 'How was your night?' she asked, to whomever might respond. She'd never asked the question to Ed or George, but her father's presence had increased her desire to know more about their life on the street and she was less afraid to ask. She needed to know that he would be okay, as illogical as that seemed given he had been living on the streets long before she descended on his life.

'It was fine,' David responded, sensing his daughter's concern. 'Where's Rosa?' he asked, genuinely interested.

'She's had to go back to work, in Paris.'

'You going back too?' His tone was more encouraging than disappointed.

'Yes, at some point.' Eva avoided giving any details.

'Soon I hope. Seems to me you have someone important waiting for you, and a business to take care of,' he said. His words carried wisdom and his smile was reassuring. Heat rushed to Eva's cheeks.

'I want you to have this,' Eva said, handing over a small package.

David assessed her quizzically. 'What is it?' he asked.

'It's a mobile phone. Open it,' she said, holding back a smile. I want you to have it. It's pre-programmed with my number and I'll take care of the payments for the contract. If you get into any trouble, or need anything, at any time. You call me. Promise?'

David grinned. He wasn't going to get away with refusing this offer of support, and actually the idea appealed to him. 'Thank you,' he said, staring at the package.

'Open it,' Eva said, impatiently. I'll show you how it works.'

'I did have one once,' David said with a wry smile, 'but I suspect they've changed a lot since then.' He tilted his head in recognition of the passing of time. 'How do I charge it?' he asked.

Eva's face contorted. She hadn't thought about that.

'There are loads of free places across town,' Ed piped up, with a beaming smile. 'I'll show you,' he offered.

'Thanks,' David said. Eva breathed a sigh of relief.

'Will you come and visit?' Eva asked, still unable to reconcile the fact that her father would rather stay here, on the street, than live in a home.

'Maybe,' he responded, but his eyes hadn't really registered the possibility. Eva sighed deeply, and David reached for her hand. 'You have a big heart Eva, a lot like your mother.' The reference to Rowena shocked Eva. 'My life here is so very different. I wouldn't cope well with living in your world, anymore than you would in mine.' His smile was gentle, nurturing even as his eyes directed the scene around them. 'I made my choices many years ago. For right or wrong, who knows? But, I'm happy here. This is my home.'

'I know,' Eva choked down the lump in her throat.

David raised her lowered chin and looked her directly in the eye, with a firmness she hadn't seen before. 'Thank you for caring enough to find me. I promise to keep in touch, and I'll let you know where I am in case you want to visit some time,' he said with a mischievous smile. 'And I promise, if I change my mind about your offer, you'll be the first to hear about it. You've given me a good reason to stay sober,' he said. Although, Eva doubted how long that might last in her physical absence. Her eyes confirmed her understanding and David released his grip, planting a kiss on her cheek. She reached up, touching the spot the rough stubble had stimulated. It was an alien feeling, and one she would remember for a long time. 'I'm moving on today,' he said.

Eva could see his eyes glassing over, and not from alcohol. 'Right,' she said, aware that this was his way of releasing her. 'Where to?' she asked.

'Over Peckham way, with Ed and George,' he said, matter-of-fact.

Eva nodded her head, biting down on her top lip to prevent the tears escaping. The lump in her throat burned fiercely. 'I'll be off then,' she said.

David pulled her into his arms and squeezed tightly, reaffirming their connection. Eva knew he would be true to his word about keeping in touch, but that didn't stop her heart feeling as if it were splitting into tiny shards. The pieces flew, fizzing into the darkness. As she watched the display, taking place in her mind; the shield over her heart splintering, separating and disappearing, she pulled out of the hold, for some inexplicable reason, feeling stronger and more complete than she had ever felt in her life.

The beaming smile on her face was met with an acknowledgement from her father that spoke volumes. He returned the smile. 'Take care of yourself and that girl of yours,' he said.

'Thanks, dad.' David's eyes shone at his daughter's use of the term, and he turned towards his compatriots to avoid the tears from falling.

Ed was rubbing his eyes and George cleared his throat before speaking. 'Nice meeting you Eva,' he said.

'Thanks for the… stuff,' Ed said, through a broken voice, petting his dog tenderly. Marco yawned, got to his feet and shook himself down. Ed stood too. 'Time to move on,' he said.

'Take care,' Eva said, squeezing her father's hand briefly, before letting them all go. She watched for a short time as they ambled down the street, before turning and heading back to the hotel. She had a few loose ends she needed to tie up before returning to Paris.

26.

The sound of the clicking camera blended into the hustling sounds on the street as Eva exited the dance studio. She was oblivious to the lens pointing in her direction. She had arranged to visit Charlie at the first opportunity, following her return from London and she had come straight from the airport, even though it was early in the day. The session had been a good one and she felt enlivened by her plans to support the men she had met in London… and her father. She hadn't been able to get them out of her mind, not without doing something to help them. The clicking continued as she pulled the dancer into a warm hug and placed a kiss on her cheek, before releasing her and skipping her way up the street to her flat. She needed to change her clothes and drop her bag.

Entering the cold flat, she shivered. The simple pewter urn still stood on the low table in the living room, reminding her of the arrangements she needed to make for her mum's ashes. 'Hi mum,' she said, dumping her bag and heading into her bedroom to shower and change. Rowena had specified the disposal details in her will, but Eva had needed to wait until the time was right. That time was fast approaching. She would make arrangements to take the ashes back to Wales and have them spread on top of her grandmother's grave. But firstly, she needed to sort out a simple plaque that could be added to the gravestone. Another thing on the list, she noted to herself as she towel dried her hair and pulled on her jeans and hoody.

She threw on her coat, grabbed her rucksack, stepped out of the flat, and headed towards the office. She stopped for a box of donuts en route, smiling wryly to herself as her mum's image came to mind, pleased to note the absence of sadness in that moment, instead, feeling reassured by her sense of Rowena's spiritual presence. It was another thing that had shifted as a result of her work with Charlie, and for that she would feel eternally grateful to have the amazing woman in her life.

Eva unlocked the office door and entered the empty room. She had expected Carine to be at her desk, but the air was cool, a clear indication that she hadn't turned up at work yet. She placed the box of donuts on the table and walked to the coffee machine. Eva opened her bag and pulled out her laptop, firing it up while the coffee hissed and popped. Having stirred the sugar, she sipped at the coffee and sat on the couch in front of the screen. She searched for memorial plaque sites and spent a few moments pondering the options, grabbing a donut as she researched. She would need to consider the inscription. She sighed, and clicked onto her emails. She wanted to update Mitch. The sound of one side of an argument, taking place in the corridor drew her attention to the office door.

Carine's smile was tightly formed on her face, as she entered the room with an unnecessary sense of urgency. She had clearly not realised Eva was at work until getting close to the office door, when the shouting had suddenly ceased. She crossed the room with only a fleeting glance in Eva's direction. 'Hi, how was London?' she asked, heading straight for the coffee machine.

'London was very good.' Eva responded, unsure how to read Carine's behaviour. She seemed pre-occupied. 'Everything okay?' she asked.

'Fine.' Carine spooned the sugar into her coffee, staring at Eva, assessing her in some way. The force behind the glare caused a wave of discomfort to strike Eva in the gut. Carine walked across the room, reached into the desk draw and pulled out a bottle of Macallan. 'Celebrate your return?' she asked. The sudden softness in tone seemed in conflict with the tension she had brought into the room.

'No thanks.' Eva said, grabbing another donut and biting into it, licking at the jam that had escaped down the side of her mouth. 'You want one?' she asked, whilst chewing and staring at her laptop screen.

'Thanks.' Carine took the couple of paces to the couch and sat, too close to Eva, deliberately brushing an arm languidly across her chest as she reached for the snack.

Eva backed off and stood up sharply, threw the remaining donut into her mouth and brushed the sugar off her fingers. She chewed briefly and swallowed hard, feeling more than a little confused at Carine's behaviour. 'You sure you're okay?' she asked.

'I've missed you,' Carine said, putting on her most seductive grin.

Eva felt the donut heave in her stomach. A tight grimace formed on her face and a rush of anxiety filtered through her body. She reflected on the fact that Rosa was unaware of her previous liaison with this woman and felt sick. She pushed down the self-disgust, and tried to put the situation between them back onto a professional footing. 'So, what's been happening?' she asked, ignoring Carine's advances. She had no desire to engage with Carine in a way that would imply anything between them - past or future.

Carine cleared her throat, stood elegantly and returned to her desk. Turning her eyes to the screen in front of her, she clicked at the keys and started to update Eva.

*

Rosa could feel the heat flushing her cheeks with the intensity of Dee's stare, across the canteen tables. The last few weeks had been strained. Rosa had made the point perfectly clear that Dee had overstepped the mark and that until she apologised to her girlfriend, they had nothing to say to each other. Working together they had remained professional with their communication, but aside from that they had hardly shared a word. Rosa missed her friend though and with Eva now, firmly back in her life, wanted more than ever for them to reconcile their differences.

But for a table of nurses just coming off shift and two patient visitors waiting for their coffee, the canteen was deserted, and relatively quiet. Dee stood, causing the metal chair to squeak, the loud noise drawing attention to her. She squirmed. The smile on Rosa's face carried across the room and Dee's mouth twitched in response. Nothing could intrude on Rosa's happiness and her eyes conveyed that message.

Dee crossed the room tentatively. 'Hi,' she said, hoping that whatever it was that made Rosa look so happy would also facilitate the forgiveness she desired, even though she hadn't been able to forgive herself yet. When she had explained what had happened to Angie, even she had ostracised her. She had been sleeping in the spare room ever since. The problem was, she hadn't been able to speak to Eva to apologise, and she really wanted to right the wrong she had done.

'Hi,' Rosa responded. She looked radiant.

'You look good,' Dee said, fidgeting her hands in her scrubs pocket. 'How's Eva?' The question stuck in her throat. It was an assumption, but one founded on the fact that the only person who had ever had that effect on Rosa was Eva.

'She's amazing, and wonderful, and I really am in love with her.'

Dee's eyes widened, and her jaw dropped a fraction. The openness with which Rosa spoke floored her momentarily. 'Wow,' she said, trying her best to sound supportive. 'I'm really pleased for you,' she continued, admiring the gleam in Rosa's eyes.

'She's coming home today. She's been in London,' Rosa started to rattle out all that Dee had missed. Dee made a move to sit and Rosa encouraged her.

'Rosa, I really am sorry about...'

'I know.' Rosa reached out and pressed a hand on Dee's arm. 'It's okay. I get it.' She squeezed Dee's arm reassuringly. 'Though an apology wouldn't go amiss,' she said. Dee nodded.

'You know her mum died just before Christmas?' Rosa asked.

Dee held her gaze. 'No, I didn't know,' she said, feeling even more shit than she already did about her actions. Her eyes lowered to the table and she rubbed at the side of her temples. Something about Eva still grated, but there was no way she could express her concerns to Rosa. The surgeon was smitten and any attempts to get her to see another side of the woman she was in love with would meet disdain. There was, apparently, nothing Eva could do wrong.

'Look, I'm sure she'll forgive you. She's like that,' Rosa said.

'Umm, maybe,' Dee responded, but she wasn't sure she wanted Eva's forgiveness. She would wait out for a couple of days and see.

'Thanks for coming over,' Rosa said, standing from the table. 'I need to get finished up,' she said, picking up her tray and putting it on the stand.

Dee stood and followed her. They sauntered down the corridor together, breaking the relative silence between them as their paths took different directions. Rosa headed to her office, Dee to the surgical ward.

*

Even though Rosa was expecting her, Eva approached the gated building with her heart pounding, her clammy hands juggling the bunch of red roses she had had specially delivered to the office earlier that afternoon.

The gate buzzed open before she reached the keypad entry system, causing her to jump, her eyes scanning Rosa's windows for evidence of her watching, as she reactively hid the bunch of flowers behind her back. She walked towards the front door, to face a beaming smile, dressed in black jeans and a white Calvin Klein sweatshirt, highlighting the tanned skin and deep brown eyes that sparkled in her direction.

'Sorry, I got back from work late,' Rosa explained, rubbing at her still wet hair with a hand-towel.

'You look stunning,' Eva responded, entranced by the wavy wet hair and the scent of bergamot and thyme drifting across her senses. Eva's broad grin lit up her face and her eyes shone in the dark evening. She presented the roses from behind her back. 'These are for you,' she said.

'I guessed,' Rosa remarked, with a teasing grin. She took the flowers in one hand and Eva's hand in the other. 'Where are your things?' she asked, noting the absence of any bags as she placed the flowers on the table by the door.

'Um, I left my stuff at the flat. I didn't want to p...'

Rosa closed the space and quieted Eva's shaky voice with an impassioned kiss. Eva's shoulders dropped as she eased into the probing tongue that danced seductively with her own. Rosa moved away gently, resting her head against Eva's. 'I want you to live here with me, now,' she said, croakily. Her flesh was alight and as she pulled back, and her eyes had darkened.

The look drove Eva to claim the swollen lips instantly, her hands exploring inside Rosa's sweatshirt, causing her to gasp. Eva's fingers traced quickly to the front of Rosa's jeans, flicking the button, and ripping down the zip to gain access.

Within a moment, Eva's fingers had found the silky wet area, begging for her touch. The contact elicited a guttural groan, and Rosa grabbed Eva forcefully, pressing their bodies together, and deepening the kiss.

Eva moved Rosa, allowing her to gain better access to the heat that was driving her own sex into delicate spasms. She pushed Rosa firmly against the wall, spread her legs with her thigh, and explored her fully, watching intently as her fingers penetrated, twisted, and teased. She reached behind Rosa and wriggled them both to help lower the jeans that were restricting her access. Lowering to her knees she pulled Rosa's hips forward, presenting the swollen bud, and in one swift move her mouth had taken control. Rosa's scent was driving her insane with desire, driving her fingers faster, and deeper. She needed this. Now. She needed to take Rosa, and never let her go. Even as Rosa rode the waves of the orgasm that had her buckling at the knees, Eva didn't stop. With the lightest of touch, she continued, building the pressure exquisitely, guiding Rosa into oblivion, pinning her to the wall with certainty and determination. Rosa was hers.

Rosa shuddered as she bathed in the sensations that had rendered her speechless. She bit down on her lip as another wave of trembling caused her to lose all strength in her legs. She started to giggle as the intensity merged with amusement at her current predicament. Eva beamed at her with a smile that had such depth it prised her heart in two. 'I love you,' Rosa said after a few moments of studying Eva intently. She had changed. She felt more confident than before, but there was something else. Something Rosa couldn't name. It just felt good, very good.

'I love you too,' Eva said, kissing Rosa tenderly.

'Well that was one hell of a homecoming,' Rosa added, with a wry smile.

Eva laughed. 'I'm glad you approve.' She winked, and her gaze gave Rosa the distinct impression that she hadn't even got started.

'Come to bed with me.' It wasn't a question and Eva didn't need to answer it. Rosa picked up the scattered items of clothing and led the way.

27.

Eva slid out of bed being careful not to disturb Rosa. She tiptoed down the stairs sporting the biggest grin, and started to make breakfast for her girlfriend. Just thinking about Rosa lying in the bed above her while she worked caused parts of her body to ache with longing.

The aroma of coffee and pancakes started to waft up the stairs, gently arousing Rosa from a light, early morning sleep. She turned into the empty space in the bed, opening her eyes suddenly with the dawning realisation that Eva wasn't there. When she tuned in to the noises coming from the kitchen, and placed the smells that had woken her, she smiled broadly. She stretched out, encroaching on the empty space next to her, before throwing back the covers and jumping out of the bed. Putting on her robe she descended the stairs and walked into the kitchen. Her grin widened when she spotted Eva scraping something off the bottom of the frying pan. 'Thought I could smell something,' she said, teasingly.

'I only took my eye off it for a second,' Eva remarked, but she too was laughing. 'Are you hungry?' she asked.

Rosa's eyebrows rose, and she bit down on her bottom lip. 'That depends.' She moved to occupy the space next to Eva, pulled her away from the sink and into her arms, placing a tender kiss on the lips that were doing strange things to her mind and body.

Eva dropped the pan and willingly succumbed to Rosa's demands. The softness and gentleness of the unhurried kiss touched her profoundly. The absence of urgency and the calmness didn't detract from the depth of emotion she was feeling. On the contrary, it added to it. The intensity was almost overpowering, and it took everything Eva possessed within her, and more, to stay open to the sensations coursing through her body. Something at the back of her mind still urged her to run, but she wouldn't. She couldn't do that to Rosa. A whimper fell from her lips with the flurry of electricity rushing down her spine.

Rosa eased out of the kiss. 'Morning,' she said, belatedly, teasing with a cheeky smile, enjoying the effect the connection they shared was having on her body.

'Pancakes are on the table,' Eva said, her voice husky from their brief interaction.

Rosa glanced in the direction of the pancakes, fruit, yogurt and coffee, sitting on the table. 'Yum.'

Eva smiled coyly. 'You need to get going or you're going to be late,' Eva stated. Rosa started to laugh. Eva had changed, and she liked it.

Rosa pressed a kiss firmly on Eva's mouth before sitting down and diving into the pancakes, leaving Eva quaking with the after-effects of her touch.

Eva watched Rosa enjoying the early breakfast for a moment, before she joined her. Within a few minutes Rosa had leapt up from the table and shot upstairs to shower and dress. By the time Eva had cleared the table, Rosa was back down again and heading towards the front door.

'I'll see you later,' Rosa said, putting on her coat. She looked blissfully happy.

Eva studied Rosa in awe. The fact that she played a big part her girlfriend's ecstatic appearance worried her more than it excited her. She had never been responsible for anyone before, and that pressure weighed heavily. She would speak to Charlie about it at their session later. She stepped into Rosa's space and kissed her forcefully, biting down on Rosa's lip as if to claim her as her own. 'Later,' she said.

Rosa was still blushing as she exited the gated complex and headed for the Metro.

'I don't know that it's appropriate,' Carine said, holding her mobile phone slightly away from her ear to avoid the wrath that might hit her from the other end of the line.

'What do you mean, appropriate?'

'I mean, now is not a good time.'

'When is a good time Carine? When is a good time for me to visit my home?' The anger in the voice on the end of the line was beginning to irritate Carine. Even though the question was a valid one, she lacked answers.

'I'll let you know. I'm really busy right now, so we wouldn't see much of each other. You might as well take a holiday out there.' It was a poor rebuff and she knew it.

'You are still my girlfriend, aren't you?' Tori said, incredulously. She hadn't expected Carine to respond negatively to the news that she was coming home for a three-week break.

'Yes, of course.' Carine responded, though in her heart she knew things between them had changed, even though she had yet to discuss those changes with Tori.

'Well you could sound a bit more enthusiastic about it, for fuck's sake.'

'Sorry. I am really under pressure here,' she lied.

'Right. And I've been under fucking pressure here for the last year. I'd like to see my partner. I was hoping we might even be able to go away for a few days.'

Carine sighed heavily.

'Well I'm glad you feel that way too,' Tori said, sarcastically.

'Sorry, it's just that I really am very busy.'

'So you said. Anyway, I'm coming home. If you can't take time off then fine, I'm sure we can find time outside of work. I can come to your networking events with you if you like, you know, like we used to do?' she offered, hoping it would make a difference to Carine's response.

The offer met with silence from the other end of the phone. The silence continued until Tori realised they had been cut off.

Carine watched the caller display disconnect as she pressed the end button on her phone. The red rage that had formed from the onset of the call, had settled into a heavy mist in front of her eyes. The last thing she wanted right now was Tori to return home, even for a day. She paced the office, trying to dissipate the boiling sensation in her head. She hated feeling out of control. What would she say to Eva? She needed to keep them apart and work out some way to ensure Tori's visit was as short as possible. She popped a pod in the coffee machine and waited. *Eva, Eva, Eva.* What had that woman done to her? A coy smile came to her face as she answered her own question, softening the mist in her mind. Whenever she thought about Eva, she felt good. They were right together.

*

Eva stepped into her cool, damp flat, shivered at the feeling of emptiness she found there, and vowed to get it cleared out and sold. She had come for one reason and one reason only. She would clear the flat on another day. She picked up the small box that had been her mum's Christmas present and studied it, rubbing her fingers across the surface of the wrapping paper. It would always be the gift her mum never got to see. She carefully opened the paper, revealing the red-cardboard gift box beneath. Removing the lid, the sight of the aquamarine stone caused her eyes to burn. It seemed bizarre to align a material object with a human life, but in that moment, that was exactly how she felt. The stone represented her mum and she felt the need to keep it close to her. She

219

lifted the pendant, and noticed how the different light on it subtly shifted its colour. She unclasped the chain and then retied it around her neck, tucking it safely under her t-shirt. Pressing her hand against the stone resting against her chest, she smiled. This way her mum would always be with her.

She grabbed the urn from the table and put it in the suitcase she had dumped after her trip to London. She would drop the suitcase at Rosa's en route to Charlie. She also needed to fit in a shopping trip, for something to wear for the christening. As she walked away from the place she had thought of as home for some years, she knew the next time she returned would be the last. She was pleased that the thought didn't come with the wave of sadness that she might have expected.

She looked back, noticing the drab appearance of the dirty building that reached too high into the sky, and a sense of something unnerving caused her to shiver. She glanced around, but there was nothing to pin her gut feeling on. Just the normal activities: people passing by, cars moving too quickly, and a couple of cyclists, all going about their business. She had a sudden urge to text her father. Maybe it was her sixth sense telling her to contact him. She pressed the send button, then pulled the wheeled case behind her down the street and into the Metro.

*

Eva was too far away to hear the clicking of the lens, or the grunting sound that emanated from the person with a keen interest in her activities. 'Bitch.' The word carried sufficient venom that, had it been injected directly into the recipient, would have surely paralysed them: the sound though, got lost in the regular city noise.

'Hey,' Charlie greeted Eva with a warm embrace.

220

'Hi.' Eva entered the familiar space and immediately relaxed. Even though she hadn't been feeling tense, something about the energy in the studio seemed to take her to an even deeper level of calmness.

'You look good,' Charlie commented as they walked along the short corridor to the stairs.

'I am, thanks.'

'I've got the plans ready,' Charlie said, as they entered the living space, with a number of documents spread out on the large table.

'Oooo, that's exciting.' Eva rubbed her hands together. Standing at the table she scanned the paperwork, briefly.

'We can go through those afterwards,' Charlie said, heading for the therapy room.

'Sure.' Eva followed her into the room and hopped eagerly onto the therapy bed. She had a lot she wanted to talk about, but first, she would enjoy the relaxation and mental space that Charlie's reiki afforded her.

*

'This is brilliant,' Eva said, her eyes soaking up the drawings, and reading through the business proposition she had discussed only briefly with Charlie on her return from London. 'You're good.'

She checked her phone. There was still no response from her father, but that wasn't unusual. She challenged the anxiety that pricked at her gut. It was hard to trust that he was okay, when the reality could be far from that fact. She didn't know if she would ever get used to the idea of him living on the street, she could only hope that her plan to help the guys would give them some respite, and a choice. By providing a shelter that would be run by homeless people, for homeless people, she hoped they would be encouraged to support each

221

other by offering food and shelter to anyone who needed it. It wasn't a novel idea, but it was one that would give her father a roof over his head on any night that he chose to stay. And that was critical. She hoped he would run the shelter, with some assistance of course. She prayed it would give him hope for a better future, but if she were truly honest with herself, it was really about satisfying her fears, her needs.

'I'm sure you can make it work,' Charlie said, sipping at her herbal tea, enjoying Eva's enthusiasm. 'You just need to find the right building,' she added, but she was smiling confidently.

'We will find the right building,' Eva said. The certainty with which she spoke left no room for doubt. She was going to make this project come to life, no matter what. Even if her father didn't want to take advantage of the opportunity, the likes of Ed and George probably would. She would introduce skills classes for the homeless people at a later date: IT, construction, and even some personal development so that they could apply for jobs in the future. Eva beamed as the idea began to take shape in her mind.

Charlie studied Eva, hoping that her plans would come to fruition.

Eva's phone pinged, raising the biggest smile to her face. 'It's my father, he's fine,' she clarified to Charlie.

28.

'Come back to bed.'

Rosa reached out and grabbed Eva by the arm, confidently, tenderly, pulling her naked body down on top of her. The intensity in her dark brown eyes pierced through Eva's thinly veiled façade, causing her nerves to fire uncontrollably. Eva moaned in pleasure as their bodies made contact. They fit together so perfectly; the softness of Rosa's tanned skin and firmness of her muscular frame melding with Eva's body at every point down her length. She felt consumed by Rosa's touch, again, and it felt so fucking good she didn't ever want it to end.

'I want you.'

The intensity of Rosa's gaze never wavered as her mouth crashed urgently into Eva's. Rosa's hands moved swiftly down Eva's body, as if this was new, exciting territory, to her. But, it wasn't. It was familiar, comfortable even. Safe. It was wonderful.

Eva's hips bucked involuntarily as Rosa's fingers swept through her folds, softly, deftly, spreading her effortlessly. The deep, earthy groan Eva emitted fuelled Rosa, and the deep thrusts she delivered created a wave of intoxication, that flowed through every cell of Eva's body. Collapsing, her mouth finding Rosa's firm breast, her tongue instantly flicking at her erect, dark nipple, she bit down hard. Rosa screamed in pleasure, her near-black eyes stared at Eva intently. Eva raised her head, locking onto the stare, finding the truth. She reached for Rosa's arms and pinned her to the bed. The look was wicked, her intentions clear, and her mouth claimed Rosa's breast again, causing her back to arch instantly. Eva had to work hard to keep Rosa from raising her arms and trying to take back control. Eva had no intention of letting that happen.

She pinned both hands above Rosa's head and reached for the belt of the robe that was still attached to the headboard. She smiled seductively as she tied Rosa's hands together. Rosa bit her top lip, never averting her gaze, writhing underneath Eva's exposed crotch. Eva groaned at the sensation coursing through her sex, lifting herself away from the contact before she lost complete control.

'Fuck me.' Rosa begged.

Eva kissed her way down Rosa, teasing her and making her repeat her request. When her mouth took Rosa, parted her, delved into her, Rosa bucked and screamed. Eva continued pressing deeply, rhythmically, until the screaming silenced and her body shook hard.

'Holy fuck! How do you do that to me?' Rosa was panting hard, her pulse thumping through her rising chest. Eva watched in adoration, circling the rising and falling nipple, tracing the goose bumps that followed her touch. A beaming grin on her face, her eyes sparkling, she pressed a tender kiss on the erect nipple.

'Enough, I can't take any more,' Rosa wriggled. 'Untie me...' Eva gave her a look. 'Please.' Eva's mouth twitched, and her head tilted, as if processing the request.

'Maybe I'll leave you there all day,' she said, watching for Rosa's response.

'You can't, we've got a christening to go to,' Rosa smirked.

Eva grinned wickedly.

'You wouldn't...' Rosa started to frown and wriggled to free her hands.

'Oh no you don't. I haven't finished with you yet.' Eva pinned them in place and pressed a deep kiss on Rosa's swollen lips. Rosa responded, taken in by the tenderness and longing the kiss delivered. She jumped at the unexpected touch to her shaved sex, and groaned as Eva entered her and moved her rhythmically into another intense orgasm.

'Jesus Christ, Eva stop... please,' Rosa begged, through her body's shuddering response. She started to laugh uncontrollably. 'Seriously, we've got to get going or we'll be late.'

'I'll remind you, it was you who pulled me back to bed,' Eva quipped, jumping up from the bed and heading for the shower.

'Hey, untie me.' Eva turned her head, winked, and ignored Rosa's request. 'You little shit,' Rosa shouted, in jest, wriggling intently to release her hands from the tie. She worked her way free and jumped out of bed, immediately struck by light-headedness, that struck her from being prone for so long. Steadying herself, she chased after Eva into the bathroom.

Eva had stepped out of the shower before Rosa and dressed quickly. 'Come on, we need to get going,' she shouted up the stairs, just as Rosa started to descend.

'Well, if you hadn't delayed me then I would have been out already,' Rosa teased, on her way down, pulling Eva into her and kissing her firmly as she reached the bottom. Eva groaned at the sensation on her lips, pulling away to hand Rosa her coat. 'Later,' Rosa said.

'Perfect timing,' Eva said, with the beeping of the horn. Stepping into the taxi she pulled Rosa into her shoulder. They would be at the barn in an hour.

*

'It looks fabulous, darling,' Lisa said, admiring the display inside the gazebo-style tent that had been constructed for the christening. The tented corridor leading from the house had been adorned with shamanic images and inside the tent sat several shamanic drums and bells. The white-smoke of burning herbs still wafted around the quaint space, from the earlier cleansing and purifying rituals.

'I love it,' Anna said, squeezing her mum's arm. 'Martine has set it up beautifully.'

Lisa smiled, with a tear in her eye. 'It is spectacular,' she said, leaning into Anna, with an arm around her daughter's waist. 'Right, let's see what the chefs are up to.'

They wandered back up the short corridor, into the hallway and through to the kitchen, picking up the delicate aroma of baked bread and cake. Lauren and Vivian were up to their elbows in flour, chatting away as if they had all the time in the world. Anna smiled, watching the two women. She loved that they got on so well, but more than that, the sight of Lauren with flour across her cheek caused tingles to run down her spine. 'You look...'

'A mess,' Lauren interrupted, rubbing the cuff of her shirt across her face.

'Hot, I was going to say.' Anna rubbed at the flour and pressed a kiss on Lauren's cheek. 'And you've got about half an hour before people start to arrive,' Anna added.

'Anything I can do?' Valerie asked, sauntering into the kitchen looking the picture of elegance.

'Don't come near here or you'll end up covered,' Lauren said with a laugh.

'Champagne's in the fridge,' Vivian added, nodding towards the cabinet. 'I'm ready if you are,' she suggested.

Valerie looked at her watch out of principle, but with little regard for the time of day. 'Of course, darling,' she said, with a flirtatious wink in Vivian's direction. She pulled the bottle from the fridge and handed it to Vivian who elicited a soft pop from the cork, muffling the sound with a tea towel. She started pouring and handed Valerie a flute.

Lauren and Anna sniggered at the harmless banter between their mothers, enjoying the fact that they all slotted together so well. 'I'll have one,' Lauren said, placing the final batch of bread rolls into the oven. Anna nudged her in the arm and tutted, then took the flute that had been offered to Lauren and marched out of the kitchen with it, sipping happily. 'Hey,' Lauren called after her. They were giggling.

Anna stepped straight into Martine's path. She was waving a stick of smoking herbs and blowing the white smoke around the hallway, chanting as she went. She blew the smoke into the corners of the room and then made her way into the kitchen. Anna laughed as she watched the others exit the room at great haste, taking care not to spill their drinks.

'Is that really necessary?' Valerie grumped, somewhat bemused at the excessive ritual. Anna shrugged, placed a kiss on the older woman's cheek, and ushered her gently into the living room, where the crackling fire, Henri, Antoine and Chico's company might feel a little more comfortable. Vivian and Lisa followed, and she shut the door behind them, breathing a sigh of relief.

'I'm going to get changed,' Lauren said, smiling with her eyes at the antics, and Anna's ability to soften Valerie's temperament.

'I'll let Martine know to avoid the living room,' she said.

Lauren sniggered, taking the steps two at a time. She jumped into the shower, and was dressed in no time at all. Pulling on her white tuxedo jacket, the sound of a snuffling Emilie caught her ear. The noises coming from the baby room melted her. She peaked around the door to see Emilie trying to pull herself up in her cot. She watched the struggle for a short while, until Emilie spotted her and started to giggle. 'Hello sweetheart,' she said, softly approaching the cot and reaching out to collect her daughter into her arms.

Emilie was already clothed, in a white dress, but her socks lay in the cot having been kicked off during her short nap. Lauren picked them up and carried both child and socks down the stairs, unaware of Anna's presence in the foyer below.

'You look hot,' Anna said, unable to take her eyes off of Lauren, eyeing her from top to bottom. She was biting on her bottom lip and by the time their eyes connected her pupils had darkened. *Fuck.* Anna swallowed hard and tried to curb the desire that had rendered her mind numb. Lauren's smile floored her though, and an unplanned groan escaped Anna, the heat moving down her body causing her knees to go weak.

'My thoughts exactly,' Lauren remarked. Her eyes were wide, and her smile ran deep. She turned her attention to Emilie. 'Doesn't mummy look lovely,' she said to her.

Anna brushed a finger softly down her daughter's cheek. 'And doesn't mummy look hot,' she said in a child-like voice. Her other hand tracing determinedly down the centre of Lauren's tuxedo jacket, popping a button and slipping inside to get just a little closer to the flesh that tempted her.

Emilie gurgled, and Anna kissed her softly on the cheek. 'Want me to take her?' she asked, removing her hand from Lauren's firm abs, having clearly expressed her intentions for later.

'Sure.' Lauren handed Emilie over.

'Let's go and see Nana and Grannies,' she said, bouncing Emilie in her arms.

'I'll get that.' Lauren said, at the sound of the ringing doorbell.

*

Lauren pulled the door wide open, just as Eva and Rosa's taxi crunched its way back down the gravel driveway, leaving them standing at the front door. 'Hi.' Lauren said, her expression slightly reserved, from a few moments ago.

'Hi Lauren.' Rosa stepped up and pulled Lauren into a tight embrace, breaking the distance that seemed to sit between them.

'Hi,' Eva said, waving her hand by way of greeting. Rosa released Lauren and put her arm around Eva's waist. Entering the foyer area, a smile appeared on her face when she caught sight of Anna.

Anna rushed at Eva giving her a big hug. 'I'm so glad you could make it,' she said, releasing her and assessing Eva from top to toe. 'How are you?' she asked, watching Eva's response intently. She looked good.

'I'm great,' Eva responded, reaching for Rosa's hand. Her smile was genuine, and Anna noticed a different quality emanating from her best friend. She seemed settled and a lot less edgy than she had ever known.

'Come in, come in,' Anna said, dragging Eva and Rosa into the kitchen. 'What can I get you?' she asked.

'Water's fine thanks,' Eva responded, gaining a quizzical look from Anna. 'I stopped drinking,' Eva added, with a soft smile.

'Wow. What have you done to her?' she asked Rosa, who shrugged, squeezing Eva's hand firmly. Eva brushed a thumb across the back of the hand in hers. *What had Rosa done?* But the truth was more than that, and they both knew it.

'I'll have a water too please,' Rosa added.

Anna handed them both a tumbler and a bottle of spring water. 'Come through. Emilie will be so excited to see you.'

*

The delicate sound of chanting filtered into the living room, causing the voices inside the room to quiet. Valerie's eyes widened, and she reached for Henri's firm hand for some sense of normality.

'I think that's the call for us to move into the room for the ceremony,' Lauren said, addressing everyone. She led the way.

Aside from Emilie's mumbled sounds, they entered the tented space in silence and took their seats, which formed a semi-circle around a large bowl of smoking herbs, facing a table upon which lay a range of instruments: bells of different sizes, and two drums. Martine continued to chant oblivious to the guests who had just entered the room. Anna and Lauren sat in the centre of the group, with Emilie taking a position on Anna's knee.

The chanting stopped suddenly. Emilie continued to chatter, in her own language, drawing a smile from the older people in the room. 'Welcome,' Martine greeted the small gathering, in her soft French accent. 'We are blessed to be here today to celebrate the birth of Emilie. I invite you to think of a personal quality that you would wish for Emilie to help her in her life. Then at the end of the ceremony, you will stand and tell the group the quality you have chosen for her. This is a special gift that only you can give to her.' Lisa rubbed her hands with glee at the idea. Valerie's eyes widened, and she paled. Henri put a calming hand on her knee and she grabbed at it like a lifeline. Anna stared into Lauren's watering eyes and brushed a thumb tenderly over her cheek.

Martine continued. 'Firstly, I will conduct the cleansing. Please stay seated and I will come around with the herbs and clean you.' Valerie's mouth dropped open and Chico stifled a giggle, receiving a nudge in the ribs from Antoine. Martine began to chant again and moved from person to person wafting the fine mist of smoke over them, from head to toe.

Lisa entered into a trance, savouring every moment and Vivian sat with her hands clasped in her lap.

Once the cleansing had taken place, Martine reached for the large drum and began to bang in a rhythmical pattern as she walked around the room. 'I am calling the ancestors to join us,' she explained. Chico started to snigger again, but the boom of the drum next to his right ear silenced him instantly. Emilie's eyes widened and followed the banging sound around the room. The drumming ritual continued until the energy in the room had shifted. Valerie had relaxed into the rhythmical sound and was even beginning to enjoy herself.

'I am going to undertake a blessing now, using the bells and chanting. Please think of the quality you would like for Emilie to grow up with, that will be with her in her lifetime.' With that, Martine stood behind the table and started to bellow, raising her hands as she spoke. Lauren glanced around the room. Everyone's eyes were shut, except Emilie's. She smiled to herself, and keeping one eye on her daughter she pondered the quality she would wish for her to take through her life.

As the bells ceased, each guest was invited to stand and share their quality with the group. Anna's eyes watered and she couldn't prevent the tears from falling. Lauren took her hand, also allowing the tears to roll down her cheeks. Chico wiped at his eyes with the back of his hand and Valerie cleared her throat before stating her gift.

'Love,' she stated emphatically.

Emilie started to wriggle and complain.

'I love you,' Lauren whispered into Anna's ear.

'Thank you everyone,' Martine said once they had all given their gift to Emilie. 'The ceremony is concluded.' The guests sat in stunned silence for a few moments before Lisa bounded to her feet.

'Magnificent,' she declared, breaking the trance.

*

'That was amazing,' Rosa exclaimed.

'Awesome,' Eva said, rising from her seat and nodding her approval of the shamanistic ceremony that had captivated the small group. They were the last to stand, the other guests having already vacated to the living room. 'I'm still tingling from the bells,' she added, wrapping an arm around Rosa's waist and pulling her close. She looked longingly into the dark irises staring back at her. The kiss she planted took Rosa's breath away.

'Hey you two,' Lauren interrupted. 'Time to cut the cake.' She ushered them into the living room, just as Anna popped the cork on another bottle of champagne.

Anna shouted, 'Cheers!' Her eyes sparkled as she focused on Lauren. She looked stunning, and hot. Her tanned skin and shoulder length curls contrasting perfectly with the white tuxedo. Anna licked her lips. Handing Lauren a flute, her fingers lingered on Lauren's before she released the glass to her. 'Mmm,' she whispered, her hot breath causing the hairs on Lauren's neck to rise.

Lauren's face was flushed when Anna moved away, and she took a long sip of the fizzy drink, which did nothing to quench the thirst pinching in the back of her throat. The bubbles tickled her, resulting in a light cough.

Rosa smiled knowingly at the display, squeezing the hand that rested in her own. She knew how Lauren felt. She turned her eyes to find Eva staring straight at her. The message was clear. Heat rose to her face and she too struggled to breathe. She took the offered flute of champagne. Eva declined, and Rosa put her untouched drink on the mantelpiece. She smiled coyly at Eva. Then, suddenly she was thrust out of the trance by the rhythmical, banging of a drum.

232

The room went silent and all eyes were on Martine as she underwent a ritual of blessing for the cake. Chico raised his brows and tried not to laugh, squirming when Antoine poked him in the ribs with his elbow for a second time. Valerie started humming along to the sound, much to Lauren's amusement. Emilie's eyes widened at the now familiar sound and she mumbled her own words, clinging on to Lisa as she watched, until the point at which Martine started dancing around the room waving feathers, which resulted in her chuckling merrily and pointing a finger at the strange movements. As the ritual came to an end, Lauren picked up the sharp blade and sliced through the cake.

'I want you,' Eva breathed into Rosa's ear, as they waited for a plate to come their way.

Rosa swallowed hard. 'Let's go home,' she whispered, with a tilt of her head.

'Soon,' Eva responded.

'Thanks,' Rosa said, in a slightly broken voice, taking the offered cake from a tutting, but grinning Anna.

29.

Rosa stared at the screen of medical data, finding it hard to concentrate and unable to wipe the beaming smile from her face. Her thoughts drifted to Eva, the christening ceremony, and the time they had spent together since she had turned up at the hotel in London. She clicked on a couple of keys before stopping, standing, and gazing out the window. Lost in a dream of the future, the pinging of her phone thrust her out of her reverie. Warmth invaded her body at the message.

I love you xx

She smiled, responding to the text with her own declaration of love. Admonishing herself for her mental absence, she sat back in her seat and began the process of going through her mail. Her interest was piqued at the manila envelope. Her name was hand-written, the hospital address wasn't written out in full and it hadn't been franked by the postal services. She ripped open the seal with vigour and reached inside, pulling out the contents. Four photographs dropped from her hand, and she stopped breathing. *No, no, no.* She gulped for air, but the feeling of strangulation increased with every second that passed. The word repeated itself like a mantra playing out in her mind. Surely there was a mistake. She couldn't bring herself to touch the images that seemed to ram the facts into her face. Even the obscured photos were too painful to reveal. She stood as if to remove herself from the scene staring up at her. Who was being kissed she couldn't make out. But the one doing the kissing was very clear. Eva!

Rosa's hands shook as she picked up the top image, revealing a second that was equally as disturbing. Spreading out the four pictures, she studied them, working hard not to allow her legs to buckle beneath her. She slumped into the chair, fighting the tears that vied with the rising anger in her chest. They collided in the lump in her throat, making it hard for her to swallow. The door to her office opened at the same time as the knock that jolted her eyes towards Dee, but her mind was engaged in an entirely different awareness.

Dee stopped in her tracks. Their relationship had suffered, for sure, as a result of her actions against Eva, but right now, if looks could kill she would have been struck down dead. 'Are you okay?' she asked, tentatively moving inside the room, and shutting the door. Rosa's mouth opened, but no words came out. The shaking in her hands had reached the rest of her body. She was shuddering violently. 'Rosa, what's happened?' Feeling more reassured that her life wasn't under imminent threat Dee rushed towards Rosa, and knelt facing her. Her eyes were drawn to the images adorning the table and she swallowed down hard, unsure of what to say. She took Rosa's hands in her own, and rubbed her thumbs across their backs. 'I'm so sorry,' she offered, even though she could have predicted the turn of events.

'I...' Rosa started to speak, but the choking sensation in the back of her throat stopped her. Dee pulled Rosa into her arms and Rosa let her, albeit she rested stiffly. Rosa tried to process the new reality and pulled back sharply. 'Did you do this?' she asked. The anger in her voice caused Dee to stand abruptly and back off.

'No.' Dee said, her tone quieter, her face flushing with the idea that it was something she might be accused of, given her history with Eva. 'No, I didn't,' she said, more firmly. 'I really am sorry Rosa.' Dee's eyes lowered to the floor as she grappled with how to handle the situation. She wanted to exit the room, but she couldn't leave Rosa in a state of distress. 'How can I help?' she offered.

Tears had already started to fall down Rosa's cheeks as her eyes re-focused on the images in front of her. Disbelief warred with the possibility that the pictures of Eva in a clearly impassioned kiss actually reflected the reality of the situation. *Surely not?* The words pursued Rosa. *After their recent time together, how could this be true?* Yet, the images were dated, and were taken on the day Eva returned from London. Rosa studied the photographs further. It looked like early morning. Eva had said she would be arriving on the early flight and going into work. It hadn't mattered that she wasn't able to see Rosa first, since Rosa had needed to be in work for 6am. But who was this woman? As Rosa played out the scene over and over, her heart sank deeper and deeper, until the feeling of disgust rose within her. She threw the pictures back into the envelope and held her head in her hands. 'Give me a moment,' she said. Dee nodded, standing perfectly still. Rosa breathed deeply and allowed the long breath out slowly. She repeated the process several times and then stood. 'I need to get to work,' she said, and marched out of the room.

*

Eva sat at the kitchen table sipping at her morning coffee, checking her emails. She had risen not long after Rosa left for the hospital, having kept her in bed for as long as she could get away with. That thought brought a smile to her face and as she sipped the heat caught her lip. *Ouch.* With nothing urgent that needed dealing with, she shut the laptop and stood. She finished the last of the espresso and packed her rucksack with the files she needed to drop off with Carine. The business had been going well in her short absence. For all her faults, Carine certainly knew her stuff. Eva smiled as she shut the front door, immediately missing the scent of the town house that was now home, and ambled into the wet Paris morning. Hoping onto the Metro, she made her way the short distance to the stop that served both the office and Carine's flat. Knocking on the door, she became aware of the sound of raised voices coming from inside, one of which was getting louder.

The door swung open. Eva recognised the face from one of the pictures she had seen lying around the flat. The jet-black haired woman assessed her through almond shaped eyes. She wasn't smiling. Eva could see Carine approaching behind the shorter woman and smiled weakly. 'Hi,' she said with as much warmth as she could muster, trying to placate the clearly fractious situation she had intruded upon.

'And you are?' The woman asked in a soft American accent. She was clearly aware that Carine and this woman knocking on their door knew each other.

'Sorry, I'm Eva,' Eva responded, holding out a hand. The woman took it. Her grip was soft, and in contrast with the atmosphere she had been party to creating with Carine.

'Eva, hello.' Carine's eyes were on Eva's, delivering a message she didn't understand, even though her tone seemed pleasing enough. She never used the word *hello* with her, Eva noted.

'Tori,' the dark-haired woman said, by way of introduction. Her tone had softened, and the fact that Carine had what appeared to be a hand tenderly caressing the small of the woman's back didn't go unnoticed to Eva.

Eva took a half-pace backwards. 'Look, I'm sorry to have disturbed you,' she started. 'I bought the files over. I didn't expect...'

'It's okay, I'll take them,' Carine interrupted her, stepping in front of Tori, staring intensely at Eva to get the message and go. Carine offered her hand and Eva placed the files from the rucksack in it. 'I'll catch you later then?' she asked, turning to leave.

237

Carine took a pace back into the flat. 'I'll be in around 10,' she said.

'Nice meeting you,' Tori said, but Carine was already closing the door. The sound of raised voices followed Eva out of the building.

Eva wandered out onto the street feeling confused. Carine had said that Tori and she had split up some time ago. If it wasn't for the raised voices she might have assumed that they were back together again. Shaking her head, trying to find an explanation for Carine's strange behaviour, she made her way down the street.

Eva clicked at the keys on her phone with a smile that lit up her face. She watched her screen for a while waiting, hoping, for a response before reaching the conclusion that Rosa must be in theatre. The thought of not being able to see or touch Rosa for at least another eight-hours caused a wave of disappointment to pass through her. Maybe she would make a surprise visit about lunchtime, after her meeting with Charlie? She pondered the idea, enjoying the feeling of excitement that it brought. She would have to accept that Rosa might be in theatre though. Having agreed with herself she could handle it if Rosa couldn't see her, she skipped her way through the park.

*

'So, she's the latest,' Tori accused, thrusting out of Carine's grip and storming her way into the living room.

'No, she's not,' Carine screamed after her, her arms flailing above her head as if doing so might make her defence more believable.

Tori stopped and stared incredulously at her girlfriend. 'When will you stop yourself from lying, Carine?' she asked, the calmness in her voice reaching deeper than any screaming rant could ever hope to penetrate.

Carine's arms lowered, and she turned away sharply. 'You bitch,' she said, feeling the pain of the knife that had been firmly implanted by the words. 'You...'

'I what?' Tori asked, not waiting for an answer. 'I drove you to it. Oh for fuck sake Carine, grow up. I didn't drive you to anything.'

Carine turned to face the dark eyes and thinning lips, with her own thunderous glare. 'You had an affair,' she spat, her skin darkened by the rage fuelling her.

Tori's head was shaking gently back and forth as she watched Carine's display of anger. She crossed her arms and breathed in deeply. 'Is that the story you keep telling any poor bastard who will listen to you?' Again, the calm delivery struck Carine and she started to shake.

'It's fucking true and you know it,' Carine bellowed. Picking up the nearest thing to hand, she threw it in Tori's direction.

Tori ducked effortlessly and turned to see her mobile phone connect with the open brick-styled wall, missing the window by inches. The phone fell to the floor, the screen smashed. Tori turned and made a move towards Carine, but then stopped. 'You will pay for that,' she said, pointing to the device before going and picking it up from the floor. 'You need some serious help,' she said, walking past Carine and out into the hallway.

'Fuck off,' Carine shouted.

Tori stopped and looked back towards Carine. It still touched her deeply to see the woman she loved in such pain. But there was only so much she could take, and Carine seemed to be getting worse the older she got. In the beginning, her self-deception had been part of the game they had played together, but the closer she had become to Carine, the more she had realised there was more to it than the role-playing that had drawn them together. Carine didn't seem to know where to stop and the lies had started to impact their life together. Taking the job in New York had provided the space that they both needed. But Tori had never strayed, even though she had had the opportunity to do so on many occasions. The latest trip had taken its toll though. They hadn't been apart for this length of time before now, and this homecoming had been far from pleasurable.

'We're done,' Tori said. Turning, she walked into the bedroom and started to pack.

*

Eva's plan to surprise Rosa hadn't materialised, having needed to spend longer with Charlie than she had originally thought. She stopped by the local store on the way back to Rosa's and picked up a range of ingredients. She would make them something fun to eat.

Turning the key in the lock, something irked her. She stepped into the hallway and placed the bags on the floor. The light was on in the kitchen and she wandered through the door. Her heart hit the back of her throat at the sight of Rosa sitting on the floor, leaning against the fridge. She was swigging from a newly opened bottle of wine. 'Jesus Rosa, what's happened?' The voice full of concern met with a stern glare.

Rosa threw the envelope at Eva, who stumbled backwards, grabbing the work surface for support. 'Don't deny it. I don't think I could stand that.' Rosa said.

Eva's eyes widened. Her pulse raced, and her mouth felt as dry as bone. She couldn't breathe. 'What are you talking about?'

'Look for yourself,' Rosa said, taking a long swig from the bottle.

'Stop, please,' Eva said, making a move to take the bottle from her.

'Fuck you, Eva. Don't you fucking dare take...' the tears were beginning to fall.

Eva dropped the envelope and fell to her knees, pleading Rosa to make some sense. 'Rosa, what's happened. I don't understand.'

Rosa's eyes searched out the envelope.

Eva reached for it, sliding into a seated position on the floor opposite her girlfriend. As her eyes registered one image, she flicked through to the next one. Her shoulders rose, and her eyes widened. 'This isn't...'

'You? Of course it's you.' Rosa interjected.

'Yes, it's me.' Eva sighed deeply, rolling her eyes to the ceiling. Rosa had started to sob.

'No Rosa. Yes, it's me, but this is Charlie, and this isn't what it looks like.' Rosa continued to cry, but her desire to believe that Eva was being honest had piqued her interest sufficiently for her to stop drinking. 'This has been made to look like something its not.' Rosa wanted to latch onto the words, wanted them to be true. The tears stopped and waited for Eva to continue. 'I've been working with Charlie for some time now. She's helped me get clean.' Eva pinched at the bridge of her nose as to prevent the anger that was beginning to infiltrate her veins. *Who would do this?* 'She's also been helping me with a business idea that I'm putting together to help the guys, and my dad, in London.' She turned her head to assess Rosa's response. The sadness in Rosa's eyes ripped through her and she couldn't hold back the tears that surfaced in an instant. 'I wouldn't do this to you,' she cried, holding out the picture. 'This was a kiss on the cheek and it's been made to

241

look like a full-on snog. I don't understand who would do this,' she said, shaking her head.

Rosa watched. Deep down she knew that Eva wasn't lying. 'Who could be so cruel?' she asked, feeling her own surge of adrenaline.

Eva shrugged her shoulders, working hard to not pick up the bottle of wine and drink it herself. She stood to remove herself from temptation. The desire to withdraw, even from Rosa, burned deep in her solar plexus, but she stood her ground and held out her hand. Rosa took it, stumbling as she got to her feet. Eva pulled her into her arms and held her tightly.

'I'm so sorry,' Rosa said. 'I wanted to believe...'

'Shhh,' Eva whispered, rubbing her hand through Rosa's hair, kissing her on the forehead, tenderly. 'It's okay.' Eva sighed, as her brain worked through the options. She pulled back suddenly. 'Dee,' she said.

Rosa shook her head. 'I asked her. I know what she did to you was out of order, and she knows that too. But really, I don't think she is capable of this,' Rosa said, sniffling into the cuff of her sleeve.

Eva trawled through her memories. Surely Mitch wouldn't do such a thing. *Why would she?* Then, the penny dropped. 'Carine,' she blurted. 'Wait here. I'll be back in a bit,' she said, releasing Rosa and racing to the door. She had exited the building before Rosa had processed the fact that she had gone.

30.

Eva opened the door to the office. The space was empty. She walked across the road to Carine's flat and banged heavily on the door. She banged again and only silence came back at her. She walked down the street, glancing into the local bars as she passed. Nothing. She popped into Frank's, but he hadn't seen Carine for at least a couple of weeks. He was looking good, she thought, but she didn't have time to chat and excused herself before he tried to convince her to dine. Intent on finding Carine, she took a cab to *Le So What.*

'Hello stranger,' Ali's friendly voice came from behind the bar.

'Hi,' Eva responded, her eyes searching the bar with desperation.

'Looking for someone?' the astute woman asked.

'Yeah, Carine. You remember, tall, long blonde hair, Parisian woman. We came in a while ago,' Eva explained to a nodding Ali.

'I remember,' she said. 'She came in a while ago. Sat over there in the corner booth,' she said, pointing into the darkest corner in the room.

'Thanks,' Eva said, stepping out at pace across the dance floor. Other than a couple sat at the other side of the bar, the place was empty. But then it was still early, and most people wouldn't be out and about until later. She was grateful for the fact since she didn't want to make a scene, but she had no idea how Carine was going to react to her presence. Since returning from London, the woman had been behaving quite strangely towards her. Approaching the bench-seat, she could see the blonde hair covering Carine's face, her head resting in her hands and hanging over her empty glass.

Her eyes rose up, but her head barely moved. 'Hello,' she said. The word was slurred and as she motioned to move, her elbow slipped off the table causing her to almost fall off her seat. She righted herself and motioned for Eva to sit.

'You're drunk,' Eva said, ignoring the request.

'Yes. I'm afraid so,' Carine responded sarcastically, trying to deliver her words with sophistication.

'Why did you do it?' Eva asked, calmly.

'Jealousy,' Carine replied honestly, knowing exactly the topic of conversation to which they were both referring.

'But why would you want to hurt me?' Eva asked, unable to reconcile Carine's obvious affection for her with an act that was so destructive.

Carine was shaking her head as Eva posed the question. 'I don't. I love you. I want… wanted you.' Carine sat upright, but her eyes refused to focus. She stared through Eva. 'You're gorgeous, and I fell in love with you. I'm sorry. I was stupid, pathetic. I thought if she threw you out once and for all, we could be happy together.' Carine's eyes wandered around the bar as she spoke.

Eva slumped into the seat opposite Carine and rubbed her hands across her face, contemplating her next move. 'No.' The word that came out was barely audible.

'I know. It was stupid of me.'

'What about Tori?' Eva asked. She wanted to know the truth about Carine's relationship with the American woman.

Carine shrugged, and her eyes lowered to the table. 'I haven't been entirely honest,' she admitted. She didn't notice Eva's eyes widen.

'What do you mean?' Eva asked. She needed to know the details before she decided whether to sack the woman sitting opposite her. She felt torn. Carine looked older than her forty-four years, and the elegance she normally carried so well had deserted her. But, she had been there when Eva was at

244

her lowest point and she was good at what she did. She at least owed her the opportunity to explain herself.

'I wanted you to feel sorry for me. I wanted you to care. I wanted you to feel about me the way I feel about you. Tori never had an affair. There were no other women and we hadn't split up then,' she explained. 'She was always faithful, and I never deserved her anyway.'

Eva recognised the fact that Carine was talking in the past tense. 'So, what about now?' she asked.

'She's gone,' Carine slurred, sinking back into the seat, trying to hold Eva's strong gaze.

'I'm sorry,' Eva said.

'I deserve it,' Carine responded. She wasn't feeling sorry for herself. She wasn't feeling anything. 'My life's a mess and I've created it.'

Eva admired the honest self-reflection, but was still reeling at Carine's deliberate attempts to sabotage her relationship with Rosa. 'I still don't get it.'

'I can't cope with the idea of getting older. I cling on to stuff… people, work, power, to make me feel better, but it never lasts.'

Eva leaned back in her seat, 'But you're not old,' she said.

'Yes, I know. I'm not that old, but the idea of it obsesses me,' she said.

'You need to talk to someone,' Eva said, reflecting on the help Charlie had been at a time when she felt so low.

'I'm talking to you,' Carine said.

'No, not me. I'm not the person you need to talk to. You need to talk to someone professionally.'

'Ah my darling, such a great idea, but that would involve me revealing my weaknesses to a stranger, and that, is a step too far.' She held up her glass, swilled the remaining whiskey before downing it in one go and wincing at the burning sensation in her throat.

Eva stood. 'Think about it,' she said. 'In fact, you seeing someone is a condition of you keeping your job,' she added. 'You're good at what you do Carine, but you can't stay at the agency unless you learn to handle whatever it is that is… poisoning your brain,' she waved a hand in Carine's direction. 'You and I were never an item and we never will be,' she added.

'I know,' Carine responded, despondently.

'Let me know what you decide. And, an apology will be expected… to Rosa, not me,' she clarified. Turning sharply, she walked out of the bar, leaving Carine slouched in the seat.

Carine staggered to the bar and ordered another whiskey. 'This will be your last tonight,' Ali said. Carine downed the amber liquid in one hit and walked out the door into the dark evening chill.

*

Eva unlocked the front door, taken aback by the aroma that wafted out with the heat, into the night. She had walked for an hour before returning home. She hadn't decided what to do about retaining Carine, but she had calmed down. Rosa met her at the door and she fell into the warm embrace. 'I'm so sorry,' Eva said.

'I'm sorry too,' Rosa said. Her tone was flat, exhausted by the stress that had worn her down with worry throughout the day. The light sense of relief had yet to exert a fully positive effect. 'I should have trusted you,' she said, placing a tender kiss to Eva's cheek.

The spot burned on Eva's skin and sent a fiery trail down her neck and back. 'It was Carine,' she confirmed. 'I need to talk to you.' It was now or never, but if they had a future

246

together Eva needed to let Rosa know what had transpired between her and Carine.

Rosa took Eva's hand and led her through to the kitchen. She served up two plates of the stew she had prepared and placed them on the table. 'Sit down,' she said. She had all the time in the world and no matter what it was Eva needed to get off her chest, it wouldn't change the way she felt about her. Whatever it was, she vowed to work it through.

Eva sat, her eyes lowered to the glorious aroma of food rising from the plate. 'This smells great,' she said, drawing her eyes back up to meet Rosa's gaze. The smile on her girlfriend's face provided the reassurance she needed. Taking a deep breath and releasing it, she started to talk, watching Rosa's every move. Rosa didn't look away or tear up, and she didn't look heartbroken at the fact that Eva had slept with Carine. The only emotion Eva could read was compassion, and when Rosa took her hand and rubbed her fingers tenderly, it was Eva's floodgates that opened, and it was Eva who wept.

Rosa moved around the table and pulled Eva into her arms. 'Thank you for telling me, and you need to know that it doesn't matter. We weren't together then, remember. But we are now, and I love you,' she said. 'Now, and the future is what matters.' Cupping Eva's face, holding her eyes with her own, she closed the gap between them. The soft sensation on Eva's lips sparked every nerve in her body and she flinched. She had never felt more vulnerable, more exposed, and then she also felt an overwhelming sense of safety.

Eva pulled out of the kiss. Rosa's eyes were as dark as the night sky and her lips swollen from the lightest of touches. 'Will you marry me?' Eva asked. The words came out broken, but the sincerity was never in question.

'Yes.' The response came quickly and without hesitation, followed by a clashing of teeth as their mouths met with a charged urgency that continued long into the night.

*

Eva sat on the slightly damp grass, fingering the gold embossed lettering on the ornate plaque. The sun sat brightly in the early spring sky. Even the daffodils had already started to bloom. Eva laid a bunch of them on the grave of Elsie Jones, directly below the plaque. Rosa rested a hand on Eva's shoulder. They read the words on the plaque in silence.

Rowena Adams (Nee Jones).
Born 12th January 1959, Died 22nd December 2016.
Daughter of Elsie and Ewen Jones.
Loving mum to Eva Adams.

The gravestone behind the plaque, belonging to Rowena's parents, looked weathered and the stone engraving had lost its clarity over the years. Rosa squeezed Eva's shoulder, turning her head.

'It's a lovely spot,' Eva remarked, looking out over the waters of the Bristol Channel. The breeze was still cool, but it was the situation that caused Eva to shiver. She stood and tucked herself into Rosa's arm. 'I'm so glad you're here,' she said.

Rosa squeezed her tightly. 'There's nowhere else I'd rather be,' she said, kissing the top of Eva's head. They stared at the urn sitting on top of the grave. 'Do we need to tip the ashes?' Rosa asked.

Eva sighed, 'I guess,' she said, with a heavy heart.

'Only when you're ready,' Rosa said. 'We've got time.'

'Your mum's waiting for us,' Eva said.

'And your dad,' Rosa reminded her, not that Eva needed to be reminded of their visit to see the boys and David en route to Brigitte's.

Eva touched her hand to her chest, making contact with the pendant underneath her coat. Standing taller, having regained her composure, she traced her finger down the side of Rosa's cheek. 'I'm so in love with you,' she declared.

Rosa pulled her close. 'I'm in love with you too,' she said.

Eva broke the hold and bent down to pick up the urn. She undid the lid and started to pour her mum's ashes onto her grandmother's grave, allowing the tears to fall freely and the wind to whisk away the lighter dust as it fell. When she turned to face Rosa, she too was crying. Eva leant in, and kissed her full on the lips. 'Let's go see your mum,' she said.

'She's going to love you,' Rosa said, as they linked arms, ambled across the grass, and out through the cemetery gates.

About Emma Nichols

Emma Nichols lives in Buckinghamshire with her partner and two children. She served for 12 years in the British Army, studied Psychology, and published several non-fiction books under another name, before dipping her toes into the world of lesbian fiction. You can contact her through her website and social media:

www.emmanicholsauthor.com
www.facebook.com/EmmaNicholsAuthor
www.twitter.com/ENichols_Author

And do please leave a review if you enjoyed this book. Reviews really help independent authors to promote their work. Thank you.

COMING SOON...

Beyond Duty will be published in Spring 2018.

Please register at **www.emmanicholsauthor.com** for news about the release of Beyond Duty and other Emma Nichols titles.

32289136R00145

Printed in Great Britain
by Amazon